DAVID FREED

**sang like an angel in the synagogue and
fought like a veteran in the gang-held streets.**

*His "golden" voice was the sole support of
his impoverished, devout family; his religious
faith was a fortress against the bitter inse-
curity of the Depression. But the tragedies
involving a memorable Italian family, the
shameless hypocrisy of a famous cantor, and
a shocking crisis in his own household drive
David from a safe and comfortable child-
hood.*

No longer a boy, not yet a man, he must
abandon his old faith for a new one—a lonely, courageous belief in himself.

Don't Miss These Outstanding Books
Available in Paperback for the First Time
in SIGNET Editions

The Song of
David Freed

By ABRAHAM ROTHBERG

A SIGNET BOOK

Published by
THE NEW AMERICAN LIBRARY

Parts of this Novel appeared, in slightly different form, in the *Antioch Review* and the *Pacific Spectator*.

Library of Congress Catalog Card Number: 68-12110

This is an authorized reprint of a hardcover edition published by G. P. Putnam's Sons and published simultaneously in the Dominion of Canada by Longmans Canada Limited, Toronto.

SIGNET TRADEMARK REG. U.S. PAT. OFF. AND FOREIGN COUNTRIES
REGISTERED TRADEMARK—MARCA REGISTRADA
HECHO EN CHICAGO, U.S.A.

SIGNET BOOKS are published by
The New American Library, Inc.,
1301 Avenue of the Americas, New York, New York 1001

FIRST PRINTING, JANUARY, 1969

PRINTED IN THE UNITED STATES OF AMERICA

TO ESTHER

for all the good years

And your sons and your daughters shall prophesy,
Your old men shall dream dreams,
Your young men shall see visions.

The Song of David Freed

WHEN public school was over, David Freed came home for his Hebrew school books and his afternoon milk and crackers. He would rather have remained to play indoor baseball in the schoolyard, and he sat in the small, dark kitchen, dawdling with his milk until his mother hurried him along. "David, you'll be late again for Talmud Torah! Do you want Rebi Greenberg to tell Papa that you were late again this week?" Remembering his father's angry face and Mr. Greenberg's pinching, ear-pulling little fingers, David gulped the rest of his milk and went for his books. At the door his mother caught him, picked up his black silk skullcap, embroidered with the blue Star of David, and quickly brushed his hair into place. "Now remember," she said, her brown eyes large and serious, "no fighting. Your father said that if *they* want to fight, you mind your business and go to the Talmud Torah." David nodded hopelessly. What was the use of explaining again that you couldn't go past them? His parents didn't understand that there was no use talking to the Forty Thieves, because *they* wanted to fight, not talk. Their favorite hangout was on the street before the Talmud Torah, so that they could get at all the Jewish boys who had to pass them to go to Hebrew school. And there were always fights, every day. As he was leaving the house, his mother called after him from upstairs, "Don't forget what I said, David. *No fighting!* And I want you home right after Talmud Torah. Papa will be hungry, and I don't want to wait with supper."

David didn't answer. He went quickly, closing the door silently behind him, so it would seem he had already gone when she had called him. Outside, Sonny Richter, eating an apple, was waiting. He and Sonny had just worked out a way of going through the back alleys so that they didn't have to pass D'Aquino's candy store, where the Forty Thieves always waited. It was always at D'Aquino's that the fights started. The Jewish kids went in twos, usually because so many of them had been beaten up, but even that was no good because the Forty Thieves came in fours and fives now.

"Did you do the homework?" Sonny asked, taking another bite of his apple.

David nodded.

"I didn't do mine. No time," Sonny said. "Wanna bite?" He proffered the apple but David refused. "Tell me about the homework, huh?"

"Oh, it's Joshua blowing the trumpets and the walls of Jericho falling down," David replied.

"Again?"

"It's one of Greenberg's favorites."

They walked down the street, ducked into the alleyway behind Jiggs' apartment house, through the backyard of D'Aquino's, under the twisted little crabapple trees and past the Italian grocery store on the corner. Then it was only a dash across the avenue, and they were half a block from the Talmud Torah and safely past the Forty Thieves. "That's a good way," Sonny said, beginning to gnaw his apple again. "They didn't even see us. Look, they're in front of D'Aquino's, turned the other way."

David wheeled and saw in the front of the candy store four of the Forty Thieves: Banana Nose, Fonzi, Sal and Petey. "They'll see us someday and catch us behind D'Aquino's, and that'll be worse," he said. "Besides, I hate to sneak."

"You wanna fight with them every day? Two against four? Two against five? Not me."

David shrugged. "I don't know."

"You know what your father said about fighting them. And my father, too. Boy, he gave it to me last time, too, when Fonzi tore my shirt."

"I ain't scared of 'em," David said.

"You ain't scared, huh? You look plenty scared," Sonny said.

"Maybe I am scared, then," David replied after a moment, "but I still don't like running away."

"But you can't talk to those guys. You know that. Schloime tried last week, so they tore up his Bible and burned his skullcap with matches, and beat him up anyway."

They walked down the few stairs that led to the Talmud Torah. Mr. Greenberg had already started the lesson when they opened the classroom door. "Oho, *trombeniks,* you're here already? Good evening to you." He made them a mock bow and then picked up the blackboard pointer while they hurried to their seats. David opened his book to the place and hunched over it, still thinking of the Forty Thieves. Someday they were going to get it, all of them, and get it good.

"Dovid?" Mr. Greenberg stood next to him.

"Yes, Rebi Greenberg."

"Where is the place?"

"Here." David pointed and Mr. Greenberg brought the pointer down across his knuckles. "That's for coming late. Now translate!"

His knuckles were like fire and he almost got up to hit back, the way Nadie Rosen had done when Mr. Greenberg hit him before Rosh Hashanah, but he remembered what his father had told him. There was to be no more trouble with Mr. Greenberg and the Hebrew school. If there was, his father had promised that *he* would get it, and good, so David just looked his hatred at Mr. Greenberg's thin, pale face, with the little silver-rimmed glasses and the wispy mustache and sideburns.

"Translate!" Mr. Greenberg repeated. "Are you deaf on an ear?"

David began to translate:

So the people shouted when the priests blew the trumpets and it came to pass that when the people heard the sound of the trumpet, they shouted a great shout so that the wall fell down flat and the people went into the city without trouble and they took the city. . . .

When he was finished, Mr. Greenberg called on Sonny, gave him the pointer across the knuckles for coming late too, and then hurried Sonny's translation. David hated Mr. Greenberg's teaching. It wasn't like public school, where the teachers got mad and maybe made you stay after school or do extra homework, or even wear a dunce cap. Mr. Greenberg was always hitting, with the pointer or with his hands, on the knuckles, the back, the legs, pinching an arm, or twisting an ear with his strong, hairy fingers. Now, because Sonny had missed a word, because he hadn't done the homework, Mr. Greenberg twisted his ear while Sonny tried to pull his head away and finish his

translation at the same time. He was halfway out of his
seat when the unfinished half of his apple fell out of his
pocket and rolled on the floor, and the class burst into
laughter. "Silence!" Rebi Greenberg roared, and after an
extra, final tweak, he let go of Sonny's ear and finished the
translation himself:

> And Joshua commanded them, saying, Cursed be the man
> before God who shall come and rebuild this city of Jericho:
> the foundation of it shall lay in his first-born, and on his
> youngest son shall he set up its gates.

It was a long time until the lesson was over, and David
left the classroom quickly, rushing as if he had to get into
the open to breathe again. He went up the stairs two at a
time until he was outside the synagogue. Evening had
come quickly, fallen like a haze of darkened snow. The air
was clean and cool in his mouth, and he swallowed it until
Sonny and Nadie Rosen came upstairs, and Nadie said,
"You let him hit yuh again, Davie." It was half a question, half an accusation.

David said nothing.

"His old man said he'd give it to him if he started up
with Greenberg again," Sonny explained for him.

"He musta been talking to my old man," Nadie said. "I
seen them in the synagogue together on Shabbos. I told
my old man that no matter what he said, Greenberg
better not lay a hand on me anymore. Great! So he gets
mad and says that if Greenberg don't, he will. He give me
some shellackin', too."

"Did you cry?" Sonny asked.

"Whaddyu think, I'm a crybaby?" Nadie asked. Then,
changing the subject, he went on. "That Greenberg. He
loves that Book of Joshua better than all the rest together,
because there's war and killin', and the Jews conquering
the Amorites and the Perizzites and the Jebusites."

"Be a lot better if he could tell us how to conquer the
Forty Thieves," David interjected. "Now."

"Oh, that," Sonny laughed. "That's easy. Just get your
trumpet and we'll blow 'em down, just like Jericho."

"Big joke," Nadie said disgustedly, "but it aint funny."

At the corner, Sonny, suddenly confidential, said to
Nadie, "Listen, we've got a special way to get past the
Forty Thieves. You want us to show you?"

Nadie looked at him for a moment, his shoulders
hunching under his brown suede jacket. "I'm not runnin'

away from them, or from Greenberg, or from anybody," he said, his smooth brown face stiffening and his jaws working.

Sonny stopped. "Well, I don't care about you, but Davie and I are going our way," he said defensively.

"Okay, who's stoppin' yuh?"

"I'm going past D'Aquino's with Nadie," David said, after a moment of silence, sorry to see Sonny's face fall and his eyes go wide with fright. He knew there was no use in ducking through the alley anyway. The Forty Thieves would find out and pretty soon they'd just wait there, so what difference did it make? Might as well go the regular way.

"You guys nuts?" Sonny asked. "You remember what your father said about fights, Davie. You better go with me."

"Scared cat," Nadie said.

"I ain't scared. It's just dumb to fight."

"Come on, Davie," Nadie said, "let's go."

They stepped off the curb and began to cross the street. "Okay, okay," Sonny called. "Wait for me. If you guys go, I'll go too." They waited, and when he caught up to them, they walked three abreast across the street, and then across the avenue to the side D'Aquino's was on.

"Make believe we're talkin'," Nadie said, "like we don't even notice 'em."

"Sure, but they're waiting. Four of 'em," Sonny said. "Banana Nose, Fonzi, Sal and Petey."

"Hey, Freed, yuh sheeny," Banana Nose called, "yuh running home to Mama to do yuh homewoik?"

"Listen, you Banana Nose guinea," Nadie replied, "you too dumb to do your homework. You can't even read."

"He wasn't talkin' to you," Fonzi cut in. "He was talkin' to little Davie there. You mind your business."

They were at D'Aquino's now, and Fonzi and Banana Nose had stepped out on the sidewalk to block their way, and Petey and Sal stood at the side, leaning against the Indian-nut and poppy-seed machines.

"Look, Fonzi, we're in a hurry. We gotta get home for supper," Sonny said, pleading, but Nadie looked at him and he shut up.

"You gonna let us past, Joe?" David asked Banana Nose, calling him by his school name.

"My name's Banana Nose to you, sheeny, see?" he said, pushing his finger into David's chest and bringing his face so close that David could feel his own eyes pull together to watch Banana Nose's big nose quivering and his dark eyes brimming with hatred.

"Look, Banana Nose," David said, "we didn't come here to fight, but you better not say sheeny again."

"D'yuh hear that, Petey?" Banana Nose half-turned to the two still leaning and watching. "He ain't come here to fight, and we better not say that doity woid sheeny." He turned to David, pushed his face close again, and yelled, "Sheeny, sheeny, sheeny yella belly!" and then slapped David's face with a loud-sounding open palm that was like a paper bag blown up and burst. David felt the same burning pain in his face he had felt in his knuckles when Mr. Greenberg had hit him, and he punched Banana Nose's head. The fight was on. Nadie rushed Fonzi, and Petey and Sal jumped on Sonny and began to punch him while he tried to cover his face. After that, David had eyes only for Banana Nose. Banana Nose hit him in the stomach, and David felt sick and breathless together. A fist hit his nose, stinging and painful, and he felt the blood run salty over his lips. He put his hand up to his face and wiped the blood away. The sight of it, red and rivuleted on his hand, made him crazy mad. He jumped at Banana Nose, hit him on the ear, punched his head again, slammed him in the stomach, and then threw him on the sidewalk. Banana Nose pulled his ankles and David went down on the sidewalk with him, rolling over and over as they punched each other's ribs and backs.

Above the roar of his anger and the beat of his blood, David heard two voices shouting together, and hands pulled him away from Banana Nose and Banana Nose away from him, while both of them kept trying to punch. "Thick heads," a voice cried, "Calabrian thick heads! Sicilian bandits! What the hell you do in front of my store? You wanna bring tha police here?" It was Mr. D'Aquino, two hundred and fifty pounds of him, his big belly hanging over his thin belt and baggy pants, pulling Petey and Sal off Sonny. The other voice was yelling in Yiddish, *"Trombeniks!* Gangsters! You are thieves and carriage drivers, to fight like this in the street?" And in the midst of Nadie and Fonzi, still fighting, David saw Mr. Greenberg, his black caftan flying and his black felt hat on the ground, knocked off his head by Fonzi to reveal his white embroidered skullcap. In a few minutes, it was all over. Banana Nose, Fonzi, Sal and Petey were lined up behind Mr. D'Aquino's huge bulk, and Sonny, Nadie and David were behind Mr. Greenberg's caftan. D'Aquino and

Mr. Greenberg were talking simultaneously, and their words were mixed in David's ears. "Now, whaddyu wanna fight for, huh? . . . You know what you'll get when your parents hear you fight in the streets like hoodlums . . . Whatsamatta, not enough trouble ina woild fa you? . . . How many times in class I have told you that fighting is bad. . . ." There was a sudden silence as they stopped together. "Now, you betta go home, no hang around my store no more, you hear," Mr. D'Aquino said. "If I see you fighting again, I give you five extra pages to translate," Mr. Greenberg warned, picking his hat up and brushing the dust from the nap with his sleeve, before he set the hat straight and awkward on his head. "Now, go home!"

As they turned to leave, Banana Nose yelled, "Whatsamatta, yella bellies, need your sheeny teacher to help yuh fight?"

David turned back, Nadie right behind him, but Mr. Greenberg stepped in front of them. "It is enough," he said in Yiddish. "Go home. You will not make them think better of you, or of me, by hitting them."

"Yuch gekitchmerougarabovok," Banana Nose mimicked the Yiddish. "Whyn't yuh speak English, yuh forriners?"

"Let be ssha!" Mr. Greenberg ordered them, his face sterner than David had ever seen it before. None of them dared to answer.

As a parting shot, Banana Nose shouted, "We'll wait for yuh in the schoolyard tonight to finish this, yella bellies."

"You better be there too," Fonzi added, "or we come and drag you outta tha house."

"G'wan with you big mouths," Mr. D'Aquino said, lifting his huge hands. "G'wan, before I make you little mouth."

"You big fat slob," Fonzi called.

"You think you own the whole street because you gotta stinkin' candy store," Petey added.

"Scram out!" Mr. D'Aquino shouted, stamping his foot, and the Forty Thieves fell back.

"Don't forget, sheenies," Banana Nose shouted again. "The handball courts at half past eight." Then the four of them slouched to the corner and were gone.

"Go home, already," Mr. Greenberg commanded, and they began to walk toward the other corner, while Mr. Greenberg turned back to Mr. D'Aquino. As they walked away, David heard Mr. D'Aquino say, "Whaddyu gonna do with sucha kids?" and Mr. Greenberg's answer, "When they are men, grown, maybe they are smarter?"

Nadie, Sonny and David walked up the street in silence, trying to straighten their clothing, wipe their faces clean with their handkerchiefs, and smooth their hair with their pocket combs. David's shirt was covered with blood and dirt, and he knew that unless he could get into the bathroom and get cleaned up without his mother seeing him, the whole thing would start all over again, only this time his father would punish him for fighting, because Jewish boys were not supposed to fight. They got to David's house before Sonny asked, "You gonna be there tonight?"

"Where?" David asked.

"The schoolyard," Nadie answered. "Sure he's gonna be there. And me, too. You better be there, too."

"Whaddyu mean?"

"Just be there," Nadie repeated. "I'm gonna bring Maxie Jonas along, too—he's a good fighter—so it's four to four, even."

"All right," David said. He hadn't thought of going, but maybe that would settle it once and for all. "Meet you at the schoolyard, our side of the street, about half past eight."

Upstairs, David opened the door quietly, and hearing his mother in the bedroom, slipped into the bathroom and locked the door.

"Davie?" his mother called.

"Yeh, Ma, I'm in the toilet."

"Hurry up and get out of there. Papa'll be home any minute."

When he had washed all the blood and dirt away, David took off his bloodied shirt and put it at the bottom of the hamper, covering it over with all the other soiled laundry. Then he opened the bathroom door, went into his bedroom and put on a clean shirt. He heard his father come in, his mother's, "Jakob?" and his father's grunted, "Yah, Leah." David sat down with his Bible and tried to do the translations for the next day's lesson in Talmud Torah, but he couldn't concentrate. If he went to the schoolyard and fought, his father would find out and beat him for fighting. If he stayed home and didn't go, the boys would think he was a coward, and the Forty Thieves would make it miserable for him every time he passed D'Aquino's, and even in public school. And what if he did beat up Banana Nose? What difference did it make? You couldn't talk to the Forty Thieves, but you couldn't beat them either. They liked to fight, and it would mean fights and more fights with Banana Nose, with Fonzi, with Sal, and all the rest of them until he got licked. You just couldn't win. He tried not to think of it, to concentrate on Joshua and the Amorites.

> Then Joshua spoke to the Lord on the day when the Lord delivered the Amorites to the children of Israel, and he said before the eyes of Israel, Sun, stand still over Gibeon; and Moon, in the valley of Ajalon.

> And the sun stood still, and the moon stood still, until the people had avenged themselves upon their enemies.

But David knew that the Lord would not deliver the Forty Thieves to them, nor would the sun stand still on their street, nor the moon stand still over the handball courts of the schoolyard. At half past eight they'd all be there, waiting, and he would have to go.

"Dovid?" his father called.

"Yes, Pa, I'm in the bedroom."

"Come to the table," his mother said.

"What is he doing in there?" his father asked his mother in Yiddish.

"I'm doing my Talmud Torah homework for tomorrow," David answered in English as he came into the kitchen.

"How is it in Talmud Torah?" his father asked in Yiddish when he sat down at the table. Only recently, his father had begun to talk to him in Yiddish, as if he now suddenly and overnight understood the language for the first time. "I saw Rebi Greenberg in synagogue tonight, at *maariv,* but he did not have time to talk with me." David said he was doing all right, and wondered what luck had kept his father from talking to Mr. Greenberg. His mother came to the table with hot *borscht,* quartered potatoes and sliced, hard-boiled eggs swimming in it, and his father began to eat. There was halibut dipped in egg and fried brown and tender, a salad of red cabbage, strips of orange carrot, light pink tomatoes and cool green lettuce, and finally blintzes, with the soft cheese inside the thin browned dough. When his mother brought the coffee, his father spoke. "Mr. Rosen told me that his son, Nadie, is a big fighter. He is your friend, no?"

David nodded, swallowing a bit of blintze too quickly, so that his throat hurt, and he could not trust himself to speak.

"I do not want to hear you made yourself cheap fighting in the street like a hooligan," his father said slowly.

"But, Pa," David protested, "even in the Bible the Jews fought. I just finished Joshua's battle with the Amorites, where the sun and moon stood still, and tonight in Talmud Torah we read about the fall of Jericho."

"That was another time, a long time ago, and another country," his father said, his eyes faraway. "It was different."

"You must fight sometimes," David insisted, "they won't let you alone."

"*They? They* will always let you alone if you let them alone."

His mother glanced at both of them and looked down at the slim gold band of her wedding ring. "It's that your father knows you cannot fight and win," she said quietly. "It is only by *not* fighting that you win."

"I don't understand. How can you win by not fighting?"

"By being living," his father replied. "It is sometimes braver to turn away than to fight and be killed."

"But, Pa, if they call you dirty Jew and sheeny, and beat you, you can't just turn away. They think you are a coward and treat you like dirt. And you feel dirty too, inside. They'll only do it more, anyway, more and more, until you can't stand it."

"Let them speak their filthy words," his mother said, twisting her ring on her finger. "They are dirtied by such words, not you."

"But I am dirtied too, if I let them speak so to me."

"But you live," his father said. "Is it necessary to care what they think? Do you want them to pay you honor?"

"Yes, I want them to pay me honor," David said stubbornly. "Why shouldn't they? Am I dog, to be kicked and stoned and spat on? I'm a man!"

His mother smiled at that, but his father's face remained grave, the lines around his eyes cut deep into the skin, the eyes dark in the hollows and tired. "You are a man, perhaps, but a young one. You do not understand that this honor is *their* honor, and whether you fight or not, they will kick and stone and spit. And if you fight, they will kill you. Not the first time, maybe, or even the second, but they will kill you sometime."

"Why? why?"

"Because, my son, *their* honor is a thing decided with blows and ours is—and yours should also be—an honor which has to do with righteousness."

"If they call us names and beat us, then are we not righteous to defend ourselves, to return their—"

"Blows? What does a blow prove, David? That you are right, or that you have a stronger fist?"

His mother began to clear away dishes and his father sat quietly, almost sadly, David thought, smoking his little brown cigarettes. He didn't know why the talk had made his father so sad and quiet. His father might be right, but he was not like his father, he could not live that way. He could not suffer Banana Nose and Fonzi and the others to think him a coward, nor would he suffer them to abuse him. He would fight for *their* honor, even if it were only the honor of a fist and an honor not worth believing in or fighting for. He got up from the table and went to the bedroom. He put on his old leather jacket and his oldest pants. If they fought, he might tear his clothes, and it would be better to tear old clothes. His mother would not be so angry then. When he came out of the bedroom, he saw his father staring into a cloud of cigarette smoke that hung about his head and over the whole kitchen table. As David went to the door, his father spoke in English for the first time that evening, and said, "Where do you go?"

And David, speaking also in English, replied that he was going out to play. His mother wanted to know if he had homework, and when he said he had done it, she warned him to be back before ten o'clock and then let him go. He closed the door behind him and went down to the street. Outside, the streetlamps cast pale yellow spots of light that made the darkness around seem darker. Above, a few scattered gray clouds were like rags of smoke in the sky, and as he walked toward the school-yard, David remembered how, when he was little, his mother had told him that the stars were the eyes of God in heaven, always watching you no matter where you were or what you did. Somehow, tonight, the stars seemed very far away and like blind eyes staring down, without knowing and without caring what went on beneath them.

Nadie Rosen and Maxie Jonas were waiting at the schoolyard. They said hello, and he asked for Sonny. Maxie smiled and Nadie said he didn't think Sonny would show up. David suggested that they climb the fence and wait inside, and Nadie agreed, saying that the Forty

Thieves would probably come from their side of the street. As they got to the top of the fence and were about to go down into the schoolyard, Sonny arrived. "Hey, wait for me," he called in a hoarse whisper. "I'm coming with you."

"It's about time," Maxie said.

"What're you shivering and whispering for?" Nadie asked irritably. "Fonzi got your tongue?"

Sonny climbed over the iron spiked fence and joined them. They walked silently toward the middle of the handball courts where there was a small yellow night-light, the only light in the whole of the darkened school-yard. As they came up to it, Banana Nose stepped into the circle of light and said, "I didn't think you guys was gonna show up. You tree minutes late." David was surprised to find himself calm. Or was it calm that he felt? It was like a dead circle of cold air in his chest and stomach, but he did not feel shaky. "Dyu bring your boys?" Banana Nose asked.

"Three of them," David said, "but this is between you and me, and I don't want them mixing in."

"Yuh mean this is a grudge fight?" Banana Nose seemed surprised. "And you ain't gonna let my boys have some fun beatin' your gang up?"

"No, just you and me. Who you got with you?"

"Fonzi, Sal, and Petey, same as before."

"Never mind the talk," Fonzi interrupted, sticking his head into the light. "You gonna fight or ain't yuh?"

"Butt out, Fonzi," Banana Nose answered. "Don't you worry, we gonna fight." He turned to David. "We fight in the light and they watch, your boys and mine."

"Okay," David replied. He stepped into the light and put his hands up, crouching in the way that Mr. Kay, the gym teacher, had taught him. Banana Nose's arm reached out of the circle of light into the darkness behind him. There was a glint and then the arm came back into the light, and the hand had a knife in it. Banana Nose pressed the spring, and the long blade sprang out with a loud click.

"Say, wait a minute." Nadie burst into the light, horrified. "We didn't come for a knife fight."

"Whatsamatta, Nadie, yella?" Fonzi taunted.

"You want Davie to fight Banana Nose bare-handed against a knife?" Nadie asked. "He ain't got no knife." He shook his head at David.

"Naw, we give him an even break," Banana Nose said after a minute. "Give him your sticker, Petey." There was a fumbling silence, and then Petey slid a long pearl-handled knife along the ground into the circle of yellow light. David looked at it, unable to touch it, and Nadie called for time out. He pulled David out of the light, but David couldn't take his eyes off that knife.

"You know how to knife-fight?" Nadie whispered in his ear. David tried to answer, but his throat was dry and tight and he couldn't, so he shook his head. "Listen," Nadie advised, "keep your left arm up so if he cuts you, he cuts your arm. That's not so bad." David nodded and began to move back toward the light, his eyes still on the knife. "Don't forget," Nadie hissed his final counsel. "Test the knife to see if it's sharp."

David moved into the circle of light where Banana Nose was waiting. He stopped, picked up the knife and touched the spring button. The blade leaped out like a live, shining thing. He looked around at Fonzi and Sal and Petey, whose faces were ghostlike in the shadows behind Banana Nose, and as he did so, he hefted the knife in his open palm, as he had seen them do in the moving pictures. He tried to keep the choking sense of airlessness down in him, but it had spread until he felt his whole body empty except for a dull booming beat in his hands and chest that he suddenly knew for the frightened beating of his heart and blood. He looked straight at Banana Nose and the ghostly faces behind him, and the words came out of his mouth without his even knowing what he was going to say. "Till one of us is dead."

Banana Nose's voice squeaked. "Dead?"

"Dead," David repeated in a flat voice, and then he said, "Like this," intending to run the knife-edge along his thumb to see if it was sharp. But his shaking hand drew the knife deep into the flesh, and the blood welled out of the skin and darkened the brightness of the blade. "Like that," he repeated dully, showing them his hand and the blade. All of them looked at the bleeding hand, and then Fonzi's voice came out of the dark, high-pitched and screechy. "Madonna, he cut himself!" And then Petey's low, scared, "He gonna kill you, Banana Nose. He crazy brave to cut hisself with that knife. It some sharp sticker. I know, 'cause I sharpen it myself."

David lifted his bleeding left hand, palm up, in front of him, crouched, and with the knife in his right hand advanced toward Banana Nose. For a moment, Banana Nose stood staring at him, his face recast from disbelief to terror; then there was the sudden sound of feet running and a shout, "I'm gettin' outta here!" that was Fonzi's, and Banana Nose, hearing his friends running away, took one more look at David's hand, his face shifting from hope to despair, before he dropped his knife and ran into the darkness. David stood still crouched, the knife clutched in his wet palm, listening to their running and the sounds of their climbing the fence mingling with the dripping of his blood on the concrete handball court. It was a moment before anyone spoke. Then Nadie came into the light and said admiringly, "Boy, you got some guts, Davie. We ain't gonna have no trouble with those guys no more." He bent and picked up Banana Nose's knife. David turned, feeling suddenly shaky in the knees, and handed him the other knife. "Don't you want it?" Nadie asked, surprised. "You sure deserve it." David said nothing; only he never wanted to see another knife again. "Give it to Sonny or Maxie, whoever wants it," he said, carefully shaping the words to keep them from trembling out of his shaking insides. They walked back and climbed over the fence back onto their street.

There Sonny stopped them and picked up the bleeding hand, took a clean white handkerchief from his pocket, and tied David's hand up with it. For the first time, David felt the pain of the cut. At David's house they all said good night, their eyes fixed on the white handkerchief and the slow spreading stain on it. After they had gone, David sat down on the stoop and looked up at the night sky, breathing deeply until he felt the shaking hollowness quiet and fill inside him. He held his hands out in front of him and looked down at Sonny's red-stained handkerchief, feeling his blood flow out of his flesh and over his palm beneath it.

A sudden brightness mounted in his throat and choked him with happiness. He had won! He had fought the Forty Thieves their own way, with the fist and the knife, with *their* honor, and he had won! He wanted to cry out his victory loud and strong, but his voice came out softly sobbing, so that no one could hear him. He would tell them, though, his father and mother and Rebi Greenberg: he was right and they were wrong. He had won! They wouldn't dare scold him for his cut hand or punish him for fighting now. Like Joshua in the Bible, he had flourished the knife and the Forty Thieves had fallen down before him.

When he came into the house, his mother and father were in the parlor, and he could easily have walked into the bedroom without their seeing him, but instead he went into the parlor and stretched out his bleeding hand. For a moment his parents sat staring at it, not moving. Then his father got up and took him to the bathroom, and his mother followed. His father took Sonny's handkerchief off, washed the hand with cold water, and then put iodine on the cut. David felt the sear all the way inside him and the nausea in the pit of his stomach, but he didn't cry out. He would cry out only his victory, not his pain. "It's deep but it's clean," his father said, as if to himself, and taped the gauze over. They stood there, the three of them, looking at the bandaged hand, and then his mother picked up Sonny's bloodied handkerchief and wiped the wash-basin clean.

"Why don't they say something?" a voice inside him cried. "Why don't they ask me what happened?" David looked at them, standing over him and staring at his bandaged hand. They thought he had lost! That was it, and why they were saying nothing. They believed that they were right and he, David, was wrong.

They went back into the kitchen and sat down at the kitchen table in silence, still looking at the hand, until his father lit a cigarette and suggested that they have some tea and jam, and his mother got up to bring it. Well, he would tell them what happened, about the knife and the blood and Banana Nose in the schoolyard. His bloody hand was not a wound, or a defeat; it was a victory. Sitting there, waiting for his mother to bring the tea, David tried to put the battle into words for them, careful-ly shaping and memorizing them, as he sometimes did for Rebi Greenberg with his translations of the Bible, but somehow the words would not stay together and make sense, but kept blurring and being washed over with blood.

David looked at his father's face across the table, seri-ous and remote, and tried to smile, but although he could see that his father was trying to answer with a smile, he couldn't quite manage it. Instead, he reached his big hand over and covered David's white-bandaged hand with his own, and blew so much smoke from his quivering nostrils that the table was covered with a little cloud of gray. Then, seeing the pain in his father's face and the little dancing muscles under the skin, David suddenly knew he hadn't won at all, and it seemed as if he had known all along that it was a funny cut with a knife that had fooled and frightened the others. Just like the priests blowing

their horns and the walls of Jericho falling down. A fluke.
A lucky break. He hadn't beaten anybody, and neither had
they. The walls had fallen, just as the Forty Thieves had
been chased, by luck, by accident.

The memory of Banana Nose and the schoolyard and
the circle of light came back to him, so he could see the
shine of the knives and hear the dripping of his blood on
the concrete. No, he reminded himself, not by accident.
By luck, but not by accident. He had gone out to fight in
the schoolyard and taken the knife in his hands, just as the
priests had gone out before Jericho and taken the
trumpets in theirs.

His mother brought the old teakettle and put it on the
table, its spout steaming. David watched her set out the
cups and saucers and then pour each of them a cup,
carefully putting a teaspoonful of prune jelly in first.
When she sat down, they stirred the jelly in the cups in
unison, and David looked at their faces and saw their sad
eyes and quiet, pursed mouths. He realized then that they,
too, had once gone out to fight and maybe even won a
victory, not the same victory he had won, but one of their
own, one that had lasted twice as long as he had lived,
and more. They'd been trying to tell him about it, trying
in their own way to explain how it was, so that he
wouldn't have to go out to fight Banana Nose and cut
himself to find out. And then, for the first time, he knew
their silence for what it was, and he was glad.

He reached for his cup and sipped the tea, but it was
too hot, and burned his lips and the roof of his mouth.
"It's too hot," he said, not thinking.

"What did you expect it to be?" his mother asked.

"Put the cup down," his father said quietly. "If you
wait, it will soon be cool enough to drink."

David saw old man Vecchione for the first time in the
front garden of the house, bent over turned-up clumps of
webbed earth, and he did not look up when David, going
to Hebrew school, passed. They had just moved into the
old, two-family house, and David liked the bigness and the
way the house sat by itself, away from the others, with the
gardens in front and back, and the spreading magnolia
tree that had not yet blossomed. His father had not liked
the move, although it was only a block and a half from
their old apartment house, and said so to his mother.
"Why must we move into *their* house, Leah? We cannot
move among our own?"

"But, Jakob," his mother had said patiently, the words worn smooth as white stones, "it is a good place, and they are good people. There is light and sun all day, and plenty of room for the boy to play."

"Play! Agh!" his father grated. "He is old enough to be studying Talmud. He is too old to be playing like a child."

But they moved anyway, and his father was already fond of the new house, even if the Vecchiones did live downstairs and were the landlords, because he had a room to himself where he could keep all his books, and where he could sit, alone or with his friends, and study. David, too, had a room where he could draw and read and do his homework, a big room at the back of the house, far from his mother and father's room, so he could get up early and make noise if he liked, and sit and look out of the big double windows. And looking out was the best of all in the new house, for beneath the windows was a hoed field that his mother told him was Mr. Vecchione's garden. Beyond it was a long, narrow strip of hard ground, beaten down by many feet and outlined by a thin ribbon of wooden planks. There the old Italian men played a strange game with little black balls, rolling them from one end of the field to the other, running after them, and sometimes yelling and raising their hands in question or in triumph, their fingers all together, and their hands in the distance flitting like brown sparrows. After the games, they sat around a wooden table just outside the borderline of planks, shaded by four twisted peach trees and a faded orange umbrella that rose out of the table like a mushroom, drinking wine and talking, and sometimes watching others play the game.

On their first Sabbath in the Vecchione house, David came home and found his mother preparing the usual meal. The house had its special Friday night quiet, as if he would have to whisper if he had anything to say. His mother moved silently around the dining room, setting the long, braided *challah* on the round table, the log-shaped *kugel*, its odor of baked noodles and white raisins filling his head and making his mouth water; the *gefilte* fish, white and snowball-shaped, lay in a deep dish, and all of it shone on the icy-white tablecloth that was starched stiff beneath. His mother set the three-pronged candelabrum in the center of the table, sparkling in the last light of the spring sunset, and put the white linen napkin on her head as she intoned the prayer blessing the candles, moving her long brown hands over them in small circles that set something shivering inside of him, too. Something good, as if the house were filled with a white light that came from the fish and the tablecloth and the bright silver of the candelabrum and its three flames, and David felt a lingering peace inside.

And the white quiet remained with him until his father, hungry and irritable from having waited so long for the evening prayer at synagogue, came in. When they were gathered around the table and about to begin the Sabbath meal, they sang the ritual *"Sholom Aleichem,"* the song he had always loved but that now seemed part of the whiteness and silence in him turned to melody, which rose up pure and strong and floated from him, soprano, over the food and the candles:

Sholom aleichem, malache hashores, malache el yon . . .

> Peace be unto you, you ministering angels,
> Messengers of the Most High. . . .
> May your coming be in peace. . . .
> Bless me with peace. . . .

Not until he had finished the third stanza did he realize that his father and mother had stopped singing, and when he opened his eyes, he saw them exchanging looks and staring at him. "Your voice," his mother said, softly and surprised, "why, it's beautiful."

"He sings like"—his father, hesitating, groped for words—"like a cantor." His father looked pleased and puzzled, as if suddenly he had found something precious in the street, where he had never expected to find it, and didn't know why he had been chosen to discover it.

They stood there looking at him, until David felt his cheeks grow hot and looked down at the shimmering table.

"Never have I heard you sing like that, David," his mother said, reaching toward him with a caress that smoothed his hair and straightened his skullcap at the same time. "You must sing some more for us."

"He must sing in the synagogue, Leah," his father said, "with the choir, on the altar. One day—who knows?—he will maybe be a cantor. Tomorrow, I will speak to Chazan Barrt." His father smiled at him. "You would like to study with him?"

David knew his father wanted him to say yes, but he couldn't. Nor would he say no. He looked down at the tablecloth again, anxious, because it was the same voice he had always sung with, only he had not sung much before his parents. His father came around the table and put his hands on his shoulders, so that David could feel his own blood beating against his father's palms. "You will sing like an angel, the *kiddush, neilah, Kol Nidre,* like Yossele Rosenblatt." His father's fingers tightened. "My son, Dov-id." His father sounded proud of him, as he almost never did, and David was happy for that. But when they sang the last stanza together:

> May your departure be in peace, you messengers of peace,
> Messengers of the Most High, the supreme King of Kings,
> Holy and blessed is He.

the white quiet inside him had gone.

After supper, David went out into the backyard and looked at the moon, white and quiet on old man Vecchione's field, but the feeling did not come back, and he felt only the pinch of the pickets of the fence as he leaned his arms between them.

The voice behind him was strange and hoarse, but it did not startle him when he heard it. Even without turning, he knew it was old man Vecchione.

"That was you, upastairs, singing?" the old man asked.

David nodded.

"You sing vera fine. You study musica?"

David turned, and was surprised to find the old man's face on a level with his own, because the old man was bent over like a jackknife with the blade left half open. That was the way he stood and walked. The quiet gray-blue eyes were like marbles in the wrinkled sand of the skin, and fixed him. "No," David said, "I do not study music."

"You like," he asked, the full, chapped lips suddenly smiling, and David knew he meant the music, not the study.

"I like," David replied, smiling back.

"Come." The old man motioned for him to follow, and then, abruptly, he turned and said, "Whatsa you name?"

"David. David Freed."

"My name Vincenzo Vecchione, but everyone callsa me Pop. You calla me Pop. Okay?"

"Okay"—David laughed—"Pop."

Pop led him through the back entrance of the house into the cellar. There, under a dim, green-shaded yellow bulb that hung over a table, four men were playing cards. "Those my sons: Joseph, he'sa the oldest, and then Vito and Carmine. The other, he—how you say?—stay with us. Rent a room upstairs. His name John Strigari." He called to the men in his rasping voice, "Hey, boys, thisa here is new boy, lives upastairs. David."

They waved and called hello but did not look up from their game. David followed Pop past the staircase that led up to the Vecchiones' apartment on the first floor, and walked into a front room furnished like a parlor, with a rug and a couch and a big victrola. The old man went to the victrola cabinet and opened it, almost patting the dark, polished top into place. David saw painted on the open cover a black-and-white dog sitting next to a megaphone. "This machine could be you best frien'," Pop said, talking almost to himself. "When you sad, she makes you music so sad is more easy, and you be happy by and by. When you tired, she make you rest. She a ver good frien'." He motioned. "Come ona here. I show you how she works."

Carefully, the old man explained and David watched how the victrola was to be wound with the metal arm that came out of its mahogany side, how new needles were to be taken out of a little metal pit and put in the head of the phonograph arm, how the old needles went into another little pit, and finally, how the shiny black record with the red label was set down on the felt turntable and the arm and needle brought gently down on it. "Is Caruso," Pop Vecchione said, putting the first record on. "A big record. The biggest. He's tenor. You listen, eh?"

David nodded, and sat on the old couch. First, there was only a little scraping sound, like a cat scratching the door at night, and then the music came, and a sad, slow, lonely, crying voice, and David forgot the scratching and the dusty smell of the couch and the sounds of the card players in the next room. He even forgot about Pop Vecchione, standing next to the victrola, his white head lifted from his doubled-up body as if it no longer belonged to it. And David felt as he sometimes did when he ran wildly down the streets into the wind, the air rushing against his face and into his lungs, until he felt he was flying. All he could hear was the rising and falling of the voice, its turning in and flowing out, loud, soft, in words he did not recognize, but speaking a language he knew without words, a speech that ran through him and lifted him like the wind.

When the music ended, there was again the cat-scratching, then silence, and the old man, tears in his eyes, stood looking at him. "You like," he managed to say, without its being a question.

David nodded, not trusting his voice to speak for him, not wanting to break the other sounds with his voice, unwilling to come down from the flying and the wind-whirling. Never had he heard anything like it. It was even better than the *Kol Nidre,* or the *Umipenay Chatoenu* in the synagogue.

"Someday, maybe, you sing like him?" Pop smiled.

David shook his head. No other voice could ever be like that. Surely not his.

"But you try?"

"I will try," David said, finding his voice in his throat, new and trembling. "What is the name of the music?"

"I don't know how you call him in English," Pop said, running his earth-colored hands through his snowy hair. "Hey, Carmine," he called, "how you call the music in English?"

"It's called *The Pearl Fishers'* aria, Papa," a summery-soft girl's voice answered.

"Oho, is Antoinette," Pop said, turning to the door. "Is the youngest, my daughter, Toni."

In the doorway stood a tall young woman in a white dress, in the dimness looking like a fragment of the moon that had walked into the cellar. David was surprised at the wild yellow of her hair and the coal-glow eyes beneath. It wasn't until she came into the room and took her father's arm, erect and lithe next to his gnarled body, that David saw she was only a girl, no more than fourteen or fifteen. A light behind Pop Vecchione's face glowed when he looked at her, proud and admiring, the way his mother sometimes looked at him, and the old man's head seemed to lift again from his bent body.

"Toni, is new boy from upstairs, David."

"Hello, David," Toni said.

"Hello, Toni," David answered, unable to look directly at her moonlit beauty.

"Why you no sing for me and my Toni?" Pop requested.

"Don't be bashful," Toni coaxed, in her summery voice, and David knew he had to sing, because it was as if he had swallowed a little piece of her, her wild yellow hair and her quiet, dark voice that was a song. Into his throat, unbidden, came an old tune his mother often sang, "The Three Sisters," and in Yiddish he sang:

> In England there is a town Leicester,
> In London is the same named square,
> And there we find three sisters,
> Of whose lives none are aware.
> The eldest she sells her bright flowers,
> The second sells laces for pelf,
> And late in the night we see coming
> The youngest who sells only herself.

When he finished, Pop and Toni applauded together, and David could hear separately the thick, callous sounds of Pop's palms and the whisper of Toni's soft hands.

"What do the words mean, David?" Toni asked, her eyes dark-glistening and faraway.

"It's just a song about three sisters in England. My mother always sings it."

"It sounds so sad."

"I guess it is. The music is sad, but I don't think the words are so sad," David replied.

A sudden embarrassed silence settled over them; the only sound was the wax slap of cards on the table in the next room.

"Let's go outside and look at Pop's tomato plants," Toni suggested quickly, extending her arm for him to take and pulling her father along with her. "He's even prouder of them than his victrola records."

Arm in arm, the three of them walked sideways through the narrow doorway into the back room, just as the Vecchione brothers and John Strigari were getting up from their card table.

"You through?" Toni asked.

"Your brothers weren't satisfied with the rent money your mother gets," John Strigari said—David noticed him for the first time, a short, slender man with hair so black it looked wet—"so they decided to win some more playing cards."

"He'sa not so good witha cards, eh, Vito?" Pop said. "Mebbe, Johnny, you betta stick by painting houses for living."

Outside, in the spring air that still had the chill of winter on it, they all walked to the picket fence separating the backyard from the field beyond that was plowed with furrows of dark and light. Johnny Strigari lighted a crooked little black cigar. They stood silently for a few moments, and then from behind them came a new voice. "You keep you Papa in the night cold and make bad his rheumatiz. You good sons and daughter."

They all turned together, and David saw Mrs. Vecchione, short, almost square, but with faded blond hair that once must have been wild and bright as Toni's, and with the same dark skin and eyes. Pop said something in swift Italian, and they all laughed.

"You laugh," Mrs. Vecchione said, "but it'sa not funny."

"Okay, okay, I go inside," Pop said. "But I like for you to say hello the upastairs boy, David."

"Hello," David said.

"You sing *musica* before?" Mrs. Vecchione asked.

"It'sa him, all right. He sings like little Caruso," Pop said proudly.

"D—a—a—v—i—d!" His mother was calling, and David realized how late it was. He let go of Toni's arm, called a quick good night to all of them, and bolted down the alley toward the front of the house.

In the morning David found Toni waiting for him next to the magnolia tree, which overnight had unfurled into a cloud of petals over the garden, and they walked to school together. Although she was more than two years older than he was, David was only a year behind her because he had skipped three grades, and they went to the same junior high school. That afternoon, when David came home from Hebrew school, Joe Vecchione was in the backyard, leaning against the picket fence and watching the old men playing the game with the black balls. "Hello," David said shyly, not sure that Pop Vecchione's tall, thin-faced son would remember him from the night before.

"Hi, David," Joe said, mussing his hair. "Where've you been all afternoon?"

"Hebrew school."

"Oh. I used to go to one of those when I was your age."

"Hebrew school?" David asked, surprised, trying to imagine Joe's dark Italian face in the synagogue.

"No." Joe laughed. "Catholic school, but we learned the same kind of things."

"Oh, but you didn't study Talmud and Gemora," David said, certain it was different.

"No." Joe laughed again. "What's it like in your school?"

David told him about the Hebrew school, about Rabbi Eisner and Rebi Greenberg, and how he was studying Gemora and Rashi. He would have told him more, but Toni arrived.

"I thought you were going to wait for me after school, David," Toni said.

"I didn't know you wanted me to," David said, remembering how he had hesitated and gone on alone, because Toni was with some of the older boys and he was sure she didn't want to walk with him. "But I'll wait for you tomorrow," he offered eagerly, "if you want me to."

"Okay, then, it's a date."

The three of them went into the cellar to the victrola room, and after Joe played the record twice, David sang with it the third time, singing only the melody of *"Una furtiva lagrima"* because he didn't know the words. Afterward, Toni and Joe taught him to play an Italian card game, *brisca,* and he won seventeen cents from Joe, but wouldn't take it, not even when Toni assured him that Joe was a schoolteacher and could afford it.

After that, David came to expect their walk to and from school under the arches of the new, spring-green trees, enjoying the way people turned to look at Toni and the way the other boys in his class teased him about his "girl friend." As the silent spring days passed, David came to know the Vecchiones almost as well as his own family. Sometimes he almost wished he had been born into their family instead of his own, and when he did, he was ashamed and tried to be especially dutiful when his father asked him about Hebrew school, or when his mother wanted him to run an errand. With Mama Vecchione he always had fun. They sat together on the benches in the backyard, and David helped her clean the snap beans and cut them, or peel and slice potatoes, or mix the dough for cakes, rubbing it the way his mother had taught him, while Mama Vecchione sang the old songs she remembered from Italy, songs that vaguely reminded him of the Yiddish ones his mother sang. Sometimes he would sing her his mother's songs from the old country, because she would ask him to, and then ask her for the ones in Italian, the whirling dances she told him were called *tarantelle,* and the slow, stately ones that were like the victrola records. She sang them all in a low, breathy alto, like Toni's voice grown old, and he loved to listen. And always, Mama Vecchione fed him, saying, "You gotta eat, David. You gonna be big man." Although his father warned him about eating unkosher food and often complained to his mother that he would become a *shegetz,* a *goy,* from being always with the Italians downstairs, David liked to eat with the Vecchiones. He did not tell his parents that he ate the thick, doughy, butter-colored macaroni and spicy red sauce, the crisp beanlike chick-peas and salty anchovies, the earth-flavored lentils and bitter, crisp escarole, and the flat, dry provolone. But he did not eat their meat, the unkosher ham and pork and bacon whose fat, sweet smell made him sick.

In the dusky late afternoons, Carmine and Vito played baseball with him after they came from work, and Joe sat in the backyard with him after school and read from books David had never heard of. But the stories and poems touched him, as the victrola music had, and he would lie on the wooden bench and listen to Joe's quiet voice reading about other times and places. Sometimes, at night, they sat in the backyard, Vito with his concertina and Carmine with his guitar, and Mama Vecchione and he would sing, separately or together, in Italian or Yiddish or English, and Pop would clap his hands and stamp his feet, and Joe would drum with his fingers. Only Johnny Strigari, when he was there, was quiet, smoking his dark-smelling cigars. Toni would sing too, in her summery-soft voice, the lonely little Italian songs that hurt in his throat, and the others would grow quiet, their faces soft and open as they watched her. He knew they all loved Toni in a special way, perhaps because she was a girl, or because she was so beautiful, but in a way that made all their dark faces light when she sang and tossed her wild yellow hair. Once, Joe said they loved her best because she was their hope. David asked him what that meant, but Joe only smiled and went back to reading him a poem. The way they looked at him when he sang was good too, and he knew they liked him, as he liked them, but with Toni it was different, especially for Pop, who looked at her in a way he couldn't describe, except that Pop always seemed straighter when he did, and his old body seemed for a moment younger.

And it was with Pop he liked most to be. Sometimes, in the afternoon, David helped him in the garden, while the old man showed him corn and cabbages and his prize tomatoes. Or Pop took him to watch the old men playing the game with the black balls, called *boccie,* and even gave him a sip of the sour Chianti they drank. And with him, David felt at home.

Other times, he went to the Vecchione cellar by himself, and played the old victrola and sang along with the melodies. Soon he knew the names on the records as well as the music: *La Traviata, La Forza del Destino, La Bohème, Il Trovatore;* but most of all, he liked *The Pearl Fishers'* aria, and he played the record over and over again until he knew it by heart.

One evening, when he had already eaten at the Vecchiones' and couldn't get his mother's dinner down, his father looked first at him and then at his mother. "He is eating unkosher food, Leah," his father said heavily.

David shook his head, not daring to speak, but he knew his father did not believe him. His mother, not speaking, took the plate away from in front of him.

"Always he is down there with *them,* singing and making a fool of himself, just like them. He will grow up to be a taxi driver or a house painter."

David was surprised that his father knew Carmine was a taxi driver and Vito and Johnny Strigari were house painters. But why didn't he say that Joe was a teacher, too?

"The boy is lonely, and there are young people there. It is good," his mother said in his defense. "And he learns about the earth and planting from the old one."

"Who will teach him Talmud there, and Jewishness?" his father asked, and no one answered. "They will teach him to sing their music, and for the holy songs his mouth will be unkosher and dumb."

David wanted to tell his father that he loved the cantillations and the holy songs, that they were as sweet in his mouth and throat as the other music. But he was sure his father didn't care about that, as long as he could tell his friends that his son David sang with Cantor Barrt, and was even a soloist at weddings.

The week the magnolia tree's roof of white blossoms fell into the garden and petals skipped on the pavements, David's father came home and said he was to study with Cantor Barrt. And so, in the afternoons, while the azaleas were red and then blew off in the spring winds and rains, David went to Cantor Barrt's house to practice and study. It was a green and white wooden house with a wide front porch, where David waited until the cantor was ready and called him into the long, red-carpeted living room to practice scales and the cantorial melodies for the Sabbath and the High Holy Days, but most of all the songs that he hated, the songs for the weddings: "I love you truly, truly dear.... Because God made thee mine, I'll cherish thee. . . . O promise me that some day you and I. . . . When the dawn breaks in the sky, I love you...." And Cantor Barrt accompanied him at the mahogany grand piano, correcting him, teaching him, but never quite talking *to* him, until David felt like a victrola the cantor had wound up and was listening to, his head tilted to one side, his gray hair showing beneath his black skullcap, his big curved nose quivering when he sang bass corrections to David's soprano mistakes.

When he was finished, David raced home and into the Vecchione cellar to try to wipe away the memory of the wedding songs by listening to the victrola, or playing *brisca* with Toni or Joe, or learning to play *boccie* with Pop and then helping him with his tomato vines, tying the stalks up on sticks. But it was like trying to drink the sour taste of Parmesan cheese out of his mouth with water, or even wine; he couldn't do it.

Often, when the spring was full outside, David lay awake in bed, tasting the sourness in his mouth and wishing he never had to go to Cantor Barrt's again. And one night when he could not sleep, he went to sit at the window. The moon was low and heavy and golden in the violet sky, and a pale gold mist was on the fields and the twisted flowering peach trees near the *boccie* alley. David opened the window quietly and leaned out, enjoying the soft, wet night air and the spring mist that had no chill. As he was looking up at the faraway specks of stars, he thought he heard rustling and a whisper light as the mist, and when he looked down he was sure there were shadows in the stairwell that led to the Vecchione cellar. For an instant, David thought there was a flash of yellow hair and he called, "Toni?" in a soft, hoarse whisper, but there was no answer, and when he leaned farther out of the window, he could see no one there.

In the morning, walking to school, David asked, "Was that you in the backyard last night?"

Toni turned to him, her face very straight, and then, in a minute, grinning and mussing his hair, asked, "Now what would I be doing in the backyard last night?"

"I thought maybe you couldn't sleep—like me."

"I sleep fine," Toni answered, "not like you. I don't have all your brains to keep me awake."

When the term was in its last week and Pop's tomatoes were red-ripe on the vine, Toni was late one morning and they had to hurry. Halfway to school, her dark face went pale and loose and sick. Then, suddenly, she stopped and leaned over a garden hedge they were passing. David took her books and turned away as he heard her gasp. When she turned back from the hedge, her forehead glistened damp and her eyes were frightened. David wiped her forehead and her mouth gently with his handkerchief, and they stood together quietly, Toni, soft and still smelling of sleep, leaning heavily against him.

"You want me to go home with you?" David asked.

"I'll be all right in a minute," Toni managed in a hidden voice.

Walking home after school, Toni was quiet. David tried to tease and joke with her, as he usually did, but she didn't seem to hear him. After his singing lesson, he ran all the way home, but in the cellar, Toni was in the victrola room with Johnny Strigari, her cheeks hot-looking and her yellow hair tangled. Even Johnny's wet black hair was mussed, and when David ran in, he jumped up from the couch next to Toni and said, "Don't you ever knock before you come in?"

"What?" David asked, not understanding why Johnny seemed so angry.

"Nothing," Toni said. "Johnny's joking."

"Oh."

"It's having the afternoon off that makes him so funny," Toni said, smiling with a stiff mouth.

After a moment, David asked, "Are you okay now, Toni?"

Johnny wheeled, his usual little black cigar unlit in his mouth, a match flickering in his hand. "What?"

"Oh, it's nothing," Toni said. "Just the *scallopini* Mama made last night. I didn't feel so good this morning, so I threw it up going to school."

"No! God, no!" Johnny said. "Is that the first time?"

"No. That's what's funny," Toni said thoughtfully. "I've been feeling like that in the mornings now, every day, here." She placed her long tanned hand under her heart. "But it goes away, usually, after lunch."

"Holy Mother!" Johnny Strigari exclaimed. He threw his cigar on the floor and stamped on it with his feet, grinding the tobacco into the rug. "Holy Mother!"

The next morning, while he was waiting for Toni to come out and walk to school, David saw Mama Vecchione there instead. Her face was stiff, as if she had just pressed it into shape with her hands before opening the door, and her eyes were swollen and red. "You no wait for my Antoinette," she said, not looking at him. "She no go to school today."

"Toni's sick?"

"Yeh, she sick."

"Tell her I'll come to see her after school," David said. "And I'll tell Miss Kendall she's sick and get her home-work."

"You no see her. You no say nothing to teach," Mama Vecchione said flatly. "She no go school no more." Then the old woman turned, her eyes still faraway, and walked slowly back into the house.

David stood there, wanting to run after her and ask what was wrong. Was she angry with him? He had done nothing. At least, he couldn't remember anything he had done. In school he couldn't sit still all day. He missed his recitation in Latin and got a zero for not paying attention in history, as well as a zero in algebra for not working two examples at the blackboard. That afternoon, he couldn't concentrate on Cantor Barrt's teaching. When they re-hearsed "O Promise Me," he laughed out loud because again the cantor sang: "Those first sweet *w*iolets of early spring," and was so angry when David sang "*v*iolets" that he hit David's knuckles with the baton he always kept on the piano. But the pain was less than what he had seen and felt in Mama Vecchione's face that morning. Toni was in trouble. Toni needed help. The Vecchiones were all in trouble and needed help. But what trouble he didn't know, or what he could do to help.

It was raining when he left the cantor's house, and he walked slowly through the rain, letting it soak through his jacket and hair and run down his face. The clouds were low over the housetops, and it was almost dark when he slipped quietly into the Vecchione cellar. No one heard him. There, near the green-shaded yellow light, Pop and Joe were standing with their backs to him, and Carmine and Vito were holding Johnny Strigari, facing them. John-ny's face was ashen, his black hair plastered over his forehead, and one eye was closed and purplish. His thick lips were cut and his bared teeth bloodied.

"Why you do it?" Pop was asking. "You live with us. We treat you like son. Why? Why you had to do to us?"

"Aw, what's the use of talking, Pop?" Carmine said. "Let Vito and me finish up what we started."

"I no want you touch him," the old man said. "You unnerstand? I no want you put finger on Johnny. He gonna marry you sister."

"You're crazy." Joe spoke for the first time. "He's no good. Send him away, and we'll take Toni to a doctor."

"He'sa no good. You right, Joe. But no take my Antoinette, my little girl, to doctor. He gonna marry—"

"That's what you think," Johnny began, but Vito hit him and Carmine held his arms.

The old man said something to Joe that David couldn't hear, and then to Vito and Carmine, "No hit him no more, I say!"

"But, Pop," Joe protested, "Toni's a baby. She's not even sixteen yet. You can't make her marry. You'll ruin her life. She's too young."

"Ina old country, is old enough to marry twelve years."

"This isn't the old country," Joe insisted.

Johnny began to struggle, shouting, "I ain't gonna, you hear. I ain't! I ain't! She wanted to as much as I did. It's . . . ."

The old man stepped up and slapped him once, sharp across the mouth. "Shaddup. Shaddup. You hear. You no talk about my Toni. And no make so much noise. You gonna go upastairs now and tell Mama and Toni."

"Pop," Joe said, stepping between the old man and Johnny Strigari. "You just got to listen to me. You can't do this. Toni's your only daughter. You can't make her marry this . . . this . . . She didn't know what she was doing—" Joe broke off.

"No know?" the old man laughed, painful and rasping. "She not too young for . . ." he said something in Italian that David did not understand. "She not too young." There was a moment of quiet. "No more talk now. We go upastairs."

Between them, Carmine and Vito forced Johnny up the stairs and Pop and Joe followed, Joe still talking, pleading, until their footsteps and voices faded into the apartment upstairs, and David could not hear anything anymore. They had not even noticed him. For a long time, he stood there in the puddle of rain that had dripped around his shoes from his wet clothes, trying to figure out what he had seen. Then he went out into the rain, around to the front of the house and up to his own apartment. His mother was preparing supper, and was angry because he was soaked to the skin. She sent him to his bedroom to change into dry clothing, and David heard her in the kitchen, singing to herself an old Jewish song about a man going home to the house he had lived in as a boy and finding everything strange, and no one in his hometown who remembered him.

When his father came home, David saw that he was troubled. He did not say *"Shalom,"* nor did he kiss the *mezuzah* on the doorjamb when he came through the doorway. His mother, too, knew immediately and asked in Yiddish, "What is, Jakob?"

"Nothing, Leah, nothing."

"Tell me what is, Jakob. I know something goes badly."

"Ach! It is the old Italian from downstairs. My heart is twisted for him," his father said, taking his wet coat off slowly and heavily and hanging it on the open closet door to dry. "The boarder, the dark one, has led away his daughter."

"She is?"

"What else? Yuh."

"I should go down. . . ."

"No, Leah, it is not our business. We should not mix in." And after a moment, "The old one makes them married."

"That is not wise. She is so young, too young."

"Sure. Of course, it is not wise," his father replied abruptly, and it seemed to David, unreasonably angrily. "And what else should he do? He should make them a party?"

"He should maybe help the girl to—"

"Ssha! The small one doesn't understand."

And David knew they were talking deliberately so that he could not understand, and he hated it. Although he did not understand, he said loudly, "I do so understand," but when his parents coaxed him to say more, to say what he understood, he would stubbornly say no more.

He sat in his bedroom alone for a long time, unable to hear what his parents were saying, but from the rise and fall of their voices, he knew they were talking about the Vecchiones. One sentence floated into his room in his father's voice. "We should not mix ourselves in." Downstairs, there were strange noises from the open windows, shouting and crying and heavy falling noises, like furniture being moved. Out on the *boccie* field the old men came like shadows, gathered in little knots under the night-lights, their brown hands flying, their heads turned toward the Vecchiones' house, and then went away without rolling the little black balls.

Later, when the light in his parents' room went out, David sneaked downstairs in his pajamas. Quietly, he scratched at the Vecchiones' door. There was a sudden silence behind it, then a whispering, before the door was opened a crack, and Joe's thin, dark face looked out.

"It's me, David."

For a moment, Joe stood there, looking at him as if he were a stranger. "Go back upstairs," he said finally, in a slow, choked voice.

David opened his mouth to speak, but Joe was suddenly seeing him, recognizing him, mussing his hair and saying: "It's got nothing to do with you, David. You're still our little friend. Now, go back to bed." He gave him a slight pat on the cheek. "Go on, there isn't anything you can do," Joe said, and then softly closed the door. David stole back upstairs to his bedroom, wondering how to get to Pop and tell him what he felt and how he wanted to help.

In the middle of the night he awoke suddenly, feeling feverishly hot, and unaware that noises had awakened him until he heard sounds like the faraway chopping of trees. At the open window he saw Pop Vecchione out in the fields, bent double, head down, with a hoe in his hand, furiously beating another row of his tomatoes into bloody splotches on the moon-pale earth. David wanted to shout to him, to call out his comfort, assure Pop that everything would be all right, just as it used to be. As he watched the hoe flash in the moonlight, he wished he could sing out— something, anything!—loud and clear and strong, like a pulse up toward the blind eyes of the stars and down to the jackknifed figure of the old man. He remembered the music they had listened to together, the music the old man had taught him about, and the sounds of the aria from *The Pearl Fishers* went singing themselves through his head, but now the aria was filled with torn and broken sounds, as if it were being sobbed, not sung. Strangely, in his mind, it seemed less like the smooth Italian sadness of the aria and more like the bitter Hebraic mourning of *Eli, Eli* . . . *"God, O God, why hast thou forsaken me?"* And then he knew that no song would help, nothing he could do for or say to Pop Vecchione would help. He heard his father's running footsteps behind and felt his deep-breathing, sleep-warm figure behind his back, but he could not turn to him to speak.

So he stood staring out at the old man and the *boccie* alley, the strange tangle of *The Pearl Fishers* and *Eli, Eli* a dark flame in his mind and a bitterness in his mouth and throat, until he saw his father, looking like a scarecrow in his flapping bathrobe and white skullcap, climb the backyard picket fence and run across the furrowed field to the old man. When he got there, David saw him take the hoe from Pop Vecchione's hands and throw it to the ground. Then he began to help the old man across the field back to the house. Together they went over the fence, his father almost lifting the old man over the pickets, and finally, when they were beneath the window, in the darkness of the stairwell, David heard the crushed crying of the old man and his father's "Sssha," sounding as it had when as a child he had awakened from a nightmare and his father had come to comfort him.

And now, in the silence of the night, he was frightened, cold and trembling. Beneath the twisted peach trees, the black *boccie* balls looked strange and ominous, and the tomatoes on the ground were spattered blood. He felt someone behind him and when he turned, his father was there, smiling down and patting his shoulder.

"The old man, Pop, is all right now. And Toni will be too, maybe," his father murmured quietly. "Come to bed now, my son. There is nothing more to be done."

David got into bed and covered himself, aware that his father had called the Vecchiones by their first names for the first time, names David hadn't even known his father knew, because his father had always called them "they." In the doorway, his father stopped and looked back, and David could not see his face clearly in the darkness, but he could hear his words plainly: "It will be very hard for them. We will do what we can." Then, with the warmth and gratitude for his father in him sudden and intense as pain, David heard the sharp closing of his door, and the silence of the night thickened and the night went slowly back to sleep.

Although he knew it had been on for three years and had read about it in the newspapers he had to clip every day for his civics class, a thing he had been doing ever since grammar school, it seemed it was only that spring after school was over that David heard the word *Depression*. The word was familiar, like a song he had known and forgotten or a word spoken by a familiar voice in another room, but he couldn't quite place it. But this time it remained in his mind because his father had spoken it bitterly in a Yiddish sentence, and the English word stood out like a piece of broken glass stuck in the smooth top of a wall. It had come up at the dinner table when his mother said, "Maybe we should send him to camp for a few weeks, Jakob?"

"With what?" his father replied curtly, between spoonfuls of potato soup and dumplings. "With my troubles?"

"It would be better now, especially," his mother's voice lowered, "with the downstairs one having the baby."

"Sure, Leah." His father nodded. "It would be better. It would be better also if there was no Depression."

"What's a depression?" David asked, looking up from his dumplings. He didn't care about the camp, but he wondered why he couldn't go and what this depression had to do with it.

His father stared at him for a long while in the undecided way he had when he wasn't sure whether to give a grown-up's answer or a child's. Slowly, he ran his big hand around his mouth, smoothing his mustache and his beard into shape, and then pushed his skullcap back on his head, as he always did when he was thinking or studying. "It's when there is not enough work for people," he said in Yiddish, "and they cannot earn enough money for their families. Then there is much unhappiness."

At the fence after supper, watching the old men play *boccie* in the warm spring evening, David asked Joe Vecchione what a depression was.

"Which kind?" Joe asked.

"Are there different kinds?" David answered, surprised.

"Well, there are at least two kinds, anyway," Joe said. "One is when business is bad, and the other is when you feel bad in here." He touched his heart and then his head.

"You mean, like Pop and Mama Vecchione since . . . since—" but he couldn't finish the sentence and he stopped, seeing Joe's face move and his eyes go past into the dark. David remembered the day Toni and Johnny Strigari had been married, how beautiful she looked in her white dress and veil, and how he had sneaked over to the Catholic church to throw rice at her and Johnny Strigari, not telling his parents, because they wouldn't like his being at a church. He remembered the Vecchiones' faces, all of them stiff and white as his mother's starched Sabbath tablecloths, and old, bent-over Pop Vecchione looking more than ever like a half-open penknife. Only Joe had seemed alive to him that day, only Joe's face a real face that he knew, and it had been twisted and crying.

Joe looked down at him and tousled his hair. "You're a pretty moxie kid, aren't you?"

"Moxie?" David asked, not quite listening, but glad Joe's face had come back.

"Well, this is a vocabulary lesson today, isn't it? It's an old word I liked when I was a kid. It means, well, it's being smart and seeing things other people don't see."

David smelled the old man even before he knew he was standing there beside him, the smell of earth and tobacco and garlic, and then he saw the earth-colored hands close around the pickets next to him, silently bunching until the knuckles showed white. They stood there, the three of them, looking out across the tomatoes and cabbages greening in the furrowed field to the hard, foot-beaten ground where the old men played *boccie* under the lights. One, the fat Ferrara, stood under the peach trees next to the tables and the umbrella and waved his hand. His voice in the night air and from the distance came small from a man so big and fat.

Beside him, out of the corner of his eye, David saw one of Pop's hands open around the picket, a single opening of the fingers as if an invisible bird had flown quickly out of his hand. A puff of smoke from the corncob pipe came past his ear too, but no words, no sounds. David waited for the old man to say something, hoping it would be as it had been before, before Toni and Johnny Strigari had done something that Toni was being punished for. She'd been married to Johnny and was having a baby. He could tell she was being punished by the way none of them except Joe—Pop and Mama Vecchione, Carmine and Vito, and even the neighbors—talked about Toni, and the way she didn't come out of the house to shop, or sit in the backyard, or play *brisca* with him, or sing, as she used to. Even when he came down to the cellar, it was different. Old Pop spoke less to him and played the victrola more and more, the slow, sad Italian songs, never the quick *tarantelle,* and Mama Vecchione never sang them anymore in the soft, hoarse voice that was like Toni's. Pop still asked him to sing often, the sad, hurting songs in Yiddish he knew from his mother and the mournful ancient Hebrew cantillations. The old man did not play *boccie* with the old Italian men who were his friends, or sit drinking with them the sour, dry Chianti from the green bottles in the straw baskets. His voice no longer joined their high-pitched arguing about the black balls under the twisted peach trees and laughing, laughing, in the quiet nights.

"Hola," the sound of Ferrara's voice came again,

closer, and then at the fence. Mr. Ferrara had his big blue plaid handkerchief out and was mopping the sweat from his big face and the shaking chins that made him look like he had the mumps. "How'sa by you?" he asked Pop, nodding at the same time to Joe and David.

Pop shrugged and took the pipe out of his mouth. "More or less," he said in a dry voice, "only more or less."

"Is bad with us. No jobs nowhere. In winter is for shovel snow. Now, long time, is nothing. Is gonna be long time Depression, you think?"

Pop blew a puff of pipe smoke across the pickets toward Mr. Ferrara and said between his teeth, "Aska the teach. My Joe, he got answer fa everythin'."

While Mr. Ferrara looked at Joe, his eyes shadowed with worry and too close together in the big face, David heard Joe's voice explain that the Depression would last a long time, and wondered if Joe meant the inside depression or the outside. Jobs were hard to get, Joe was saying, and it would probably get worse, although maybe this new President, Roosevelt, would help.

"What this country needs is Mussolini," Johnny Strigari said from behind them. David turned and saw Johnny leaning against the wall of the house, smoking one of his little dark cigars, his black hair and white teeth shining wet in the moonlight. "He's going pretty good in the old country. Maybe he's gonna give us a hand here."

"Mebbe you right," Mr. Ferrara said, wiping his shaking chins again. His cousin in Naples had written to him, he said, to tell him to come back to the old country. The *Duce* was making a new *Italia,* new houses, new roads, new plenty of jobs. But he was too old, though maybe his boys would go.

"Sure," Johnny Strigari said, "that Mussolini's one big man. He knows what he's doing, all right."

"You betcha my life," Mr. Ferrara said, holding his chins with the blue handkerchief as if he could keep them from shaking and sweating.

"That's just what you'd be doing, betting your life, if you went back to Italy," Joe said.

"Big man, *Duce,* he give plenty . . . castor oil. Old country look good . . . from new country," Pop Vecchione said between pipe puffs. "You wanna work this country, you find work. Only lazy like him"—he shook his head at Johnny Strigari, not turning, his back stiff to him—"no work. Even old man like me work, an' work steady."

"Whaddyu want?" Johnny Strigari rose. "I go out look-

ng every day, don' I? I can't find nuthin'. I paint rooms,
houses. Nobody's paintin' now, nobody's buildin' now.
Nobody's got no money. Everybody's damn glad if they
got enough money for rent and eats."

"You wan' work, you find," Pop repeated.

"It's not so easy, Pop," Joe said softly. "The Ferraras
can't find jobs. All the Andreozzis are out of work except
Mario. The Di Stefanos are on relief. The Scaleses closed
up the barbershop last week. No more customers, no more
money. People are cutting their hair in the house."

"Big talk. All time big talk. He'sa lazy. No wanna
work. He'sa married man. Gonna be Poppa soon. What he
does?" the old man was shouting. "Sit ina cella, smoke Di
Napoli cigars."

"Your boys ain't doin' no better," Johnny Strigari said
angrily. "Sure, Joe's got his teachin' job, but even he ain't
got no summer-school job this year. And Vito ain't paintin' no more houses than me. And cabbies ain't makin' no
hay either, so Carmine ain't gettin' no pickups. People's
takin' the train or the trolley car, even walkin'. Your Vito
and Carmine lazy, too?"

Slowly, Pop turned from the picket fence and took his
pipe from his mouth. He looked at Johnny Strigari, first at
his shoes, then at his belt buckle, his face, and finally over
his head, as if he saw something on the building behind
him, and for a moment David, following his glance,
thought he caught a glimpse of yellow hair behind the
window shade.

"They single," the old man hissed. "They no married."

Johnny Strigari threw his black cigar down and ground
the bright, hot ember with his heel into the concrete.
"You're right. They're single and I wish I was, too." His
voice went flat and hard. "And I would be, too, if it
wasn't for your dumb ideas."

"You . . . you!" Pop spat and lunged at him like a
jackknife suddenly sprung open, but Joe was there between them and held the old man. Pop pushed against his
son's arms. "I show you," he rasped at Johnny.

"Go for a walk," Joe pleaded with Johnny, "will you?"

"Fa Chrissakes," Johnny Strigari answered, "look at
him, will ya? The old guy thinks he's Jack Sharkey."

Pop threw himself against Joe's arms again and his pipe
went clattering on the concrete.

"Go on," Joe yelled, "get out of here and go for a
walk!"

"Awright, dammit, awright," Johnny said. He turned and went down the alleyway.

They stood that way, the old man straining against Joe's arms, Mr. Ferrara, eyes wide, holding his shaking chins, until Johnny Strigari's footsteps died away in the quiet night. Then Pop Vecchione slumped down, a jackknife snapped shut, and Joe let him free. David picked up the stained corncob from the concrete and handed it to him. Pop stretched his hand out, and as David handed him the still-warm bowl, patted his head. "You good boy, David," he said. Without looking either at Joe or Mr. Ferrara, he grinned weakly and whispered, "Come on, we go see our frien'." It was their joke about the victrola, the *musica* that Pop Vecchione had told him was their best friend.

They went down through the back entrance into the cellar, to the front room where the old victrola stood. Pop went to it, bent over the dark-bellied front, his big hands taking records out, then gently putting them on the turn-table and starting one. When the first cat-scratching sounds began, he came to sit next to David on the couch. The music began softly, and then the room was filled with *"Cruda funesta smania tu m'hai svegliato in petto!"* It was *Lucia di Lammermoor* and its "Torments of hate and vengeance now in my heart awaken!" and then "If thou plead'st for her, I scorn thee, cast thee from me...." As David read the English, from the record notes, Pop sat, his white head in his earth-colored hands, listening, and each time he got up to change a record, David saw the glisten-ing wetness of his palms as he tensed them open and wiped them on his trousers, and could not tell whether it was sweat or tears. After the music was done, it was still in the room until he heard Toni come in, and behind her Joe's careful, heavier footsteps—and then the music was gone.

The old man went stiff next to him, his face frozen down around the pipe and then turned up from his hands like a dark flower. "Whaddyu here fa?" he asked.

Toni said hello to David, that she thought it was he singing, but she said nothing to her father.

"I'm fine," David said, his face warm. "How are *you?*" But he saw how she was, her wild yellow hair darker and pulled back behind her ears, so her face seemed longer and thinner and paler, and her eyes like a darkness in the streets. Her body was thick as Mr. Ferrara's, and she walked slowly, as if she were tired. She sat down with a sigh and Joe took a chair near hers, his eyes turned toward her. The needle scratched on the record, and when he couldn't stand the quiet and the scratching, David stopped the victrola. "Miss Kendall asked about you in school," he said, "and lots of the kids, too. They wanted to know if you would come back next term."

Toni laughed, hoarse and coughing. "No," she said, "not next term, or the term after, or ever."

"But you didn't graduate," David protested. "You won't get your diploma."

"She'sa graduate. She'sa gotta big diplom," Pop said, deliberately staring at her belly.

"Sing something for us, David," Joe said, too quickly.

"Yes," Toni added, "I haven't heard you sing for a long time."

David looked at the old man, still puffing the tobacco alight in his pipe, and Pop nodded permission. "You wanna sing, you sing. You gotta sometin' sing fa, you sing."

The song he wanted to sing was lively but it did not sound right in his head, and instead he sang an old Yiddish song his mother always sang when she was very tired:

> Belz, my little village Belz,
> My small hometown, where I spent
> My childhood years so long ago. . . .
>
> Every Sabbath I used to run
> Straightaway from the synagogue home,
> Just to sit on the bright green grass
> Over near the old great stone. . . .
>
> Have you ever been to Belz?
>
> The eaves are crooked,
> The walls are out of plumb,
> You'd never know it now,
> Belz, my hometown Belz,
> Where long ago I spent
> The years of my childhood.

Vito came in as he was singing the last stanza, and Pop sat up straight and stopped listening. When he was through, Joe and Toni applauded softly and Toni, in her summery voice, said, "Beautiful, beautiful." But as Vito turned to go, the old man called to him.

"Yeh, Pa," Vito answered, cupping his hands over both ears to slick his black hair back so that for a minute it looked as if he were covering his ears so he wouldn't have to listen to what Pop was going to say. Then he turned.

"I heah," the old man said hoarsely, pointing his corncob with its wisp of smoke at Vito, "you hangin' ona corner with Giuseppe Russo and Mario Pastore. Whaddyu gonna be, painter or gangster, ha?"

"Joe Russo and Mario are okay," Vito said, looking down at his shoes. "Whaddyu want me to do? Sit around here all day and play *boccie* with the old men?"

"I like you look fa job, *paintin'!*"

"How many times did I tell you there ain't no paintin' jobs nowhere. Ask Johnny, he'll tell ya, too."

"You gonna be lazy like him, you no gonna stay my house. My boy no gonna be whatchumacallit—candy-store cowboy. No gangster, neither."

"Aw, let me alone, will ya?" Vito yelled, and rushed out of the room. His footsteps rang on the stairs up to the Vecchione apartment.

There was silence again until Joe said, "Go easy on him, Pa. He's only a kid. It's hard on him without a job, no money for girls or for an extra pack of cigarettes."

"Alla time you go easy. You big smart teach. Look ina lotta books, but go easy"—he pointed to Toni, sitting with her hands folded over her big belly—"you getta that."

Toni looked at him and began to cry. The tears ran down her cheeks, her mouth trembled, her body shook, but there was no word, no sound. Nor did the old man's face change from its set lines. Joe reached slowly over and put his arm around her, turned her still-wild yellow hair against his shoulder to hide her face, and patted her back and shoulders.

The next morning, in the synagogue with his father, when David was saying the morning service, "Blessed are Thou, O Lord our God, King of the Universe, who has not made me a woman," and thinking of Toni and her sound-less tears, he was grateful for being able to speak the line. The next prayer was a blessing to the Lord for opening the eyes of the blind, but his own eyes were caught on the line before, which only women said, "Blessed are Thou, O Lord our God, King of the Universe, who has made me according to Thy will." In Yiddish, David asked his father, "Papa, why do we thank God for not making us women, and women thank Him only for making them according to His will?"

His father looked down at him, his face once again

deciding between the serious and childish answers, and said irritably, "Men thank God that they do not have to endure the pain of childbirth."

"But the Lord said, 'Be fruitful and multiply,' so women giving birth should be good."

"Pray! Pray!" his father said impatiently, and David knew he would not answer further because he was worried. What about, David didn't know, but as he let the prayers speak themselves out of his mouth, having said them so often they seemed almost not to make words or sense, David wondered if his father too was worried about the Depression.

After the synagogue, they walked back to the house under the green arch of spring trees. By the way his father held his prayer sack, shifting it from one hand to another, squeezing it between his fingers as if to make sure that the prayer shawl and prayer book and phylacteries were still inside, David knew he was upset. He felt his own fingers begin nervously to probe his own blue velvet, yellow-starred sack, but he knew that speaking would only make his father angry and that he would give answers as though to a child, the hard, foolish answers that David knew meant not to ask more questions.

Only after breakfast, when his mother, not speaking, had finished serving them hot farina with butter melting into it and coffee, did he understand. His father stood up, rubbed his hands together as if washing them, went to the room where he studied, and quietly closed the door. His mother stood staring at the door with her face open and hurting, and David asked, "Is Papa sick?" although he knew the answer already.

She shook her head.

"Isn't he going to work today?"

Her face and eyes came away from the door gradually to look at him, and again, very slowly, she shook her head. She took the coffeepot, brought it to the table and poured herself a cup. "There is no work," she said heavily, looking over his head at the wall, and, almost as if to herself, she added in Yiddish, "The work has flown away."

It was the same almost every morning after that, except when, because he had slept late, he said the morning prayer at home and did not go with his father to the synagogue, or on the few days his father did have some work. Those days, his steps from the synagogue were quicker and longer so that David had to run to keep up, and there was no shifting of the prayer sack and groping for prayer shawl, book and phylacteries. But those days were few, and his father was slower and slower walking from the synagogue, staying longer and longer in the room with his books. More and more of his friends, also out of work, came to study with him, but it was not like the old days, when their voices would rise singsong through the house like a wind of joy and remind him of the happiness of *Adon Olam*, when Sabbath services were ending. Even with the words muffled by the thick closed door, their voices were now like the weak wind crying in the spring nights before rain.

In the afternoons, he went to Chazan Barrt's to practice. There were weddings, many weddings, in the spring, now that Lag b'Omer was over, and Barrt took him through the songs he hated. "Diaphragma," he would shout, ". . . *because you speak to me in accents sweet,*" his bass voice boomed. "From here! here!" He slapped his stomach, held his big nose, then twisted his face and said, as if he had a cold in his head, "Not from there. Now, once more, Dovid. Sing as if yourself were in love." He grinned, his big, tobacco-stained teeth over his lip. "Love"—he pronounced it *luff*—"you are old enough already to know what that means, no?" He struck the tuning fork, held it, vibrating, to his hairy ear, then hummed, "Hmmm! Begin." And David sang,

> Because God made thee mine, I'll cherish thee,
> And hold your hands and lift mine eyes above. . . .
>
> Because you speak to me in accents sweet.
> I find the roses waiting at my feet. . . .

He enjoyed rehearsing the synagogue cantillations, and often when he sang with the choir, solo or in chorus, or even in duet with Chazan Barrt, all of him seemed to be music, air, floating, flying. But always he had to return to "O Promise Me" and "When the Dawn Flames in the Sky."

Saturday and Sunday nights he sang at three or four weddings, and sometimes two or three more on Sunday afternoons. He sang everywhere, from Brooklyn to the Bronx, and in Jersey and on Long Island, and he went however he could, in Chazan Barrt's square-nosed Huppmobile, by subway, train or taxi, alone, with the whole choir, with Barrt, or with other soloists and musicians and rabbis, and they all seemed strangers to him, their faces blurred and their names jumbled in his memory. He grew to hate the smoke and the noise and the sentimental songs with a bitterness he could taste and barely keep out of his singing. Sometimes his "first sweet violets of early spring" sounded sarcastic to his own ears, and he could see Chazan Barrt's nostrils quiver at the sound, so he had to force his voice to sing true.

There were tiny cramped chapels with folding chairs, row upon row on bare floors, and huge, red-carpeted synagogues with polished wooden seats and pews rising in banks. Here there were flowers—gardenias, gladiolas, roses—around the altar, in wicker baskets on the aisles, around the menorahs and the lights; there they were bare and naked-looking. At some, there were bridesmaids in flowing bright gowns and ushers in somber tuxedoes and tails or morning coats, little flower girls and page boys; at others, only the bride and groom, without even parents to lead them to the altar and cry for them. There were well-dressed and clean-shaven, dirty caftans with earlocks and beards uncombed, men and women mixing, men and women separate, food and no food, music and no music, but all of it seemed the same—and ugly. It was like a show with everyone looking. Only one sameness gave him real pleasure: the altar and the marriage canopy before the Ark of the Covenant, and the burning, blood-red eternal light that made all the rest seem frayed and shabby and artificial.

The rabbi would intone the marriage ceremonial and the cantor would chant, and the choir, and he, as soloist, would sing out. The people would turn to see him in his white skullcap and robe, going "oh" and "ah," like an organ being warmed, saying in Yiddish or in English, "Isn't he sweet . . . cute . . . a darling . . . sings like an angel . . . just like Yossele Rosenblatt." Sometimes they spoke in languages he recognized as Russian or German or Hungarian but did not understand, yet he knew all the same what their words meant. He hated their staring and talking, and most of all he hated their foolishness in comparing him to the great cantor whose voice in the cantillations was as wonderful as the voice of Caruso on Pop Vecchione's records.

Many of the weddings were at Chazan Barrt's house because that was cheaper than most of the wedding halls, and now everyone was suffering from the Depression. On the first floor of his house, Barrt had a brown-carpeted living room with many chairs where he performed the ceremony under a tiny *chuppah*. In the back room the receptions were held. There, huge tables were set up, planked tops on wooden saw horses covered with tablecloths, and then loaded with food: mounds of honey cake, seedcake, sponge cake; pyramids of *gefilte* fish, layers of smoked salmon, whitefish and carp; boats in which pickled, tomato and *schmaltz* herrings lay; and long braids of *challah*, yellow with eggs on the inside and covered with caraway seeds on the brown crusts. But Chazan Barrt wouldn't let them eat any of it. There was never enough, he said, either for him or for the other choirboys, even when they had been there all day, singing at three or four ceremonies. Chazan Barrt sent them to the cellar to play cards, or read tattered old Nick Carters and Frank Merriwells, or sit, doing nothing but waiting for the next wedding. . . .

David had rehearsed all morning and half the afternoon, with Chazan Barrt more irritable than usual, shouting, making him repeat phrases until he was hoarse, his mouth parched, and he couldn't hear his voice any longer. Sonny Richter and Nadie Rosen were on Sonny's stoop playing Seven and a Half when he came up, and Nadie was asking, "You got the King of Matz?"

"Well, look who's here," Sonny said, his melon-cheeked face split by a grin, "the boy cantor, Chazan Freed himself."

"Yeh," Nadie said, raking in the cards, "just in time for a game. Got any money?"

"No," David replied, "my father's not working," the words out of his mouth before he had considered them.

"Oh," Nadie said, shaking his head sympathetically, "too bad. Mine's been outta work for weeks . . . and weeks."

"Jeez, nobody's got money," Sonny said. "If my father didn't work for my uncle, he wouldn't have no job either. But he cut my allowance anyway."

"It's this Depression," David said.

"Depression?" Nadie asked.

"Sure," Sonny said. "Don't you remember Miss Lingaard telling us it's got something to do with the stock-market crash?"

"No," Nadie replied. "Where?"

"In civics class, yuh dope."

Nadie riffled the deck, let the cards fan out in one hand, then flipped them together, riffled again, and made the cards jump from his right hand to his left in a stream. "Pretty good, huh?" He looked up at them.

"Sure is," Sonny said respectfully. "Where'd yuh learn?"

"Oh, around."

"Come on, where?" Sonny persisted.

"You know those guys who hang around Jay's candy store? They play cards in the empty store next door— remember where the tailor store used to be?—they play cards, and sometimes I run an' get 'em cigarettes or maybe a three cents' seltzer, so they let me watch."

"They play for money?" Sonny asked.

"Sure, yuh dope, whaddyu expect 'em to play for, beer tops?"

"What games do they play?"

"Oh, poker and a game like Seven and a Half they call blackjack, but you gotta make twenty-one instead of seven and a half. And they play an Italian game—you know what I mean, Davie?"

"Brisca?"

"Yeh, *brisk*, that's it. You know how to play it?"

"No," David answered, not ready to say that he knew, because they might ask him to teach them, and he didn't want to. He wanted *brisca* to be the game between him and the Vecchiones.

"Toni's brother's the guy likes that game," Nadie said.

"You mean Vito?"

"Well, I don't mean your old man," Nadie replied, riffling the cards and beginning to deal them out. "Yeh, and I hear that your Toni's got herself knocked up, that boarder guy—what's his name?—with the black hair?"

"Johnny Strigari," David said, wondering what knocked up was, not asking, but waiting for Nadie to say more, so he'd have a clue. He looked at his cards. He had a four dark and a three showing. Sonny had a deuce showing, Nadie a jack.

"Pull for two," Sonny said.

Nadie threw the deck on the steps. "Nuts. What's the use of playing with you guys? You ain't got no money." He swept the deck and their cards together and slipped them all into his back pocket. Then he stood up. "Come on, let's go over to the schoolyard. Maybe we can get up a game of indoor or something."

The schoolyard gate was open because summer school had started. The handball courts were all filled, but they were choosing up an indoor game when they got to the diamond, and Fonzi had just thrown the bat to Banana

Nose to choose up sides. Mr. McLean was there too, watching, to see that they all got to play. He was the summer-school teacher in charge of the gym and the courts and the showers, and seeing him again for the first time that year, David was surprised at how red his hair was, how dark his freckles, so that his blue eyes seemed pale as the summer sky. He was skinny, not very tall, but strong, and the kids said he'd been a wrestling champ, but you couldn't tell because he never talked about it. Although he was Irish himself, he treated all the kids the same way: Irish, Italian, Scandinavian and Jew, and you could never tell which kids he liked. He umpired the games, refereed the fights, called balls and strikes, saying, "You play the game according to the rules," and repeating it when anyone questioned his decisions, as if that answered all the questions.

It was a good game, and David forgot about the Depression and Chazan Barrt and the weddings. He even forgot he was playing third base on Fonzi's team, with Sal and Petey on his side, and Banana Nose, Louie, and some of the other Forty Thieves on the other team. He got a triple and a single, and stole second on the single. Banana Nose got so sore when he did that he threw the ball past Louie, who was playing second, and David went all the way home for the run. When it was over and his team had won, David went to the shower room upstairs in the school building with the rest of the kids. In the showers, Fonzi was yelling to Banana Nose, "Them Jew boys play pretty good indoor, hah?"

"Lucky sheeny bastids," Banana Nose growled, soaping himself.

"Mebbe we can get 'em on our regular team," Fonzi went on.

"Yuh can have 'em," Banana Nose said, "in spades. They ony got sheeny luck."

"Luck your ass," Nadie Rosen called. "We beat the pants offa yuh. And we had plenty guineas on our team too, your pals Fonzi and Petey and Sal, fr'instance. You're just a sorehead."

"All right, you guys," Mr. McLean shouted from the towel room. "Cut out the dirty talk. It's a game, not a war. And get finished in there, you ain't got all day."

David was first out of the shower, and padded with quietly wet footsteps on the concrete floor into the locker room. Mr. McLean was putting something shiny back into his jacket, which hung in one of the dark-green metal gym lockers. David knew he was interrupting, and coughed to say he was there. Mr. McLean turned quickly and then, when he saw who it was, said, "You finished fast, didn't you? Hold it a minute." He rearranged his jacket, turned the pocket flap down, and closed the locker. Then he threw David a clean towel, and while David wiped himself, said, "You played a good game, David, especially that steal." And David felt warm inside, because Mr. McLean had remembered his name and said he had done well. He felt better than he had all day, his body tired, his muscles relaxed as they never were after rehearsing with Chazan Barrt.

In the street he waited for Sonny and Nadie. When they came down, Nadie said that Fonzi had told him what a good game they played, especially Davie, and he told them what Mr. McLean had said about stealing second.

"Aw, what the hell does that Irishman know?" Nadie said. "He drinks like a fish alla time."

"Whaddyu mean?" Sonny asked.

"Boy, you're dumb, Sonny. He drinks. You know, whiskey, *schnapps*." Nadie cupped his hand, brought it up to his mouth, threw his head back, then wiped his mouth with the back of his palm and said, trying to imitate Mr. McLean's brogue, "Aggh . . . that was pre—tty damn good."

Watching Nadie's little act, David understood what Mr. McLean had been putting into his coat pocket in the locker room, but it hadn't been the way Nadie did it.

At supper it was silent. His father had not worked for a long time and came to the table looking as if he had not slept, his eyes red and his hair uncombed. He made the blessings of washing the hands, of bread and wine, quickly, without enjoyment, as if the blessings were things he did not wish to speak. His mother served the soup. They'd been having soup a lot, and the thin slabs of farina his mother cooked, jelled, cut into cubes and dropped into the soup because "they were nourishing." David didn't mind, but his father disliked soup and had often said so. Lately, though, he had not remarked on how often they ate soup, and now he only leaned over it, looking into it as if he expected to find something, and then, not having found it, began to eat. "Nuh," his father said after a while, speaking with effort, "what did you do today?"

David told him about the rehearsal and the ball game, and though his father nodded, David knew he was not listening. After the potatoes and sour cream, his father asked, "Did the *chazan* pay you today for the weddings?"

"Yes," David replied, upset because he knew that that was what his father had been waiting to ask, and because it was the first time his father *had* asked. "Yes," he repeated. He fumbled in his pockets and brought out the crumpled bills and assorted coins, but he could not hand them to his father, so he put them on the table, where, if he wished, his father could reach them. His father did not touch them.

"Leah," he called in Yiddish, "here's the money Dovid has brought. Almost a man's salary. Come see, count how much."

His mother brought the fish to the table, gave each of them a portion, and then without a word, swept the money into her apron pocket without counting it, without looking at it, almost without touching it. They ate in silence until his father, once again looking up from his food, said, "Did you keep money for yourself?"

David shook his head, then felt his pockets. He hadn't. "I don't need any," he said, the lump shaping in his throat. "There's no school or anything."

"Did you keep for the *pishka?*" his mother asked.

The *pishka* was a small tin box, painted blue, with the white Star of David and the stone tablets of the Ten Commandments on it, which his father had given him when he was a small boy. It stood in his bookcase, and every time he was given any money, an allowance or gift, or earned some money, he was required to give some portion of it for charity—to the *pishka*. Once he had told Joe Vecchione about it and Joe had said, oh, it was like an alms box, but David didn't like that word for it and thought of it always by its Yiddish name. Every few months an old bearded man with Orthodox earlocks, caftan and furred cap came to the house, and after drinking tea and jelly and talking of the importance of *tzdakah* for Jews, and repeating some small story or folk legend about charity, he would empty both *pishkas,* David's and his parents', to take the money away for the poor and the orphans and widows.

He was a long time thinking about the *pishka,* and his mother asked him again if he had kept any money to put in it.

"No," he replied, "I took nothing."

"Then you must," his father said, with bitterness, "at least for charity."

"Enough!" his mother said sharply. "It is wholly enough!"

"Yes, Leah," his father answered. "You are right: it is wholly enough."

They finished eating without talking, and then his father went to his study and closed the door. At the sink, washing the dishes, his mother was crying and he did not know what to say to her, so he asked if he could go downstairs to the Vecchiones. She nodded that it was all right, and then, from her apron pocket, she took the money he had put on the table and added two more bills from her change purse and gave it all to him. "Here," she said, not looking at him, "take the rent. They must need it, so little work and so big a family."

All the Vecchiones were in the cellar when he got there, because Joe's girl friend was visiting for the first time. Joe saw him come in and said, "Ah, now everybody's here." He led David to the couch where a dark-skinned, dark-haired girl was sitting. "Regina," Joe said, "this is my little friend from upstairs, David Freed. He looks like an angel, he sings like an angel, he is an angel." David felt himself blushing, but he knew Joe was joking. The girl's face and eyes seemed to be moving all the time, changing, and David couldn't catch her expression. "David," Joe continued, bowing low from the waist, "this is Regina Speranza, my girl."

David said hello and they shook hands, hers a long-fingered, cool, dry hand that was pleasant to touch, and that almost seemed not to be touching him, as her face seemed not to be looking at him.

Pop and Mama Vecchione were sitting, watching in the corner, and David went to them to say good evening.

"Isa good evenin' when son bring his girl," Pop said. For a moment he seemed like his old self.

Mama Vecchione rumpled his hair. "It'sa what you mother wait fa witha you, when you be bigga boy," she whispered in his ear.

Out of the corner of his eye, David saw Toni sitting with Johnny Strigari, and when he walked to her side, she squeezed his arm and asked, "Am I your girl, still?" David looked at her, avoiding seeing her big belly and noticing how swollen her tanned face seemed, how sunken her eyes were, as if they were moving away from the light, and he nodded, but he couldn't say she was still his girl.

"And now, ladies and gentlemen," Joe announced, "I wish to introduce to you the Vecchione trio, the Three

V's: Vito Vecchione at the concertina, Carmine Vecchione, guitarist supreme, and Joe Vecchione, my own
humble self, fiddler."

They all applauded, and then the three of them began
to play: Italian songs, operatic arias, American popular
tunes. In the middle of a *tarantella,* Pop Vecchione got
up, bent so that he seemed to bow to Mama Vecchione,
and taking her hand, led her to the middle of the floor,
where they began to dance. It seemed as if they were
suddenly made young and straight: their arms and legs
flew; their bodies, thinner-looking, whirled and turned;
and Mama Vecchione's faded blond hair seemed almost
wild and young as she and Pop spun and swayed and
twirled. Vito, Carmine and Joe kept the music going from
one *tarantella* to another until the old man, breathless,
stopped and put up his hands. "No more," he gasped.
"Too old danca lika young people." David clapped his
hands, the other applauded, even Johnny Strigari, and
Carmine strummed the guitar, Joe scraped the violin, and
Vito drew the concertina out in a roar.

Later, Mama Vecchione brought dishes down from the
upstairs kitchen, and Regina helped her serve cakes and
pies, little candies called *torrone,* and strong expresso
coffee in tiny flowered cups. Eating and drinking made
David feel sleepy. He was tired from the day's rehearsal
and the ball game, and there was another rehearsal with
Chazan Barrt in the morning. As he went to say good
night to Pop and Mama Vecchione, David remembered
the rent money and took it out to give to the old man.
"My mother sent the rent," he explained. There was an
abrupt silence in the room as he held the money out, and
Pop Vecchione stared at it. "You know, the rent," David
repeated, a little louder, thinking that the old man hadn't
heard him, or hadn't understood.

"Tha rent," Pop repeated, his gray eyes level. "I under-
stan'. But I no take no more. Tomorrow, mebbe two days,
come a agent from tha bank. Bank owns house now. You
mother, she give him tha rent."

"The house isn't yours anymore?" David asked, hearing
his voice too loud, unable to lower it.

"You no worry, David," the old man said. "It'sa too
much trouble for old man. Bank foreclose mortgage. Bank
better fa house." He reached his old, earth-colored hand
out and closed David's fist over the money. "Now, *buona
sera,* an' take you money to you mother."

After he had said good night and left the room, David

heard them all begin to talk at once behind him. "When did it happen?" Carmine. "Why didn't you tell me?" Joe. "Whadda we gonna do now?" Vito. "So, no Depression, huh?" Johnny Strigari. And then Toni's very soft, dry, "Oh, Papa, Papa!" As the voices mixed and faded, David remembered their astonished faces when Pop had spoken, all of them no longer thinking about the party, the dancing, the music, the food, Joe's fiancée, Regina, only about Pop's saying that the house was no longer theirs.

Upstairs, his mother and father were in the kitchen, drinking tea. His father looked up when he came in and said, "They were having a party?"

"Yes," David replied. He sat down at the kitchen table with them.

"You want tea?" his mother asked.

He shook his head.

"What is it?" she asked.

He unfolded his fist, in which the rent money was still crumpled, and let it fall out on the table.

"You forgot to give them the rent," his father said sternly in Yiddish. "You must go down again, now. It is already delayed three days, and they are a big family. They need it. The two sons and the son-in-law are not working, and the girl is with child."

"It's not the Vecchiones' house anymore," David said softly, in English.

"Speak sense," his father said angrily.

"Ssha!" his mother cautioned. "What are you screaming for? What is it, David? What's doing there?"

"A man from the bank will come. You give him the rent."

"Aha, they foreclosed the mortgage," his father said in English, tugging at his beard, nervous and sadder.

"That's what the old man said."

Later, alone in his bedroom, David no longer felt sleepy. The light in his parents' bedroom was out, so his mother was probably asleep, but the light from his father's study still leaked a thin film under the door on the waxed parquet floors. David got out of bed and went to the open window, propped himself on the window seat, and looked out. The moon was heavy, a blurred gold, and Pop's cabbages and tomatoes lay in quiet red and green furrows, while the first green of the peach-tree leaves near the *boccie* alley seemed almost golden. He liked this house, especially his own bedroom and being able to sit and look out at the night, rain or snow, but now, if his father didn't find work, they might have to move. And the Vecchiones might have to go too.

Maybe he could help them. He had the *pishka* money. He went to the bookcase and picked the *pishka* out from between his books. It was heavy. He took it to the bed, opened the back, and spilled the bills and coins on the blanket. He counted more than fifty dollars, a lot of money. He had been putting more in since he was singing with Chazan Barrt and earning money, and the old man had not come to empty the *pishka* for a long time. It certainly was more than he had ever had before. Maybe it could help Pop Vecchione with the mortgage. He put the money back into the *pishka*, returned it to the bookcase, and then went back to his window seat.

Below him, shadows moved in the dark at the picket fence, and he heard soft voices, Joe's and Regina's. He didn't move. Almost, he didn't breathe, because the first thing he heard was Joe saying, "First losing his job and now the house."

"He'll get another job," Regina said, "and this isn't the only house in the neighborhood or in the world."

"You don't understand, Gina. He loves this house. We were all born here. He's lived here more than thirty years. First he used to rent it, and then he bought it. His friends are here, his tomatoes, his *boccie* alley. This is his home, not just a house."

"Well, you can rent again. That's not so bad."

"It won't be the same for him. He's funny. I know him. He's not like other people. He does things harder and he takes things harder. The house and the job make him the man of the family, a *man*, the father of his brood. With this big house he can keep all his children here around him. Without them all, he'll feel like a failure, like he's nothing . . . like old fat Ferrara."

"He can go on relief," Regina said, "like the others."

"Relief? My old man? My father's sixty-seven years old, and worked since he was a boy. He's proud. He'd never go on relief. He's been riding my brother-in-law about being out of work. *Thisa country here good place. Man wanna work, get work.* That's why he didn't tell any of us he'd lost his job all these weeks, because he couldn't get another job. That's why he didn't tell us about the bank foreclosing. His back may be bent, but his spine is straight with pride. But there are thousands of carpenters out of work, good ones and younger, who can put in a harder day's work. They won't take him on another job, and he won't go on relief."

"You're a worrier, Joe," Regina said. "Something will come up. Things always work out."

Joe laughed, a short, twisted laugh. "Oh Gina, Gina, you're so damned young and optimistic. I wish I believed the way you do."

"How else can you live? I believe the way I breathe. It's natural."

There was quiet, and David leaned out to see if they were still there. They were, standing with their arms around each other and their faces pressed together. David was ashamed because he had listened, and glad, too, but more ashamed that he had seen Joe and Gina leaning against each other.

Saturday night it was weddings again, the first two in Manhattan with Chazan Barrt, the last the cantor had arranged for David alone in the Bronx. David got there late and tired. The hall was on the second floor of a two-story building, the first floor a place they made and sold tombstones, and as he came up to it, David saw the stones, gray, white and speckled, so that the hall looked as if it were built right on a cemetery. When he was closer, he saw that many of the stones were already inscribed with names, with Beloved Father, Loving Mother, Devoted Son, and his stomach turned and his breath caught.

In the anteroom, Rabbi Usher hurried him out of his coat into his white robe and skullcap, talking all the time. "Where've you been? Did you get lost? It's almost eleven o'clock. Barrt promised me you'd be here at ten, the latest. They're all waiting. We've been holding the ceremony for an hour. Well, anyway, you're here now. . . ."

David said nothing. It was always like that. Chazan Barrt arranged as many places for him to sing in a single night as possible, and if some had to wait, postpone the ceremony for a while, let the food grow cold, Barrt didn't care, especially if he himself didn't have to be there to hear the complaints. "I'm ready," David said, his robe and cap arranged. They went together into the small darkened chapel, and on the altar the rabbi began to chant the ceremony. David sang when he was supposed to, almost with another part of him that listened to Rabbi Usher and responded at the right times, thinking of his father not working, of Pop Vecchione losing his job and the house, of how his mother had said that morning that they might have to give up the telephone because it was a luxury they couldn't afford now, of how much soup they were eating and his father's face each time he saw it served, of how Pop Vecchione never talked to Toni, and how he himself had not been able to tell her that she was still his girl.

The best man came down the aisle, the maid of honor, the groom and his parents, and then the bride and her parents, and David sang for each of them the stanzas of "I Love You Truly," "When the Dawn," "Because God Made Thee Mine" and "O Promise Me." The rabbi went on with the ceremony until the final words, ". . . according to the laws of Moses and of Israel, and according to the authority vested in me by the State of New York, I pronounce you man and wife," and the groom brought his heel crashing down on the whiskey glass, shattering it in the napkin in which it was wrapped. Everyone cried out, as they always did, "Good luck . . . *mazel tov!*" The bride tore back her veil and the groom, his top hat too big for him and low over his eyes, pushed the hat back on his forehead so he could kiss the bride. The lights went up, the bride and groom marched out, and David was wearily glad it was over.

An old man he recognized as the groom's father, white-haired and with a mustache equally white, came up to him, leaning on a rubber-tipped brown cane. *"Boychick,"* he said in Yiddish, "you sing like a fine cantor."

"Thank you," David replied in English, taking off his white robe.

"Later, you can maybe sing a little cantorial piece for us?" the old man asked, gold teeth sudden beneath his white mustache and pale pink lips. "We'll pay extra, of course," he said after a moment. Remembering his father's face and the rent, David nodded.

"I'll sing something if you want," he answered, this time in Yiddish, ashamed that the money should have decided him, and also because the old man had seen his hesitation.

Leaning on his cane, the old man led him to the musicians' table. While the others ate, he ate too: the same sweetbreads, soup and dumplings, tasteless chicken and indigestible stuffed derma, browned and tough as leather, and spiced so hot it burned the roof of his mouth. When the little melting triangle of colored ice came for dessert, the old man returned, asking for the song. David kept his white skullcap on, but didn't put on the robe. First he sang *Eitz chaim hi. . . .*

It is a tree of life to them that lay hold of it,
And the supporters of it are happy.
Its ways are ways of pleasantness,
And all its paths are peace.

The wedding guests applauded, the little old man most of all, clapping his cane against the leg of his chair and crying loudly in Yiddish, "More, more." David sang a second time, the *Adon Olam,* this time for the gold-toothed old man alone:

The Lord of all did reign supreme
Before this world was made and formed,
When all was finished by His will,
Then was His Name as King proclaimed....

And one is He, and none there is
To be compared or joined to him,
Without beginning and without end
All strength and dominion are His....

My spirit I commit to His hands,
My body and all I prize,
Both when I sleep and when I wake,
He is with me, I shall not fear.

The last stanzas the wedding guests sang with him, their voices rich and rising together. When they were done, they applauded him and themselves, and then the orchestra began to play, couples got up to dance, and the faceted chandelier in the ceiling began to turn its flashes of light in the semidarkness.

David went to get his coat, the old man clumping after him into the anteroom. *"Boychick,"* he said, licking his lined pink lips, "you sang like the best. Tasty." He leaned his cane against the wall, and as David folded his white robe and skullcap away, took a worn leather change purse from his pocket and counted out some bills. "Here," he said, "this one"—he handed David a ten-dollar bill—"for the ceremony," and then, counting out five single-dollar bills into David's palm, he added, "and these for the cantorial pieces." David stared at the money. The old man pinched his cheek gently. "A beautiful thank you," he said, "and go in good health."

Ten dollars! And Chazan Barrt had told him he would be paid only three. The old man was almost into the hall before David could think to call out his thanks. "No," the old man said, turning and waving his cane at him, *"I* thank *you.* With such a singing, you made me a boy again for a few minutes. That"—he pointed his cane to the money in David's hands—"is very cheap payment for such a gift." Then he was gone.

"Which way do you go?" It was Rabbi Usher.

"To Brooklyn," David answered, without thinking.

"Sorry, I go over to the Concourse," the rabbi said. He saw the money. "Oh," he stammered, "they paid *you.*" It was not a question, and David noticed his faint blush and the hesitation when he said *you.* "It's ten dollars, no?"

David nodded.

"They were supposed to pay *me,* and I usually give it to Barrt, or mail him a check," the rabbi went on, "but I guess it's all right this way, isn't it?"

"Yes," David replied, "it's all right," and he knew that Chazan Barrt had been cheating him for a long time, that this was one time in many, and that Rabbi Usher knew too, and had helped Barrt do it before and would have again this time, except for the accident of the old man's paying him directly. "Good night," David said in English, deliberately leaving out the "rabbi."

"Come home safe," the rabbi said in Yiddish, and turned back into the hall.

The subway was deserted, without a station agent, and the four-part iron turnstile that always reminded him of a coffin made a mournful sound, half-sob, half-groan, as he went through it. Waiting, David took the money out again: it *was* five singles and a ten-dollar bill. He walked up and down the empty platform, staring at the bills, and a sudden gust of cold night air took them out of his hand. He grabbed at the bills as they floated down off the platform onto the tracks. He tried to watch where they all landed, but they had fluttered in different directions. The bills were in the middle of the station and a train might come in if he went down for them, but he needed that fifteen dollars. His parents needed them. If a train did come in, there was no place to run, and the stairways at both ends of the platform were at least a hundred yards away. The signal light was green, so no train had recently passed, and the next one would probably come racing into the station and scatter or tear the bills so he could never find them. He looked across at the uptown platform. No one there. No help. He had to go down himself. He put the bundle of his robe and skullcap down on the platform, took off his coat and jacket and laid them over it, quickly glanced again in the direction from which the train would come, and then let himself down from the edge of the platform to the tracks. Swiftly, he picked up two dollar bills from the square wooden ties, then a third, and finally a fourth and fifth from the roadbed, pocketed them, and began to search for the ten. Though he remembered which way it had gone, he couldn't see it. Looking carefully, he turned every few moments to see if a train was coming, his body tensed and waiting for the sound, the blood in his ears and the heart in his chest pounding so that he kept hearing trains where there were none.

Then he saw it, lying next to the polished steel of the third rail, just under the wooden plank that covered the electrified steel band. It was only an inch or so away from the third rail, and David realized that he would have to put his hand under the guard plank, carefully not to touch the rail, and snag the bill. In a flash, from the summer before, he remembered seeing an Irish setter, red-haired and beautiful, touch the third rail where the subway, near his house, ran on the ground. The dog had poked its snout under the protective plank and touched the third rail; a crazy barking wail, like a police siren's, had turned into a shriek, and in a second the dog was black, crisp-haired and dead. Reaching for the bill, the rail glittering like something glowing evil and threatening, David felt himself already black and burning, his own death cries in the shrieking air, and all he saw was the blackened dog.

With two fingers, he drew the bill slowly away from the third rail, out from under the plank, and when he heard the train's rumbling, thought it was, again, only his frightened blood knocking in his ears. But this time it really was a train. He jammed the ten-dollar bill into his pocket, flung himself on the edge of the platform, and struggled to pull himself to safety. The booming of the train was louder, and David didn't dare look to see if it was already lunging into the station. He tried again to pull himself up to the platform, but managed only to get his chest and arms up, his legs still dangling. With a tearing heave, feeling his fingernails crack as they clawed against the concrete platform, he bellied himself onto the platform like a snake, and lay exhausted, his breath stony in his throat, his heart resounding against the cool concrete beneath his shirt. The train flung itself into the station then, but it was going the other way, on the uptown side. Lying there, his head twisted to watch it, David laughed, a wild laughter that sounded in his ears like the Irish setter's shriek.

When the train on his side finally arrived, he had brushed his clothes, put on his jacket and coat, and was waiting quietly with his bundle. When the doors opened, he got on, sat down on a seat next to a window and fell asleep, but the rumbling of the train filled his dreams.

At breakfast, David was still tired. Though they had been eating hot farina every morning for breakfast, he was grateful for it and for his half-and-half coffee and hot milk. As he was drinking, his father came in. "Jakob," his mother called, "you want another coffee?"

"And why not?" his father smiled. "Dovid, are you first up, now? It's beautiful outside. A spring day, when the air feels like a *tallis* around you, silken and with tassels. Oho, you got home late, that's why! Nuh, eat hearty!" His father smiled with his even, tobacco-stained teeth, a moon between his dark graying beard and mustache. "Well, how did it go last night?" his father asked, sitting down to the coffee his mother had set in front of him.

David told him about the weddings, about the little old man with the brown cane, mentioning details that would amuse him, since he had not seen his father in good humor for weeks, and now his father seemed more curious about his singing and the weddings than ever before, but he tried to keep from telling him about the ten-dollar bill. Then, almost without willing it, the story of the old man with the cane became the story of Chazan Barrt and cheating him. "I wondered why they always paid him," David said, "not me. Now I know. He's cheating me. He tells them ten dollars for the soloist, and he tells me he got three dollars. That leaves him seven." It was so simple, clear, like the foolish arithmetic examples Miss Kendall gave them in school. It wasn't even like the algebra, where there was an x to find, an unknown.

His father's face darkened, his hand tugged his beard and smoothed a stray drop of coffee from his mustache. "Wait a minute. Don't hurry yourself." His father spoke, almost as if to himself, and as if, abruptly, the day were no longer a silken prayer shawl to be wrapped around him. "I know Chazan Barrt, and I do not think he is a dishonest man."

"He told me three dollars and they paid me ten," David repeated. "Why?"

"I don't know," his father shrugged. "Maybe a mistake.

Maybe you didn't understand right. Maybe the old man who paid didn't know the price."

"Rabbi Usher knew," David said stubbornly.

"He also could be mistaken."

His mother spoke up. "Why are you snuffling under your nose, Jakob? It's the first time you heard something funny about Barrt and money? You remember when they took up the collection in synagogue for the old people's hospital, and they gave it to him? There was money missing. The sexton said so, so maybe Barrt isn't so kosher."

"He said the *shammos* counted wrong, Leah," his father protested. "It was a mistake."

"There's too many mistakes with Barrt to be all mistakes," his mother said firmly. She turned to David. "You have more weddings this afternoon?"

David nodded.

"Then you'll ask him. You'll say, 'My mother told me to ask.' "

"Leah, you'll make the boy look foolish. So Barrt takes a few dollars. Isn't he entitled?" His father put his coffee cup down very carefully. "He tells Dovid where and sends him. This is worth a few dollars, no?"

His father was *afraid!* His father was worried, afraid he wouldn't be able to go on singing and bring home the money they needed. And his mother knew. David saw it in the way her mouth went thin, her jaw bonier. *She* wasn't afraid. Or if she was, it didn't make any difference: she would speak and have him speak, all the same. "At least he should ask," his mother insisted.

"What satisfaction is there if he asks?" His father's voice rose. "He'll have a few more dollars? And if Barrt says to him, 'All right, fine, it's true. From every ten, I take seven. You're only a boy, and *I'm* the *chazan. I* make the arrangements. *I* recommend the soloist. Isn't this worth a few dollars?' What will Dovid do then? He'll call Barrt names?"

"From children a *chazan* must also take money? From a child's throat?" his mother asked softly. "And out of our mouths? Especially now." She stopped herself, her lips closing like doors.

"It will be better if we cripple it and Barrt doesn't take the boy to sing at all? We are better off with nothing?" His father drank some more coffee. "It is not necessary to fight with him. It is not sensible."

"You are right, Jakob, it is not *sensible,* but it *is* honest and just."

They finished breakfast in silence, and his mother went to the sink to begin the dishes. David walked to his room. From the kitchen, there were no sounds except those of his mother washing the dishes. He made his bed, tidied the room, dressed, and came back into the kitchen with his coat.

"You will eat lunch before you go?" his mother asked.

"No, I'm not hungry now. I'll eat later, at the weddings."

"Some eating," she said, brushing his hair into place and straightening his skullcap.

He put on his coat and went to the door before his father's voice, from the study, called, "Dovid?"

"Yes, Papa."

"Come in here for a minute."

David went into the study reluctantly, although he loved the room with its big mahogany trestle table, polished to a dark shine, the old, yellow-paged Bible open on the lectern, as he loved the big glassed-in bookcases with their old and new Hebrew and Yiddish books: Talmud, Gemora, Midrash; Maimonides and Rashi; Peretz and Sholem Aleichem; Bialik, I. J. Singer, Bergelson, Sholem Asch, as much his father's "friends" as the records were Pop Vecchione's.

"You will speak to Chazan Barrt?"

"About what?"

"About the ten dollars . . . and the payments."

"You do not want me to?"

"No, Dovid, I do not want you to. You heard before. But you must make your own decision."

David hesitated. "I will speak to him, Father, I must."

"If you must, then you must," his father said slowly, his fingers nervously opening and closing the big *chumosh* on the table lectern, "but *must* is a very big word, Dovid. The only *must* is one *must* die." He turned away, smoothed out the pages of the Bible, and began to read. He had said all he was going to say.

Joe Vecchione was on the stoop when David went out. "Hello, David," he said, "where're you hurrying?"

"Rehearsal," David answered, "then a couple of weddings."

"You must get bored seeing so many people get married."

David nodded. "I get tired." He wanted to ask Joe about Chazan Barrt's cheating him, but it didn't seem the right thing to do. Joe was his friend, but he was an

Italian, a Gentile. What would he think of a Jewish cantor and a rabbi who cheated a choirboy? He decided to say nothing about it. Instead, he remarked, "I'll enjoy singing at your wedding, though, because I like your girl."

"You liked her? I'm glad. I like her, too."

"Mama and Pop liked her, too. I could tell," David declared.

"You could, could you? And how could you tell?"

"I don't know. I just could," David asserted, wanting to change the subject, because suddenly he remembered Joe and Regina in the backyard and the conversation he had overheard. "You know her long?"

"A couple of years, but I only started to see her regularly last year."

"That's a long time," David said.

"Oh, it's not *that* long, now," Joe grinned, then saddened, "but it's long enough."

"You gonna get married soon?" David asked. "Like Toni and Johnny?"

There was a moment of silence in which Joe seemed to be thinking the question over. "I don't know, David, I don't know. I'd like to get married, I think"—then his face changed—"but not like Toni and Johnny."

David was uncomfortable. He knew Joe was saying something sad and ugly about Toni. "I've got to go, Joe," he said, "the cantor's waiting for me."

Joe waved good-bye, but he was already thinking of something else.

Chazan Barrt was waiting for him in the parlor, seated at the piano playing scales. "Aha, you're on time." He always said that, as if he expected David to be late, and as if David always were late, although he rarely was. Without waiting for an answer, Barrt went on, "Nuh, how was last night?"

"It was all right."

"Only all right?"

"The people seemed to like it."

"That's what the rabbi told me this morning on the telephone."

So Rabbi Usher had already called and told him about the money, David thought. And the *chazan* was letting him know he wasn't going to pass the thing by as though nothing had happened. Well, he wouldn't talk about the money until Barrt spoke first.

"You sang something extra?" the cantor asked, playing

a scale, then striking one note and singing in his deep
bass, "Mi ... mi ... mi. ..."

"Yes," David answered, "two cantorial pieces." He took
his usual position at the piano for rehearsing. He cleared
his throat, coughed, and breathed deeply while the cantor
changed his note to "fa ... fa ... fa ..." and then to "do
... do ... do ..." and finally looked up, his eyes narrowed, his nostrils wide and threatening, their little clumps
of spiky white hair like tiny arrows. "They paid you?" he
asked.

"Yes," David said, avoiding his eyes.

"How much?"

"Ten dollars."

"I said three dollars, no?"

"Yes."

Barrt paused, played a run on the piano, very softly, so
that even that close to the piano, David had to strain to
hear it. "Seven is for me," Barrt said softly.

"What?" David asked, not quite sure he had heard cor-
rectly.

"Seven dollars is for me." He dropped his hands to the
piano bench, then put out his right hand, palm extended.
"Only three dollars for you."

David looked at the outstretched palm, curiously pink
and wrinkled and distasteful. "For you, why?" he asked. "I
sang. You weren't even there."

The cantor's palm folded into a fist, each knuckle white
under the skin, little bristly hairs, white, gray and black on
his fingers. "Sit down, Dovid." Chazan Barrt pointed to a
chair. "Let us talk ourselves out." When David sat on a
nearby gold-brocaded chair, Barrt continued, "I like you.
You're a nice boy and you have a nice voice." His hand
dropped back to the piano bench, folding and unfolding
over the edge. "But *I* arrange the weddings. Yes, you go
and sing without me, but the seven dollars is mine, my
commission for finding the wedding and sending you."

"But the ten dollars is *for the boy* who sings. They pay
you for your singing, too. Why does the money paid to me
for my work belong to you?"

"Look, Dovid," the cantor took another tack. "You've
heard of this Depression?"

"Yes," David acknowledged.

"Your father—I met him in synagogue only last week—
he told me there was only work one day, maybe two days
a week, no?" He let that sink in. "I can get a dozen voices
like yours," Barrt went on. "Sure, sure, yours is better,

even much better, but who'll notice? And who'll care? It's a wedding. Everybody's happy. Everybody's had a few *schnapps*. Take a young boy soprano, put him in a white skullcap and robe, and let him sing 'O Promise Me,' and everyone makes *ooh* and *ahh* and thinks it's Yossele Rosenblatt, Junior. You understand?" He held out his palm again, the fingers rigid, the palm red. "Now," he said quietly, "the money."

David sat, feeling the gold brocade of the chair with his fingertips. Barrt was right. Probably no one would know the difference, or care even if they did. Looking at the cantor's palm, he remembered his father's nervous fingers in the *chumosh*, the hopeless turn of his shoulders as he had gone back to his studying, having spoken his piece. "*Must* is a big word." Barrt took his wallet out, pulled three dollar bills from it, and laid them on the piano. "Come," he reiterated, "the ten." He pointed to the three dollar bills. "Here, this is yours." When David did not move to pick them up, Barrt went on, "Your family will need it, if work is so slow." David got out of the chair, took the ten-dollar bill out of his inside shirt pocket, smoothed it out, and laid it on the piano. Unwillingly, he took the three singles and put them in his trouser pocket.

"And from now on," Chazan Barrt said, enjoying himself, relaxed, "we won't have to have the rabbi take the money. They'll pay you, and you'll bring me my share." And as if to forestall any protest, he continued, "We understand each other, now, don't we?" He got up, patted David's shoulder and announced, "And now, a little rehearsal."

At the weddings at Chazan Barrt's that afternoon, David met Ilsa Kermitt for the first time, a tall, stocky soprano with long braids like ropes plaited around her head. "I'm Ilsa Kermitt," she introduced herself, "but you call me Ilsa and I'll call you David." Why she was there David didn't know until after he had sung his "O Promise Me," she smiled, and with a big sweep of her arm moved him behind her and boomed out in a heavy, rich soprano that was like her face and body:

> *Toujours l'amour, toujours,*
> Loved one at last I found you. . . .

After the first wedding was over, Barrt introduced them formally. "Aha," he exclaimed when he saw them talking, "you already know each other."

"Of course, Nathan, we're old troupers from Rockaway Avenue to the Grand Concourse, and old troupers are friends right away," Ilsa Kermitt said.

"Friends, yes," Barrt said, rubbing his big nose with a finger. He was amused. "Dovid," he said in Yiddish, "we call Ilsa the *shicksa*, a pretty one, no?" He reached over and playfully pinched her cheek.

"It is not right to speak Yiddish in front of those who cannot understand," David murmured.

"So who said she didn't understand?"

"I understand fine," Ilsa Kermitt said in Yiddish. "I used to sing in a trio—maybe you heard of us?—The Three Shicksas, and we sang everything in Yiddish, so I speak like a native."

"What a trio!" Cantor Barrt said, smiling with his big teeth. *"Oy vay!"* His face grew smaller and shrewder, and when he put his arm around David's shoulder, David knew he was going to say something unpleasant. "Nuh, Dovid, could you want a prettier partner? She's going to be like your partner now." He put his other arm around Ilsa Kermitt and drew them together until their three bodies were touching. "A few weddings you'll sing together, and you'll take some and Ilsa will take some, so it will be easier for both." He drew them apart and looked first at David's face, then at Ilsa Kermitt's. "A good arrangement, no?"

David remembered their morning talk, but did not answer. This was Barrt's way of telling him—no, showing him—that there were plenty of other voices, and Barrt was reducing the number of weddings he sang at, and consequently the money he made, by giving them to Ilsa Kermitt. Well, David thought spitefully, at least Barrt would have to pay her better: she would not get a mere one-third of what was paid for a soloist. But Barrt could not send her to some weddings, not to the synagogue, where neither women nor Gentiles could sing the holy cantillations.

"A good voice this beautiful girl has," Chazan Barrt said, chucking Ilsa under the chin and running his hand quickly down past her bosom.

"Yes," David assented, but he did not like her sweet, heavy singing which made the wedding songs, already flabby, flabbier.

"Between the two of you," the cantor exulted, "no one has better soloists than Barrt, huh?"

Later that evening, at a wedding in Brownsville, David, also for the first time, met the cantor they called "The Flame." It was the last wedding of the night, after two in the afternoon and two others in the evening, and his voice was husky with tiredness, but when the groom asked him to stay after the ceremony and sing *Eli, Eli,* David knew he would be paid with money he didn't have to share with Barrt, money his family needed. He began to sing slowly and was filled with an end-of-a-long-day sadness he did not understand, filled with his weariness and the way Barrt had humiliated him that morning at the piano and with Ilsa Kermitt, weary with his father's turning from him to the *chumosh* when David had spoken his *must,* and he felt the words with a special bitterness and pain:

> *Eli, Eli, lomo azaftonu*
> God, O God, why hast Thou forsaken me?

His voice rang deep and clear and rose into the room, so that the wedding guests were for a time silent, their eyes on their shoes and the scuffed ballroom floor. The musicians listened, not touching their instruments, and even the waiters stopped serving, dish towels limp and wrinkled over their stained, black-jacketed arms; not a plate rattled, not a spoon clanked. It made his sorrow greater, so that when he was finished he felt as if something had been ripped from him, and he couldn't hear the applause for the tiredness beating in his throat, or see the blur of faces in front of him. He had to drag his feet out to the cloakroom and sit there, waiting for his head to stop spinning.

When he looked up, there was a man almost six and a half feet tall standing over him, a man with a red, flaming beard and mustache, and a mane of red-gold hair that fell from under a white silk skullcap almost to his shoulders. The man put his hand under David's chin and lifted his face. "Let me look at you, boy. You have a voice! Such a voice! And a musician, too!" David was too tired to care about the open admiration he heard or the words he could barely understand. He only wanted to be left alone until he could make his head stop whirling. "What's the matter, boy? Are you all right?" the giant persisted. David nodded weakly, hoping that would make him go away. The man took another look, dropped his upturned face and went back into the ballroom. In a few moments he was back.

"Here"—he offered a small glass—"drink a little *schnapps*. You'll feel better."

David drank, coughing, and felt the liquor fall, burning, into his stomach, then rise like a heat cloud to his head. "Did you eat?" the red-haired man asked gently, and only then David remembered that he had had only a piece of honey cake all day, snatched between two of the afternoon weddings. The big man nodded, returned to the ballroom again, and brought some sliced chicken on two pieces of *challjah*, a whole tomato and a glass of red wine. "Eat," he said, tossing his mane, "but slowly, or else you will be sick." The big man watched while he ate, and when David had finished, set the plate on the floor. He took a cigarette from a gold case, put it into an ivory holder, and began to smoke. "Tell me your name," he asked, after a few puffs.

"David Freed."

"You sing in synagogue too? The cantillations?"

"Yes. I'm soloist with Chazan Barrt."

"Nathan Barrt?"

David nodded, feeling better, but still weak.

"Are you singing with him for the High Holy Days?"

"Why?" David asked, his curiosity stirred.

"I am Eleazar Flamm, the *chazan* they call The Flame," he said, bowing his head to one side and blowing a cloud of smoke.

"I've heard some of your records," David cried. "They're very good."

"You know who I am!" Flamm said delightedly. "But of course. How could you sing an *Eli, Eli* like that without having heard The Flame? If you can sing cantillations so, you must sing with me on the High Holy Days." He paused. "You could arrange that?"

"I will have to ask my parents, of course, and—"

"Nathan Barrt?" Flamm interjected.

"No. I do not ask him. I will tell him," David said quietly. "But it is a matter of money. How much will you pay me?"

"Oho, so you are a businessman too! I like that. You get right down to it, rump on the table. Good! I will give you twice what Nathan Barrt pays."

David laughed. "That's easy for you to say. You know Nathan Barrt and his paying."

Flamm laughed too, big rolling peals of bass-baritone laughter. "And you have humor too. Good! Good! I like you better every minute. All right, how much do you want?"

David took a deep breath. "Two hundred and fifty dollars for Rosh Hashanah, Yom Kippur and Slichos."

"Two hundred and fifty dollars?" Flamm struck the cigarette from his holder and ground it beneath his shoe. "Today—you've heard, no, boy, that there's a Depression? —this is a small fortune."

"It is a lot of money," David conceded, "but the time of boy sopranos is short, the voice goes quickly."

"A philosopher, too," Flamm noted, shaping his beard with a giant hand. "All right, David Freed, we'll settle for two hundred. Agreed?"

Two hundred, and Barrt had offered him only sixty. "Agreed," David said, and they shook hands, Flamm's covering his hand and most of his wrist and forearm.

"And for Succoth?" Flamm asked.

"For that you pay extra," David responded.

"And now, a small piece of cantillations."

Swiftly, and with a new feeling of confidence, David sang the opening of the mourner's *kaddish,* "Magnified and sanctified be His great Name," and watched the great red head nod before him, the eyelids come down over the bright blue eyes as The Flame listened. A waiter came out of the ballroom and interrupted. "Nuh, Chazen, enough?" he said, his white hands turned out, pleading, against his black jacket. When The Flame nodded, he went back into the ballroom.

"Give me your name and address," Flamm said after a few moments. "I will write to you after the summer."

"You can call me if you want," David said, and gave him his phone number as well.

"You have a telephone. Good."

"My mother likes it. She thinks it's very American. And it's convenient when I cannot come home, or come home late," David explained.

The Flame stood looking down at him, as if he understood that he'd just been offered a half-apology, and said, "Good night, boy. Come home safe."

On the subway, David fell asleep but awoke as the train was coming into his station. He was so sleepy he almost forgot his little bundle with the robe and skullcap. He had to run back for it, and only just managed to get out of the car before the doors slammed shut behind him. Tired and chilled by the night air, he walked toward the exit on the

empty platform, aware of how late it was and how sleepy
he was. There was a sudden clanging, like hammers on
steel, and at the bottom of the stairs that led to the street,
he heard a loud, "Chickee, someone's coming." He
climbed the two flights to the surface and, as he reached
it, heard someone dodge into the men's toilet. Then he
saw the chewing-gum machine cashbox split open and the
box empty. Some pennies were scattered on the concrete
floor beneath the gum machine. Whoever had broken into
it seemed to have left in a hurry. David bent down,
gathered the pennies and, as he straightened up, looked
directly into the eyes of Banana Nose.

"Hey, Freed," Banana Nose said, a crowbar in his
hand, "gimme them pennies."

"They yours?"

"They ain't my uncle's," Banana Nose said.

"They're ours, all right," Fonzi said, coming out behind
him from the men's toilet.

David handed him the pennies.

"You din see us," Banana Nose threatened, "get it?"

"Davie's a good guy," Fonzi said softly. "He ain't gonna
say nuthin', are yuh, Davie?"

"You guys are gonna get into trouble. If they catch
you, you go to reform school."

"First they gotta catch us," Fonzi said.

"We got more than five bucks' worth," Banana Nose
boasted, shaking his pants pocket so that the coins jingled.
"Not bad, eh? Our banker counted 'em up too, so the
count's right. No foolin'!" He called, "Hey, Nadie!" and
Nadie Rosen emerged from the men's toilet, too.

"Hi, Davie," he said, his jaws working. He looked
away.

"Nadie!" David exclaimed.

"We had another one of your boys," Fonzi said amia-
bly, "but he don' show up."

"Yeh," Banana Nose chorused, "his mudder wouldn't
let him stay out so late at night."

David stared at Nadie. "Maxie Jonas," Nadie replied.

They stood measuring each other, not speaking, until
Banana Nose grated, "What tha hell we waitin' here for?
The cops? We crazy or somethin'?" They began to run,
the pennies clanging in Banana Nose's pockets, the crowbar in his hand waving like a magician's wand. Not
knowing why and feeling guilty, David clutched his bundle
and ran with them, out of the subway station, down the
streets, running single, close against the houses, as if they

were playing "Chase the white horse," or "Ringelivio." They ran into the alley behind Jay's candy store and stopped, leaning against the damp brick wall, breathing hard. The lights were still on in the empty store next door to Jay's, and the sounds of the card game were still loud. They stood there, waiting for their breathing to become normal again, David wondering why he had run at all and why he was there, until Fonzi asked, "You wanna we should cut you in on this, Davie?"

"Whaddyu mean, cut *him* in!" Banana Nose protested. "He din do nuthin'."

"Anytime you want," Fonzi offered, "you come say so. Or you tell Nadie here."

"Yeh, Davie," Nadie seconded, "you just let me know."

"Look, fellas," David began softly, "this isn't the right thing to do."

"Nuts to that sissy stuff," Banana Nose spat.

"Divided three ways, five bucks is only a dollar sixty-six each. If they catch you, you get the reformatory for two years, at least. That's no bargain."

"Them Jews, always lookin' for bargains," Banana Nose said disgustedly. "You pretty smart at arithmetic, but you dumb anyway."

"Cut out that Jew talk," Nadie said sharply.

"Sure, sure," Banana Nose answered, "but you better tell your friend this just a small job, peanuts, fa practice."

"You talk too much," Fonzi said. He turned to David. "Your father workin'?"

"No," David said. "What's that got to do with it?"

"Your father workin', Banana Nose?"

"Naw, we on relief."

"Nadie?"

"No."

"Our fathers don' work, we don' get money. This way we get some," Fonzi explained.

"It's not worth it," David insisted.

"Easy for him to talk," Nadie bit out. "He gets enough. Sings at weddings and stuff. Probably coming from them now, loaded with money."

"Mebbe we take a little from him," Banana Nose said menacingly. "We make more than a dollar sixty-six apiece that way."

"You want to," Fonzi encouraged, "sure."

"Ain't no work at all," Banana Nose gritted. David saw the shadow of the crowbar raised in the dark, and then he heard the click that meant Banana Nose had taken his knife out and bared the blade. As the shadow of Banana Nose neared him, David saw the blade glint and heard the metallic jingle of the coins in his pocket. "I always like the idea cutting Davie Freed up a little," he said.

"I told you once before," David said loudly. "You start up with me once more, I'm gonna try to kill you, Banana Nose, or you're gonna have to kill me. You don't get a penny I got with me without killing me first."

"That's good with me," Banana Nose called.

"That's the way it's gonna be," David told Nadie's shadow. "Someday, someone's gonna try to stop you, and you're gonna kill him. Then you'll fry in the electric chair."

"You better shaddup," Banana Nose warned, moving closer. Fonzi moved back against the wall, a slim shadow, lit a cigarette, and in the flare of the match David saw his face for a moment, remote and detached, as if he were watching something happening miles away through a spyglass. And Nadie's face shone, square jaws working as if he had a toothache, afraid, but David knew he would do nothing. And Banana Nose moving slowly toward him, the knife shining, the crowbar a shadow, and his face tight with a kind of joy. As the match died, David inched his bundle up from the ground behind him, and when Banana Nose was near enough, he threw it straight at him and jumped after it. "Yah!" he yelled as the bundle hit Banana Nose's chest, and he himself struck right behind. Banana Nose grunted, fell off balance, and then David threw him to the ground. The knife went clattering away in the darkness, echoing hollowly, and the crowbar fell with a clang and struck him across the ankles. David tried to pin Banana Nose's arms and hold him, but Banana Nose twisted away and punched him in the ribs. David hit back, punching Banana Nose's head and chest until Banana Nose's face loomed abruptly close to his, the head coming like a battering ram, and pain ran through his head like ice. They rolled over and over, Banana Nose's teeth locked on his left ear, and David, tossing his head, tried to shake him loose until his forearm poked Banana Nose's Adam's apple. There was a long hissing sound, the teeth loosened, and Banana Nose lay limp on the ground.

Trembling, David got up, retrieved his bundle and the crowbar, and leaned against the wall, fighting for breath, his arms still too tired to lift the crowbar. Then, with an effort of will, he brought his right hand up to his waist and pointed the crowbar at Fonzi and Nadie. "You," he gasped, "you . . ."

"What the hell goes on there?" a voice shouted from the head of the alley.

"Cops," Nadie Rosen whispered. "C'mon, let's get out of here."

"C'mon where?" David panted. "That's the only way out."

"You comin' out of there, or do we come in and drag you out?" another voice yelled.

Fonzi knelt beside Banana Nose and slapped his face. "Get up, get up. There are cops outside."

"Okay," the voices joined, "we're comin' in after you."

David clutched his bundle and held the crowbar, flattening himself against one wall. Fonzi and Nadie flattened themselves against the other. They left Banana Nose lying on the ground. The footsteps came up the alley tentatively, probing. "When they come here, stay flat, and see if they go past. Then run, all in different directions," Fonzi advised in a whisper. The steps sounded up the alley, and then suddenly, a flashlight blinded David.

"David," a shocked voice said, "what are *you* doing here?" It was Vito Vecchione. The flashlight wavered, turned down to his shoes, moved over Banana Nose, stopping on his face, the big nose dark, the fleshy lips like split grapes, the white teeth shining like seeds in a melon.

"Christ!" the other voice said. "It's my kid brother, Joe." That was Mario Pastore. "Who gave it to him?" Mario knelt down, lifted his brother's head off the concrete, and pillowed it on his thigh. "Well, he's breathin', anyway." Mario's face went down on his brother's chest. "Heart's beatin' too. Just knocked out. Who did it?"

"I did," David said.

Mario looked up at him, the same big-nosed, dark face Banana Nose had. "Who're you?"

"My name's David Freed."

"Whaddyu do it for?"

"He started."

"This Freed kid," Fonzi said, "saw us crackin' a gum machine on the station. Said he was gonna snitch, so Banana Nose was layin' it onto him."

"He's lying," David said.

Banana Nose's eyes opened and his hands went to his throat. "Madonna," he croaked, "somebody kicked me ina neck."

"Well," Mario Pastore said, "mebbe I gotta do my kid brother's work for him. I give this little Jew boy a shellackin' so he don't forget the Pastore brothers." He got off his knees, out of the circle of the flashlight, and came toward David.

"You come near me," David called, lifting the crowbar, "and I'm gonna break your head open."

"Aw, c'mon, Mario," Vito Vecchione said, "he's only a kid. Leave him be."

"You better watch out," Banana Nose called from the ground. "He got my crowbar."

"Turn the flash on him, Vito," Mario ordered.

The spotlight wavered for another second or two on Banana Nose, squatting now, and then turned on him. David narrowed his eyes. He couldn't see their faces, but he could make out their shadows. Slowly, holding the crowbar in front of him and trying to deflect the light with his bundle, he edged along the wall, his back to it. "I'm getting out of here," David said, "and you better leave me alone." He moved quickly toward the head of the alley.

"Put that rod away." Vito's voice was sharp and urgent in the darkness. "What the hell do you think you're doing?"

"You think I'm gonna let a little kike crap me like that?" Mario Pastore grunted.

"You're nuts," Vito cried out. "You'll wake the whole damn neighborhood and get us all sent up." The flash switched off and plunged the alleyway into darkness. David felt a burst of gratitude for Vito, and then ran. He heard footsteps begin to run after him, and he turned and sent the crowbar skipping along the concrete toward the shadows behind him, and then fled. Behind, there was a cry of pain, stumbling, falling, swearing, and then he ran for his life, clutching his bundle to his chest until, breathless, he reached home.

The sun was so hot through his window that David knew it was past midday. He didn't feel like getting out of bed, and lay there listening to the sounds of his mother working in the kitchen. He was glad his father hadn't wakened him for synagogue, and he was glad that the weekend was over and there were no more weddings for a few days, and no rehearsals for that day. After a while he got up, dressed slowly, put on the phylacteries and prayer shawl, and said the morning prayer.

"D . . . a . . . v . . . i . . . d," his mother called, "are you up?"

"Yeh, Ma, in a minute."

He put the prayer shawl and phylacteries away and then counted the money from the weddings. He put some into the *pishka,* and Chazan Barrt's share into his wallet. The rest he pocketed to give to his mother. In the kitchen she was waiting for him, setting breakfast. "You came in so late?" she asked. "It's time already for lunch."

"Pretty late," David answered, "after four. Where's Papa?"

"Thank God, he had a day's work today."

Eating his farina and drinking his half-and-half coffee, David thought he might have dreamt about what had happened the night before, but he remembered it too clearly. Nadie Rosen, a Jewish boy, stealing from chewing-gum machines with the Forty Thieves. What if he was caught? Or his father found out, or Rebi Greenberg? And Vito Vecchione hanging out with Mario Pastore! That was even worse. Mario and Joe Russo were part of Georgie Harvard's gang, and if they got caught, they went to jail. It wasn't like one of the kids getting off with a warning and probation, like Jimmie di Stefano, when they caught him stealing in the A & P. They were headed for bad trouble, all of them.

A plate fell, splintering in the sink, and David saw his mother holding onto the sink with both hands, pressing herself against it, rocking gently, her face pale. "Ma?" he called. She didn't answer. He got up, and just as she reached her, she bent over the sink and was sick. David held her head, turned the tap on and rubbed cold water on her temples and wrists. Her eyes closed, she stood there shaking, then leaned her forehead against the wall over the sink. "Ma?" he asked again. "Are you all right?"

She nodded. "It's all right. I'm all right."

"Too much farina for breakfast," David said, trying to make it a joke.

She smiled weakly and gasped, "Nothing kills the poor man like his poverty—and farina for breakfast every day."

He brought her a chair, and she sat down with a quick, knee-collapsing movement that seemed like falling. For a long time, she sat staring at the wall as if he were not there, until he spoke to her again. "Can I get you a cup of tea?"

"Yes, Dovid," she said, patting his head, "tea would be good."

David watched her out of the corner of his eye as he boiled the water, made the tea and poured her a cup, but she seemed not to see him, or anything; she only stared at the wall. He put the saucer into her upturned hands before she shook her head and looked straight at him. "Thank you, son," she said, "now go outside and play."

"You're sure you're all right?"

"Yes. Sure."

"I'll be downstairs in the backyard, or maybe the cellar, if you want me."

"I'll call you if I need you," she said, sipping the tea, then stirring it. "But I'm fine now"—she smiled weakly—"fine."

Vito was waiting just outside the door, and grabbed his elbow before David saw him. "C'mere," he said, his dark head falling away from his shoulders as if he were tired, but David knew what direction Vito wanted him to go in. He went along, but Vito, limping, didn't let go of his arm. A little way from the house, Vito began, not looking at him. "Last night—you remember last night?—uh better not say anything about it to my old man. You know, about Mario and the gun, well, you know. . . ." His voice trailed off and disappeared.

"What do you think I am," David asked, "a snitcher?"

Vito let his elbow go. "Naw, I knew you were okay, but I just wanted to remind you. You promise not to tell him?"

"I promise."

They stood for a minute and then, as they walked back toward the house, Vito said, "That was a smart trick last night, but not so smart for me." He stopped and pulled his right trouser leg up. There was a long blue-black bruise on his shin, and he touched it with two uncertain fingers. "That was you," he said.

"I'm sorry, Vito, really sorry. I didn't mean it for you."

"That stupid bastard, Mario, just what he shoulda got, only across his head."

"But you got it, not him."

Vito grinned. "We both got it, him worse than me. I bet he can't even walk today."

"Good!" David smiled. "I mean about Mario. And thanks, Vito, for last night."

"Fa what?"

"For turning out the flashlight."

"Aw, that," Vito said, embarrassed. "I was just keepin' us all from getting thrown in the can. That jerk woulda had every cop in Brooklyn sitting in our laps." He dropped his trouser leg and stood erect, then touched David's elbow again. "And besides, you're a pretty good kid. Like one of the family. I couldn' let Mario rough you up."

They walked into the backyard and stood leaning against the picket fence, looking out on the *boccie* alley. Mr. Ferrara and some of the others were already playing.

"Look at 'em," Vito said, "not one of the poor old bastards has a job today. Beginnin' of the week and they're all out there, rolling black balls and wondering how they're gonna pay the rent."

"Vito?" David said hesitantly.

"Yes."

"Why don't you quit hanging out with those guys?"

"Why don't you mind your own business?"

"Because you're a good guy, too, and a Vecchione."

"You promised you wouldn't say nuthin' to my old man."

"I won't, but you know all of Georgie Harvard's boys. They end up dead, or in jail for twenty years. And you will, too, if you hang out with 'em."

"Mind yours, see!"

From the front of the house they heard a hoarse voice that sounded strange and familiar at once, calling, "*Aw, scigalate, aw, spinace, potato, potato! Quatta banda, cinga zot!*" Then, "Whoa, whoa, crazy horse, you!" When Vito and he got to the front of the house, Joe and Toni and Mama Vecchione were already there, looking up at Pop Vecchione sitting on a big wagon loaded with fruits and vegetables. The wagon was painted red and green, with banks of boxes and bags of oranges, cabbages, tomatoes, potatoes, spinach, and there was a slanting roof over all of them, and a back with big signs on brown paper bags giving the prices of fruits and vegetables. Pop, up front on the driver's seat, was alternately shouting and trying to keep the big old brown horse between the shafts from moving ahead. The horse had a funny face, with a crooked white streak over the nose and around one eye, so that he looked like something David had seen in an Our Gang comedy or like the dog painted on Pop's victrola. On its head was an old brimless fedora, sun-bleached almost to the gray-brown of dust, with holes cut in it to let two petal-shaped ears, one drooping, come through. Pop brought the horse to a standstill, got slowly down from the driver's seat, and tied the reins around the big old maple tree's trunk that stood in front of the house, growing out of a little square patch of earth in the sidewalk. Then he came around to them, his eyes alive, his hands waving to the horse and wagon and in front of them as if, like a magician, he had just made them spring out of the sidewalk before their eyes. Hoarsely, he said, "How you lika my new business?"

No answer.

"Whatsamatta fa you? You no like?"

"Your business?" Joe asked, unbelieving.

"Sure, they no wanno good carpenter, Vincenzo Vecchione, no gonna sit home an' cry, smoke Di Napoli cigars"—he looked at Toni—"gonna maka business myself, be boss myself." He went to Mama Vecchione, his eyes searching her face. "Hey, you, Mama, you wanna buy tomato, spinach, orange, potato, and ..." He put his arm around her waist, pulled her to him, and said something so quickly in Italian that David didn't catch it, but he saw Joe's mouth turn up at the corners as he tried to keep from laughing. But Toni laughed out loud, glad, and Vito exploded, "Madonna, but where did you get the money? You rob a bank?"

"No have ta robba bank. Just go in, nice an' easy, an' ask fa money. They say me, 'Fine.' Now I gotta whole business." The horse snorted, shaking itself, its tail flicking the flies on its haunches. "Oho," Pop said, "I forgetta my manners." He walked to the horse's head, picked the brimless fedora off the ears, and said, "Thisa my family, Riso." He turned to them and said, "Thisa my horse, Riso, that'sa short fa *Risorgimento*." The others laughed, and so did David because they did, although he didn't know what the word meant.

"D ... a ... v ... i ... d," his mother called from the front window.

"Yeh, Ma," David answered, looking up and waving to her, "I'm here."

"Oh, hello, Mrs. Vecchione," his mother said, "and you, too, Mr. Vecchione," seeing him next to the horse.

"Ma, Mr. Vecchione just started his own business today. This is his new horse and wagon," David called proudly, pointing to them. "He's gonna sell fruits and vegetables."

"Well," his mother smiled down on them, "then I must come down and buy something. For luck." She went inside and David turned back to the Vecchiones.

"Well," Pop said, his face almost pleading with Mama Vecchione, "so how you like?"

Mama Vecchione was quiet for a minute, watching his hands fumbling with Riso's feed bag, and then she walked to him and kissed his dark cheek. "It'sa all right," she said, "it'sa fine."

When his mother came down, she brought the tradition-al bread and salt, and insisted that all the Vecchiones take some with her for good luck. She shook hands with Pop and wished him luck; then she spoke to Mama Vecchione as if she had seen her hesitation when the wagon first came, but also had seen her kiss the old man afterward. It was a hard time to make a living, she said, and any way a man could do it was all right. She wished *his* father could start such a business, with fruits and vegetables, or any-thing, so he could be his own boss and work steady. It was the steady work even more than the money, though they all needed the money to live. Otherwise, nothing went right.

Mama Vecchione nodded. "Is no good have much time. *Must have work. Bambini* to wash, man to cook fa. Is same witha man. *Must have work.*"

"Now," his mother said, "I would like to buy some-thing. What's good?"

"Everything good," Pop replied, and they all laughed.

"He's a businessman already, Mrs. Freed," Toni said. "You can see that."

His mother bought five pounds of potatoes and the old man picked them out carefully, weighed them on the iron scale that hung from the side of the wagon, threw an extra potato into the bag. "Here," Pop said, giving the bag to David, "you carry upastairs fa you mother."

His mother counted the money out of her little purse, but Pop wouldn't take it. They quarreled for a moment, his mother insisting, forcing the coins into Pop's hand. Busi-ness was business, she said, though she appreciated the thought, but she wanted to be a steady customer and he could consider her one, but she had to pay. Otherwise, she wouldn't be able to buy. He had to make a living, too. Finally, reluctantly, Pop pocketed the coins.

"You fine people," he said, looking at his shoes, "an' gotta good boy." He put his arm around David. Then he said, "You my first customer ina new business. Maybe bring me luck."

"I hope so," his mother said sincerely, and then David followed her upstairs with the sack of potatoes.

The days followed one another so slowly, it seemed, hot

cloudless days that he could almost remember passing hour by hour, his father silently sitting in the study, not talking, not even studying, because sometimes, when the door was ajar, David could see him staring out over the books through his window. His mother moved quietly pale around the house, her eyes and forehead tight, as if she were trying to remember a recipe for something she was cooking and afraid that it might slip her mind.

Rehearsals were all the same, more wedding songs and more of Ilsa Kermitt. Barrt talked about beginning to practice for the High Holy Days, and David felt the quick, satisfying gloating of his secret arrangement with The Flame. And when he left Barrt's, he almost ran to the schoolyard to play ball—basketball, handball, indoor baseball, anything the boys were playing. Sometimes he watched the others, sitting with Mr. McLean. The summer-school teacher was always there on the sidelines in that funny crouch, like someone about to start a spring who had changed his mind about running, his elbow on his knee, his freckled face cupped in his palm. His close-cropped red, curly hair seemed to move even though there was no breeze. And once, in the locker room, after a basketball game on the indoor hardwood court, they sat on the benches, and Mr. McLean, drinking from a small silvered thermos flask of milk, he said, told him stories about when he had been at college and played lacrosse and basketball, had swum and wrestled, and what a good time it had been.

Then, once, when he was wrestling for a college championship, his last year in school, something had happened. There'd been an arm clamp and a snap roll, and the fellow he was wrestling had been hurt, something about his back and spine, and the boy was paralyzed; the doctors couldn't do anything for him at all. Mr. McLean went to visit him now and then, even sent him money, because he said it was his fault, and he didn't wrestle anymore. He didn't even like showing the kids how to do it though it was part of his summer-school job and he had to.

David said it wasn't his fault, he couldn't help it, it was an accident, but Mr. McLean said you could always help it, that it was his fault for wanting to win so much, for trying too hard. Then, later, downstairs with the other kid, he bought David an Eskimo Pie for being polite while he was just "running off at the mouth."

One hot afternoon, sitting in the backyard watching the old men play *boccie*, David told Joe Vecchione about it. It was too hot to do anything, even play ball, and Joe, lying on the bench, was reading to him, first in Italian, then in English, a poem by an Italian called Dante:

> Upon a day came sorrow in to me,
> Saying, 'I've come to stay with you a while.' ...

Joe's face came away from the book, and he propped himself up on his elbow. "Oh," he said, "was that the way it was?"

"That's what McLean said."

Joe looked at the men standing and sitting around the *boccie* alley, rolling the balls without their high-pitched talk, quietly, as if in the heat it was an effort to talk, but not to play. "Look at them," Joe said. "God, they need work, work, work!" Then, turning back to David, he continued, as if he had not interrupted himself, "The man McLean hurt was one of his best friends. Or at least, that's the way the story went."

Best of all were the afternoons he and Pop drove Riso and the wagon through the quiet streets, the sun slanting through the leaves, the shadows tired-hot on the sticky tar gutters, the creaking sound of the wagon wheels like the creaking sparrows on the electric wires. Together, they called spinach, potatoes and carrots, in a duet that made David's ear tingle so that he wanted to laugh, and then, taking baskets filled with fruits and vegetables, they went into the alleys, one on each side of the street, and yelled all over again, until women stuck their heads out of the window and told them to come up with their stuff, or to go away, they didn't want any. But more to go away, they were sorry, to go away, many of them with children hanging on their skirts and crying and looking wide-eyed at the wicker basket of fruits and vegetables that David carried. And so, when they went out, David yelled himself hoarse and ran into all the alleys and courtyards and up the stairs to see if he could help Pop Vecchione sell his fruits and vegetables, but more and more the doors were closed to him, and in the alleys and courtyards he saw thin, round-shouldered men, their eyes on the ground, singing in husky, off-key voices, or playing old, out-of-tune violins and accordions, their hats in their hands, begging for the occasional penny that dropped from the windows above, carefully wrapped in bits of newspaper.

Later, when they went back to the market and to the stables nearby, David helped Pop take Riso out of the shafts and put him into one of the rented stalls, getting the horse's feed bag, and then rubbing him down and covering him with the khaki blanket while Pop counted up the day's money. Sitting on a little box in front of the stall, counting in muttered Italian, he set the money on a second box, piles of copper pennies, silver nickels, dimes and quarters, and then the two small, green-leaf piles of one-dollar and five-dollar bills. Business was not so good, he said after each counting, carpentry was regular pay, and better than this fruit and vegetable business. Then David sat on the box while Pop talked to some of the other fruit peddlers, old Italian men, most of them, but some Greeks and Armenians, and they all shook themselves like horses twitching against the summer flies. They tugged at their mustaches, their old, sunburned faces turned down at the mouth, fingers rolling their own cigarettes, white teeth biting a chunk of plug tobacco, or pursed, chapped lips spewing a fine brown spray through the air to the stable floor. Sometimes, it seemed as if the only sounds and movements in the stables were the horses snorting and nodding up and down while they fed and the old men shaking their heads sideways, mournfully, like some other kind of animal, talking sadly of the day's business and the prospects for the next day, the next week.

With the family, Pop was always jangling the coins in his pocket, showing the roll of bills for the day, especially when Vito or Johnny Strigari was around, grinning and saying that if you wanted to work, you could make a living. But when they were not there, he sat sadly with David and listened to the records on the victrola, not speaking, and David changed the records while the old man half-sprawled on the couch until someone else came in, and he sat up as straight as his bent body permitted.

David knew that Pop Vecchione couldn't go on like that for much longer, because he was making just enough to keep going, not enough to pay for the rent on the house to the bank or for food. Joe was paying for the whole family, food and rent and all, and Pop couldn't stand that. But he wouldn't go on relief, or let Toni and Johnny go on relief, and one day when Pop jingled his coins and showed his roll of bills, Johnny Strigari said it was all stage money, phony, that they were all living off Joe's teaching salary and ought to go on relief like all the rest, and let Joe and his girl Regina get married.

Pop stood up, his face red with anger, his hands rubbing his pants as if to dry the palms, and shouted that he wasn't keeping Joe from getting married or anyone from doing anything. It was *his* house, and *he* would do as *he* saw fit. He'd like to see Joe get married and have a family the *right way*, he emphasized heavily, not like some others he knew—he glared at Johnny and Toni—and Joe could get married to Regina anytime he wanted. He'd be glad to go to the wedding and give them a wedding present, too.

"Bah!" Johnny said. "Big talk!" And he walked out of the room with Toni at his heels. David followed, wanting to leave the old man alone to recover himself, when he saw Toni trying to soothe Johnny Strigari in the next room, moving her big belly against him, so that he felt trapped between Pop in the other room and those two barring his way out. He stepped into the shadows to hide them from him and him from them. Toni was saying, "You shouldn't talk to him like that. He's an old man and my father. You should show him some respect."

Johnny turned his back and said nothing. Toni pulled his sleeve. "You hear," she repeated, "he's my father."

And then Johnny whirled, his palm flicked out to her face, hard, with a sound that echoed around the cellar walls. "You should talk about respect. Butt out, kiddo. You caused enough trouble already."

Toni leaned against the wall, her face turned away and crying, while David stood still in the shadows. Neither of them paid any attention to him, although he knew that they knew he was there.

Strigari opened the door, went halfway through, and stood there, his body cut in half by light, the other half beyond in the dark, and then Toni turned her face, red-cheeked from the slap, and called after him, "Johnny, Johnny, stay with me. I don't even see you now. You're always going out, you're always away. I don't want to be alone. Stay with me."

"Who asked you? Who needed you?" Johnny said fiercely. "You ain't even good for that, now. You can have him to keep you company," he said suddenly, pointing to David. "Maybe that'll help you out." The door slammed so that it shook for a while after he had gone, and Toni stood crying against the cellar wall.

At rehearsals, Barrt suddenly began to look at him and listen to his singing with a funny strained look on his face, as if he were waiting to hear something that he didn't yet hear. So did Ilsa Kermitt when she was there, so that one day, finally, David asked what was the matter. Barrt got up from the piano bench and came very close to him, staring at him, touching his cheek, feeling his skin for a beard, curling his earlocks over his hairy finger. "No," he said to himself, but aloud, "Not yet, not yet." He straightened up. "You've been playing ball."

"Sure," David said, "why not?"

"You've been yelling?"

"A little," David admitted, feeling himself blush.

"Your voice, it's thick, hoarse, like a pudding. I thought maybe it was changing," Barrt said hesitantly. "You must be yelling like a wild Indian."

"No," David said, knowing it was from peddling the fruits and vegetables with Pop Vecchione, not from anything else.

"You better take care of that voice," Barrt warned, touching his Adam's apple so that David gagged. "Remember, it's what you are paid for."

"Yes," David managed to get out, frightened. "I must have a little summer cold or something. It's not serious. And it's not changing." *Yet,* he said to himself.

Barrt told him to be careful, to stop playing ball and getting sweated up and screaming like a madman, and then prescribed raw eggs three times a day for the throat, so David had to tell his mother because she had to buy the eggs for him.

"What does he want you to take eggs for?" she asked.

"It's good for the throat and the voice, Ma," David replied. "I guess he wants me to be ready for the High Holy Days." He didn't tell her about The Flame either, or his father, because he knew they wouldn't like his having made the arrangements with Eleazar Flamm without telling them first, and without telling Chazan Barrt.

It was Friday night when Uncle Joe and Eva came to Sabbath dinner. Five candles were lit, the tablecloth was white, starched and stiffly ironed, and the candelabrum shone. Barrt had sung the services, and David had enjoyed the choir singing almost more than he enjoyed singing alone. He had sung only a duet with Barrt, and so well that he could see Barrt's nostrils expand with pleasure as their voices joined and rose to the vaulted synagogue ceiling. And because for a few days he had stopped yelling in the alleys with Pop Vecchione, his own voice climbed high, clear and soprano. Somehow, Uncle Joe, sitting there, and Eva, both of them smoking cigarettes at the Sabbath table, changed the fine feeling. When his father said, "Good Shabbos," Uncle Joe replied and signaled Eva to put her cigarette out as he stubbed his own into the green glass ashtray. His mother came out and took the ashtray away from the candelabrum, but his father said, *"Apikoros,* don't defile my Sabbath table with your heathenism."

"Jakob, Jakob," his uncle replied cheerfully, not taking offense, "you're the same irritable bastard, aren't you?"

"Enough of such words too, dirty mouth," his father replied. "You are not with your *trombeniks* now."

Uncle Joe laughed. "Righteous and self-righteous, too. A lecture on morality even before you say, hell, how are you, and before supper, too. What sort of appetizer is that? And after I haven't seen you for seven, maybe eight months."

"For such a brother, what did you want?" His father pointed to the telephone. "You know the number. You could call."

"You know the English is hard for me," Uncle Joe grinned. It was his way of teasing his father, because his uncle's English was so much better.

"Numbers you can read. That I know," his father answered.

"David, how are you?" his uncle asked, and came and twisted his earlocks painfully with two of his big fingers, holding his face up so that he could see only his uncle's thin, beautifully curved nose and the straight slashes of nostril, the thin-lipped, sarcastically smiling mouth beneath, almost like his father's, but turned differently so that David could tell they were brothers, but very different, very different. It was not that Uncle Joe was clean-shaven, without beard or mustache or earlocks, or that he dressed like the Gentiles and went without a hat; it was the mouth, the way it turned and talked. "How's the seminary boy?" it went on asking, shaping the words that cut like knives. "I hear you're quite a singer now, a regular little Yossele Rosenblatt."

"You hear?" his father asked the question for him.

"What then, you think he's deaf on an ear?" Eva asked.

Whenever he looked at her, David was surprised all over again that someone like his Uncle Joe, with such a beautiful face, even without a beard, could be married—his mother said they weren't really man and wife, but something she called "common law," although David didn't know exactly what that meant—to such an ugly woman. She had a big mouth with loose lips that fell away from her gums, and little white teeth, child's teeth, so she always looked as if she were grinning about a joke someone had whispered in her ear, with sandy hair through which he saw her reddened, angry scalp, as angry-looking as she was now, sitting there under the kitchen light, her face and hair and voice that always seemed to be grinning and angry at the same time, even in the candlelight.

"Sure, Jakob, you have a famous son. David Freed, the little *chazan*, the golden voice of Beth Shalom Synagogue, and of course"—his thin smile turned and twisted like a split and broken pen point—"Jakob Freed's boy. And, if only a little bit, my nephew."

He felt David's shoulders and David knew he was teasing, and serious too, in that way Joe always used for his father that made them argue, but that Joe never used to his mother. "Leah Freed," Uncle Joe had said, ever since David could remember his uncle's face bent over him and his voice booming down, "no one makes fun of. Not even Jakob. She married him so he'd be the one they'd make fun of."

"Nuh," Uncle Joe said, "so you're here, and the evening service is over, and we're hungry, and Leah's *matzo* balls are in the soup, and still you're not washed." He spun David around and pushed him toward the bathroom. "So, go, go! What are you waiting for, Chanukah?"

At the table, after they had washed, his father blessed the bread and wine, and said, "Yossel, you want to make the blessing of the wine?"

"I'll bet you think I forgot how."

His father smiled and handed Joe a black silk skullcap. "Well, if you want to, you better put the skullcap on. Even if you don't, put it on. When you eat at my table, you eat like a Jew, not like a *goy*."

But Uncle Joe didn't bless the wine; they ate instead. After dinner his uncle took out his cigarettes, then looked at his father, at the Sabbath candles, and put them away. "So, Jakob, how is it with you?" Joe asked finally.

His father shrugged and closed his fingers over his beard. "How can it be? With me it's like with the others. No work. A day here, another day there, but the shop is empty, like a synagogue after services."

"So how do you make ends meet?" Eva asked, her face grinning angrily.

"So how does the cat come over the water?" his mother replied. "Jakob makes a day here, a day there, and the boy helps."

"David is working, too?" Uncle Joe asked.

"He sings at weddings and in the synagogue."

"This is a living?" Eva persisted.

"What is a living now?" his mother answered. "A quarter here, a dollar over there. The boy makes good."

"Oho!" Uncle Joe exclaimed. "He has a golden throat *and* a golden voice."

"And how is it with you, Joe?" his mother asked.

"With the Devil's son it is never too bad. Eva still works steady in the library, so it's good. It's better here in Depression than in prosperity in Poland and Russia. Maybe, even here, there'll be a revolution and it'll be better."

"In this country they don't make revolutions so easy, Joe. That bad it isn't, yet," his father said, "and even if it was, who told you revolutions will make it better?"

"No one told me. But I'm telling you."

"You're still a crazy one. You don't remember 1905? You yelled then also that the revolution would bring everything, justice and peace and prosperity. And what did it bring? Pogroms against the Jews."

Uncle Joe's eyes hid themselves like marbles beneath his sandy eyelids. "You know who I met tonight, coming here?" he asked abruptly. Without waiting for an answer, he went on, "Aarele Greenberg. He told me about David's singing. Just think, he's now a teacher in Talmud Torah and a neighbor of yours. A small world." Uncle Joe was talking about Rebi Greenberg! David hadn't even known his first name: Aarele, little Aaron. Somehow, it didn't seem to fit.

"I know," his father said.

Uncle Joe's eyes came out of hiding, cloudy and not seeing. "1905 you said? I remember it well. Yes, we made mistakes. Who would have expected pogroms?"

"I did, and I was only a boy," his father said firmly.

"Aarele Greenberg and I. Yes, we were Socialists. It was a big word then, *Socialism*. It meant making over the world, and we could do it with these." He raised his hands and stared at them, the uncertain candlelight flickering on them, and then he dropped his hands under the table again. "But we failed. Aarele and I—God, it was funny! We went with the others to make speeches, to hold meetings on street corners, to lead strikes, with our caftans and our earlocks and our *yarmelkes*. And we fought. Oh, you never saw such a fighter as that Aarele. Small and thin he was, but like a rooster, fierce and screeching." He stopped and turned to David. "I'll bet you didn't know your Rebi was such a big fighter, did you?"

David shook his head. He hadn't known, but he didn't want to speak and interrupt the story. He loved Joe's stories. For him, Rebi Greenberg was the man of the pinched arm, the pulled earlock, the ruler across the knuckles for missing the place, and the books, the books, the memorizing and learning. But then he remembered Rebi Greenberg the night he had broken up their fight with Fonzi and Banana Nose in front of D'Aquino's. Was it then that he had said that thing about not fighting?

"You didn't know," Uncle Joe was saying. "Of course not. How could you know? But he was some fighter. Once I saw him knock down together two of those big German scabs they sent to the mills, and after that, a couple of Polacks, too. Like a windmill. One, two, three."

"And did it help?" his mother asked.

"Like a corpse is helped by cupping," his father said. "After 1905, Leah, this big socialist here"—he nodded at his brother—"became a little capitalist, a *Luftmensch* peddler. Torah? No! Talmud? Also no. Rashi? Heaven forbid! But drinking and playing cards, and"—he looked evenly at Eva—"women. These, yes. And selling—to whoever would buy, whatever they would buy, everywhere."

"Didn't he maybe also send a few *groschen* home for you to study Talmud?" Eva asked.

His father's head bent. "Yes. That Joe was a good brother for. No matter where he ran, Russia, Poland, Germany, he sent money home."

"So you could study?" Eva persisted.

"No," Uncle Joe interjected, "not for him. It was for Mama and Papa, and the other ones, who died. If there was a little left for Jakob and Torah, it wasn't so bad. He had a head for Torah, not like me."

"Yes," his father said sarcastically, "you had no head, hah!" His father turned to his mother, tapping his head with a forefinger. "A head like steel and an iron memory."

"What about Rebi Greenberg?" David asked impatiently, when a silence settled, and his uncle had again taken out and again put away his packet of cigarettes.

"Oho, so you're still awake," Uncle Joe said. "I thought maybe you were asleep already, you were so quiet."

"I was awake all the time. Now tell me about Rebi Greenberg."

"What should I tell you, Dovid? Then Aarele became no more Socialist. Even the word he hated. It became for him not an idea or a hope but a curse. Like your father, he read only Torah and Talmud after that. So he went back to the seminaries and the rabbis—and he stopped fighting."

Later, in bed in his darkened room, their voices droning comfortably in the kitchen, David thought about Rebi Greenberg the fighter, and only then he remembered Mr. Greenberg's last words to Mr. D'Aquino about fighting. "When they are men, grown," he had said, "maybe they are smarter?" His Uncle Joe went on fighting, but what kind of fighting was it he was talking about? Like fighting Banana Nose with a knife in the schoolyard or in the alley? Sleepily, he tried to listen to what the voices in the kitchen were saying. Perhaps Uncle Joe was giving an answer to what the fighting was all about, but the voices seemed like the sounds he heard when he swam underwater in the school pool, the way Mr. McLean had taught him, with his eyes open and hearing only the bubbling sounds that Mr. McLean said were his blood and his breathing.

"You better tell him," he heard his Uncle Joe say. "The boy is not stupid."

"Ssha! You'll wake him up yet," his father replied, and came to the door to see if he was sleeping.

David lay there, not moving, his eyes shut tight, until he heard his father go back through the dining room into the kitchen.

"So what have you got to lose?" Eva was asking. "It's a crime to have a baby? My God, I wish Joe and I had one. Maybe he wouldn't be so worried for the man next door, and the man who lives where the Devil says good night. He'd be worried for his own, right at home."

"It's still not too late," his mother said. "If I could be"—her voice dropped so David couldn't hear her for a moment—"then you can be so lucky also."

"From your mouth into God's ears," Eva said.

"Look, Jakob," Uncle Joe interrupted. "You *must* tell Dovid. He'll find out anyway. And Eva's right. What's to be ashamed of?"

"It's more than fourteen years' difference," his mother said.

"Still better," Joe laughed.

"Someone else's behind is always easy to slap," his father replied.

"It's not so terrible," Uncle Joe said.

And then he must have fallen asleep, realizing that, like Toni, his mother was having a baby, but why and what she was being punished for he didn't know. He slept restlessly, knowing that he was dreaming, and then, when he woke up, Joe and Eva were gone and he heard loud voices in the kitchen. The lights were still on, because, he remembered, it was Sabbath, and the candle flames and smoke threw shadows that leaped along the dining-room walls and shook and turned as if they were alive.

His mother's voice, hard and loud as he had never heard it before, burned in the darkness. "Why didn't you ask him for the money? Are you so proud?"

"I couldn't ask." His father's voice was heavy, hidden. "And stop yelling. You'll wake the boy up."

"So I'll wake him. I want *you* should wake up. Jakob, Jakob, there's no work and no money and no job, and there's a child in my belly."

"Leah, I say ssha!"

"All right, ssha, ssha! And I said you should ask for the money from Joe. Did you?"

There was silence.

"Nuh, did you?"

"No."

"We cannot afford it."

"It is God's will."

"It was not God's will that made it."

"Leah!"

"Jakob, I will not have it. Never. You will get the money, and I will go to the doctor and make it clean."

"It is not right, Leah."

"Leah, Leah. What good is Leah? The money, Jakob, the money."

His father's voice rose. "Where should I get it? Should I tear it out of my heart? Out of my lungs? Leah, what do you want from me?"

"Ask your brother Joe. Joe. What's a brother for, if not to help?"

"I can't ask him."

"So I should ask?"

"No."

"There's nobody else to ask."

"From him I can't take, Leah."

"He's got it. Joe's working. Eva's working. He doesn't need it. He'll only waste the money for his crazy ideas."

"I can't ask him."

"Jakob, the time is passing. It must be soon, quick."

"It's no use talking. Come to sleep. It's late."

"Come to sleep, come to sleep. To sleep you're fine, but for what comes from it, you are not so good."

David heard his mother crying, sobbing, his father saying, "What good is crying? Will the crying help? Leah, please stop it. Stop already. All right, all right. I'll get the money. How I don't know, but I'll get it somewhere. Now, will you stop?" David heard them go to their own bedroom, and heard the sounds of their undressing, his father's tired, discouraged dropping of his shoes, and the creaking of the bed, but his mother had still not stopped her crying.

In the mornings after that, his mother's eyes were always red and swollen, and when he asked for his father, she told him that his father had gone to New York. Though David knew it was not for work, he didn't know what it was for. His mother was sad and did not want to talk much, so he didn't talk. Sonny Richter's mother had had a baby two years before, and Sonny had a little sister. He wouldn't have minded having a sister, although Sonny sometimes complained when he had to mind the baby or wheel the carriage or even give the baby the bottle, and just when they wanted to choose up a punchball or baseball game in the summer school. Yet, there was something wrong with having a baby. It was what had happened to Toni, what Nadie Rosen called "knocked up."

In the afternoons he went out with Pop Vecchione and Riso. Pop didn't talk much and David knew he was worried about "tha biziness." One day he even stopped yelling out his melons—they had a big load of long green watermelons—as if he cared. It was very hot, and David felt the sweat running down his armpits and the small of his back. Riso was hot too, and they stopped to give him water twice. Once Pop turned a full pail of water over Riso's head, fedora and all, and the horse snorted and shook the water off like a dog, wetting them both with the spray until they too were cooler and laughing. The streets were hot and steaming, but there was a sudden sound in the trees, rushing and green, like the ocean waves on a beach. The sky went gray and overcast, and Pop, squinting up at it, murmured that it was going to rain.

They were in front of a subway station, so Pop tied Riso to a fire pump and they stood in the shelter as the rain came down, slanting into steam as it hit the burning tar streets, and then as quickly as it had come the rain was over. The day was over too, Pop said, but business was not so good. They'd sold some onions and potatoes, and some of Pop's homegrown tomatoes, cabbages and lettuce, but the melons remained. As they got up on the wagon seat to drive away, the train came from New York, and people coming home from work, sweating, dirty and tired, shirts open and ties loose, their jackets hanging limp and creased from their hands, came up out of the subway. One man yelled, "You selling those melons, old man? They look plenty good."

So Pop got down and David did too, and they went to the back of the wagon where the melons were, and before they knew it, people were pressing around them and buying, a quarter, half or whole melon, and Pop was cutting and he was taking the money, making change and wrapping. They waited for other trains until the rush was over, and they sold every melon. When they got back on the wagon and drove off, Pop was smiling and singing *"Espetta rona na stella,"* and puffing his old corncob. "We maka plenny good biziness, eh, *ragazzo?*" he said.

But when they went back to that station and some of the other stations in the neighborhood, it didn't happen again, and Pop muttered angrily, "You work hard, but it don' come, it don' come."

On Tuesdays David went up to the roof, sometimes with Pop and Mama Vecchione, sometimes with Toni and Johnny Strigari, but mostly with Joe and Regina to watch the fireworks they shot off from Coney Island every Tuesday night during the summer. David loved the long zooming candles and loping bursts of flame that exploded into stars and leaped into pinwheels and flags. He knew that the others didn't like the fireworks as well, and sometimes didn't even watch. They came to the roof to be cooler in the hot nights, and he was glad for their company. Yet each time he went, he promised himself he wouldn't go the following Tuesday, because he could hear the others who came with him, talking, saying things in the dark, under the stars and the moon that they didn't seem to say during the daytime, things that hurt them and hurt him, but he kept going back all the same.

Joe and Regina arguing about marrying . . .

"Oh, no philosophy, Joe, not now."

"What better time, Gina? Philosophy's best in hopeless situations. Sometimes that's what I think it's for, a kind of mental wrestling to keep yourself fit for actions you're unable to take."

"But it doesn't solve our problems."

"Probably it doesn't solve anybody's."

"Come down to earth, Joe. You're almost thirty. I'm twenty-five, and I want to get married and have children."

"But you heard them downstairs, Gina. You heard how the old man is doing with his wagon and his vegetables. He's working for nothing. Or for the bank, maybe, and he's just about making his bank payments. How can I even think of marrying now?"

"We've been going steady for seven months now—"

"And they've been wonderful months. And we ought to get married. But how can we? Everybody's out of work in your family except you and your kid brother, and everybody's out of work in mine except me. Carmine picks up a couple of bucks with the cab, and my father thinks he's making money with his fruit peddling, but none of it amounts to much. I even tried to get a summer job, talked to old Jock McLean, but it was too late."

"I don't care about my family. I want you."

"But I do care about mine. And you're not serious, anyway. You know you're concerned about your own family too."

"Other people are out of work. They get engaged, they get married, they have children. Why not us?"

"I'm not other people, Gina. Neither are you. I'm me. I can't answer for them. Sometimes I'm not even sure I can answer for me. But I know this: my father's losing, he's fighting a losing fight against the Depression, trying to lick it single-handed. My brother Vito's hanging around with Georgie Harvard's hoodlums. And my kid sister is going to have a baby—she's not even old enough for me to consider her more than a baby herself—with a husband who didn't want to marry her, who hasn't got a job, and who looks like he's ready to run out as soon as he gets a chance. And my mother. She gets quieter and quieter, and goes on trying to keep all of us together and from each other's throats. She makes do with what we have, and feeds us, and keeps things clean, and washes and irons. . . ."

Or Toni and Johnny Strigari.

"Please, Johnny, don't yell. They can hear you downstairs, in the backyard."

"Well, let 'em hear. What does he think I am, a horse? Like that one he drives? *Risorgimento!* He's nuts even the way he names a horse. Why can't he go on relief the way everyone else does? Whaddyu think they made relief fa? He's keeping Joe from getting married. He's keeping us on pennies. I ain't even got enough to buy cigars, and I can't stand to ask him for nothing. Nothing."

"I ask," Toni said.

"Sure, but then I have to ask you."

"You didn't use to mind asking me, before."

"Before, before! All you talk about's before. It's now, now, not before anymore."

"Listen, there's that song you used to like to have me sing to you," Toni said.

In the distance a radio played "Cuban Love Song," and behind him David heard Toni begin to sing in her hoarse, summery voice:

> One memory will always fill my heart,
> One kiss will keep us when we're apart.
> I love you, that's what my heart keeps saying. . . .

And Pop and Mama Vecchione.

"Hey, thatta one isa good," Pop said of the fireworks.

"You like, David?" Mama asked.

And then after a time:

"What you gonna do, Vincenzo?"

"I dunno."

"Mebbe you listen to tha children an' go ona relief. You an' me, Toni an' Johnny. It'sa okay. Everybody ona relief now."

"David," Pop called, "you family ona relief?"

"No."

"You see?"

And later.

"But Joe wantsa marry. He'sa good boy ana Gina's good girl."

"Who'sa stoppin'? I no tell him no get marry. Children gotta grow up an' fly away lika birds. Maka nest fa themself. No worry about Papa an' Mama."

"He'sa good boy, my Joe, lika David. No fly away like bird. He'sa man. How he fly away whena family's gotta trouble? Why you so stubborn like mule? Relief's notta crime."

"Nobody give nuthin' fa nuthin'. Give me money, tell me whatta I'm gonna keep ina icebox."

Mama Vecchione sighed, sat back in her cane chair, and looked away from where a Roman candle arched against the night, and then in the dark silence, as it burst into a pinwheel of leaping reds and blues, the old man said, "But how'ma gonna pay tha bank fa tha horse an' wagon?"

David hated the summer now, the days hot with temper, his parents not talking, the Vecchiones silent, even the Forty Thieves in the schoolyard still, all quiet like the moment before a pinwheel explodes. He felt as if he were wrapped in war bandages, like cotton, warm and soft with vaseline, his mother had bound around his face and chin when he had the mumps, like a mustard plaster burning his chest. He wished fall would come, even winter, and he dreamed of cool wind and leaves on the ground. But it seemed a part of summer and no surprise when his mother told him one day that she wouldn't be home for lunch and that maybe he would have to make his father's dinner that evening. She showed him where the food was in the icebox and told him what had to be done. His father had had a day's work and had already left the house, but that morning he had come from the synagogue dragging his feet so that David knew it was only *one* day's work, and something was still wrong between him and his mother. He heard no more crying at night or quarreling, but there was a strangeness in the house: his father longer and later at studying, no talking or joking at the dinner table, and his mother not singing softly while she worked or cooked or ironed; and now, even when his father had no work, he left the house and went to the synagogue or to New York, or to wherever he went.

His mother's face was very white and her eyes deep and dark in her head, and she didn't seem able to listen to him. She said yes, yes, and repeated what she had told him. When he asked when she would be back, she said she didn't know. Late in the afternoon, maybe, or even in the evening, and possibly tomorrow morning. And when he asked where she was going she didn't answer him, but instead bent and kissed him good-bye, as she never did during the day, holding his face in her hands and promising that she'd be back soon, for him not to worry.

"Where should I tell Papa you went?" he asked.

"If he asks you and I'm not back yet, tell him I went to see the Rabbi of Vilna." She smiled. "He'll understand. Don't worry. It's a little joke we make, your father and I."

Before he could ask what the joke meant, she had softly closed the door and was gone.

David went down to see if anyone was home at the

Vecchiones'. Pop had left on the wagon, Joe had gone to the beach with Regina, Toni was busy sewing, and Mama Vecchione was cooking and didn't know where the boys were. Only Johnny Strigari was there, and David didn't want to talk to him.

After lunch he went to the schoolyard. Sonny and Nadie Rosen were there, talking to Mr. McLean, waiting for an indoor baseball game to start. Nadie was tossing the bat up and catching it by the handle. "Hi," Sonny said, "we need another guy." He had not seen Nadie since that night in the alley with Fonzi and Banana Nose.

"Hello," David said. "How are you, Nadie?"

"Hello," Nadie answered. He kept throwing the bat and catching it around the tape, but he asked, "Wanna game?"

"Sure."

But even while they played, David was restless. Something was troubling him, something he didn't understand about his mother and father. While he was waiting for his turn to bat, Mr. McLean crouched down next to him and asked what was new.

"Nothing much."

"Sure?"

"Sure I'm sure," David replied. "Whaddyu mean?"

"There's something funny with the boys. Oh, I don't mean here in the game, or even just in the schoolyard. You don't know what it is?" His pale blue eyes went black with the question, as if he were staring at something very hard to make out its shape.

"No," David said. "I don't know, but I've gotta hunch." Mr. McLean waited for him to go on. "I think maybe that bunch is beginning to get some of our kids, too."

"What do you mean by *our* kids?" Mr. McLean asked.

"You know what I mean."

"The Jewish boys?"

David nodded. He hadn't realized that was what he meant, but when Mr. McLean said it, he knew it was and he was ashamed. *Our* kids didn't really mean just the Jewish boys at all; it was all the kids in the street, in the schoolyard, in the neighborhood. Yet, it sounded as if he were talking about only the Jewish boys, and maybe that was what he really meant.

"You think only the Jewish boys have troubles," Mr. McLean said. "Did you ever hear of the Forty Thieves?"

David said nothing.

"Well, there's a gang calls themselves that. They're trying to get all the Italian kids in the neighborhood and the Irish kids, and the Swedes and Jews, too. If the kids don't join, they beat them up. And if they do join, it's worse: stealing from stores, snatching purses, even stealing cars and holding up stores. But just practicing until they become big hoodlums."

"I know," David said. "That's what I really meant when I said they were taking some of our boys, too. Not just Jewish kids, but the *good* kids."

"How do you know?"

"I know."

"You mean you won't tell me."

"I'm not a snitcher."

"This isn't snitching. Some of those kids, friends of yours, might end up in reform school, or even in jail, if—"

"If I don't tell you? What can *you* do?" David asked bitterly, watching Mr. McLean's face go white under the freckles and the suntan. "They even tried to kill me twice."

"Kill you!"

"Sure, twice. Once right here in the schoolyard, on the handball courts at night with knives, and another time in an alley with a crowbar."

"You're dreaming."

"Okay, I'm dreaming." David shrugged.

Mr. McLean looked at him for a long time, until Sonny yelled, "You're up," and David nodded good-bye and said "I've got to bat."

He played a good game that afternoon, a triple and two doubles, and set up two double plays at second base, but his heart wasn't in it. Mr. McLean kept watching him, and he kept thinking about his mother and father, and about the Vecchiones, and all that painful talk on the roof. He missed an easy grounder, then dropped a pop fly, and knew he'd had enough. He called for a substitute and Petey, waiting on the sidelines, took his place. He waved so long to Sonny and Nadie Rosen and began to walk out of the schoolyard, but Mr. McLean waited for him at the gate and asked, "What you told me was true, wasn't it?"

"I don't lie," David said.

"I'm sorry, David," Mr. McLean apologized. "I didn't mean it that way. I only meant that you haven't been going to too many movies and maybe putting it on a little? Exaggerating?"

"You don't know the half of it."

Fonzi and Banana Nose came up, standing next to them at the gate, then walking through. "Hey," Banana Nose said, "looka who's here, our old frien', Davie. You still alive?"

"Pipe down," Fonzi said. "Hello, Davie. Hi, Mr. McLean. Gotta good game for us to get into?"

"Better ask the other boys," Mr. McLean said quietly. Then he turned and said, "So long, David, I'll think about what you said."

"Sure," David called over his shoulder, "you think about it." He laughed, seeing that the laughter hurt Mr. McLean, but he didn't care. What could McLean do about Fonzi and Banana Nose, or Mario Pastore and Joe Russo, or any of Georgie Harvard's gang or the Forty Thieves?

At the house, Carmine was sitting on the stoop, fingering his guitar and humming. "Hello, you," he said, "where yuh been?"

"Playing ball in the schoolyard."

"Do good?"

"Okay in hitting, but not so good fielding."

"It's the hitting what counts, Davie. Anybody can catch 'em, but rapping out a homer, ain't too many can do that."

"No homers," David boasted, "but I got a triple and two doubles."

"Not bad," Carmine approved, strumming his guitar louder, then softer, then so loud that the strings seemed to vibrate like thunder. "Seen your Ma come home by taxi. Boy, your family must be rich. Ridin' taxis nowadays. Ain't you heard about the Depression?" He grinned. "She shoulda asked me, I gotta taxi too, yuh know."

But David had stopped listening. He ran through the door, down the corridor and up the stairs, and only just heard Carmine shouting after him not to be mad, that he didn't mean anything, that he was only joking, honest, that he didn't even care if his mother rode in someone else's hack because it wasn't even his day on today. David closed the door on Carmine's voice and called in a hoarse, frightened whisper he scarcely recognized, "Ma? Ma? You here, Ma?" He walked into the kitchen. No one. No answer. "Ma?" His voice was louder now, the voice of a stranger. He went to the living room, his bedroom, back through the living room and kitchen, peeped into his father's study, and then his parents' bedroom, but no one was there. The bathroom door, usually open, was closed. He knocked, but no one answered. He tried to push the door open, but someone, something, was blocking it shut. He shouldered it open a crack, saw his mother's shoes on the floor and began to cry, "Ma, Ma," but she didn't answer him. He threw himself against the door with all his strength, once, twice, and the third time forced it open enough so he could squeeze through.

His mother was lying on the floor covered with blood, her perique slanted over her eyes, her skirt above her waist, her body bare and bloodied. For a moment he thought she was dead. He leaned down, heard her breathing, and quickly got from the medicine chest the smelling salts they used on Yom Kippur when someone fainted from the fasting. He put the brown bottle under her nose. She moaned. He held it there until her eyelids began to flutter, holding her head tightly as she tried to twist it away from the bottle of salts.

He went and wet a towel with cold water and wiped the cold sweat from her face. Color began to come back into her cheeks. Her perique came off in his hands and he laid it on the hamper, scattering hairpins on the floor. Her hair tumbling down, long and unexpectedly black, and David realized that he had forgotten what color her real hair was; it had been so long since he'd seen her without the perique, perhaps not since he was a child. He doused the towel again and bathed her wrists and forehead, and then gave her the smelling salts to sniff once again. Her bloodied stockings and shoes came off easily, but he tried not to look at her when he struggled with her bloodstained underwear. When he finally had that off, he washed and wiped her dry, but as he drew her skirt down, he saw that her hair had been shaved. Shaved! Somehow it made her look more naked and defenseless, but he had no more time to think about it because his mother's eyes were open. "Dovid?" she said weakly. "Dovid?"

"Yes, Ma."

"I must have eaten something that didn't agree with me," she murmured.

"Sure, Ma, sure."

"Help me into the bed, son."

He put his arm under her arm, and she leaned on him and pulled herself up. How light she was! Much lighter than he had thought: she looked so big and strong and solid. But she was light. Slowly, he helped her to the bedroom and sat her down on the bed. She fell back on the pillow, her body twisting, her eyes rolling back into her head, her mouth gasping for air, then closing. He put the smelling salts under her nose again, held them there until her eyes opened again, wet and tired, floating darkly in pools of bloody whites.

"I'm all right," she whispered, "fine."

"Let me help you get into bed," he said, beginning to unbutton her blouse.

She pushed him away. "Never mind," she insisted softly, "I'm all right. Go put up the water for tea."

In the kitchen he set the kettle to boil and prepared the tea things. When he went back to the bedroom, his mother was already in a nightgown and beneath the covers, her black hair spread out like a net on the pillow behind her. Her clothes were on the floor in a bunch. "See?" she said, her face yellow and wan as her smile. "I'm fine."

"You want me to call Papa in the shop?"

"No," she said, hesitating for just a moment. "Let him finish the day's work. He doesn't have so many days' work. I'm all right. You can see it's nothing, can't you?"

He nodded, attempting a smile to reassure her, but knew he hadn't managed.

"You're frightened? You mustn't be afraid," she said softly. "It's nothing. Only a little fainting spell, like I got a few years ago on Yom Kippur when I overworked the day before and then didn't eat. You remember? So you mustn't call Papa." She looked at him questioningly. "You promise?"

"I won't."

"And you mustn't mention this . . . sickness to anyone."

He shook his head. He wouldn't.

Relieved, she sighed and closed her eyes, the eyelids black, and said, "I think I'll sleep a little."

David stood by the bed, watching her new face, its turned-down mouth and nostrils wide with heavy breathing, the black eyelids and yellowed skin. It wasn't the face of the mother he knew, but of some other woman. She opened her eyes again, slits, and whispered, "Thirsty."

"You want some tea?"

She nodded.

He made the tea, poured a little milk into it, tasted it to see if it was cool enough, and then brought it to her. She tried to sit up to drink, but she couldn't. She was too weak. He fed her a few teaspoonfuls, but as he brought another one to her tight, pale lips, he saw tears running down her nose and cheeks. He put the cup and saucer on the night table. She didn't want him to feed her. She wanted the tea but not him to give it to her. He went to the kitchen, took two of the straws she sometimes gave him to drink his chocolate milk with, and brought them to the bedroom. He put them into the tea, bent them slightly so she could drink the tea herself if he held the cup and saucer. She opened her eyes again, took the straws gratefully, and drank. Slowly, her eyes clicking open and closed, but always faraway, she drank the cup dry. Then, the straws dangling from her mouth, she was suddenly asleep.

Gently, David took the straws from her lips and brought the tea things back into the kitchen. He picked his mother's clothes up from the bathroom floor. He held them, soaked with blood and smelling of sweat, away from him and dropped them into the bathroom clothes hamper. Blood was everywhere in the bathroom, on the floor, the washstand, around the tub and the toilet, and in the cracks of the floor tiles. Carefully he washed it all twice, filling the wash pail from the bathtub tap as he had seen his mother do, then scrubbing with the brush and soap, and finally wringing the rinse rag out in the wash-pail water. When he was finished, eveything was clean and white, but the wash-pail water was grayish blood. He stood up, a sharp ache in his back and a stinging in his knees from having been scrubbing. He picked up the wash pail to spill the water down the toilet bowl, when he saw a large red splotch, ugly and shivering. Quickly, almost automatically, he reached around and pulled the flush, saw it dart, like something quick and alive, a small blood-covered animal, down the drain. For a moment he stood there, sorry, hoping to call it back, as if a whistle or a call would do that, and then, remembering, he poured the water from the pail into the toilet, and then filled the pail from the tub tap and poured it out, and flushed, again and again, until his arm ached and the water draining out was a continuous rushing noise in his head.

When his father came home, his mother was still asleep. He looked very tired, and even before he said hello, he asked where she was. David told him that she had gone to see the Rabbi of Vilna, but his father didn't smile and David knew it was not a joke, right then, when his father, alarmed, asked, "She's back?"

"Yes, she's sleeping." David didn't tell him about the bloodstained clothes and floor, nor about the tiny red animal that had fled down the toilet. He kept his word to his mother even though it meant lying to his father. He said only that his mother had told him she ate something that didn't agree with her, watching his father's face turn and twist beneath the skin and behind his beard. His father went to the bedroom door immediately, opened it softly, and went inside. In the bedroom, the door still slightly ajar, the lamplight on now, a yellow stain on the wooden floor, he heard his mother say, "Nuh, the Rabbi of Vilna did his job."

"That is not a joke," his father replied, "certainly not to tell the boy."

"What else should I tell him?"

"You're all right, Leah?" his father asked after a minute.

"I think *it's* all right, Jakob. I'm weak. Maybe I'll have to stay in bed for a week. He told me to rest. But it's done."

"You had to do it by yourself, Leah, when I wasn't home?"

"This Rabbi of Vilna isn't your kind of rabbi, Jakob. And what would it help? You'd only worry. This way it's all over. And I had to rush; there wasn't much more time to wait."

"And if something happened?"

"Then something would happen. *You* couldn't help. No one could. That was in God's hands . . . and"—David could almost see her tired smile—"in the Rabbi of Vilna's." It was clear that his father thought him stupid, unaware, but maybe, David decided, it was better to look as if he understood nothing.

"Wouldn't it help if I was there?"

"With the money you brought yesterday, you helped. For that, Jakob, I am grateful. How and where you took it I don't know. But I know how hard it was for you to ask Joe. . . ." Her voice trailed off and there was quiet until his father said softly, as he used to say it to him when he was a child, "Sleep, Leahle, sleep."

His mother was in bed for a week and his father in the house with her except for the two days he had to work. David stayed with her even when his father was home, helping with the meals and cleaning and bed-making, and sometimes quietly playing casino with her and watching as she fell asleep in the middle of a game. The first day she was out of bed, David helped her into his bedroom, which had more sunlight than her room, and brought the rocking chair so that she could sit and look out at Pop Vecchione's vegetables and the *boccie* alley and the old Italians playing and sitting beneath the umbrellas and the fruit trees. She didn't speak, only rocked quietly in the chair, looking out, and later, when he brought her some warm milk, she was asleep with a smile on her face. Every day after that she stayed awake and out of bed a little longer, an hour, two and then three and four hours at a time.

One afternoon in the second week, the first morning his mother got up to make his father breakfast because his father had a day's work, the old man came to collect the *pishka* money, the same little creased old man with a red-brown beard and silver-rimmed glasses all the way down on his dirty, long nose. He looked as if he had walked in a cloud of dust that had left a coat all over him, his face, beard and earlocks, his caftan and black summer hat. Even his eyeglasses were filmed over so that when he pushed them back on his nose into place over his eyes, David couldn't tell what color his eyes were because they seemed the color of dust.

"Nuh," Reb Brainin said, "it's hot here like a fire."

"August is always bad," his mother answered. "But this year, truly, it's something terrible."

Reb Brainin sat down at the kitchen table.

"And what's to hear with you and Jakob Freed?"

"What's to hear? Like everyone else today. We struggle for our little bread and for enough to pay rent. It's Depression and it's bad with the dress trade."

"It's bad with everything now. Such times! Such a time! *Oy vay,* such a time should fall on my enemies like hail," Reb Brainin said. "But even in a bad time, of course, it is necessary to give charity. Always someone has it worse, who has nothing to eat and no place to lay his head."

David had never liked Reb Brainin, always talking of God and holding out his hand for money. It was not the way his father or Rebi Greenberg or Rabbi Deutsch did. They did not talk about charity with their hands out, waiting to empty a *pishka* and put the money into the worn patent leather case, like a doctor's bag, that Reb Brainin always carried. "And you, Dovidl, what is going with you? Your name is now *a name*. Wherever I go, I hear it: Dovid Freed, the Boy Chazan. For such singing, you make much money, hah?"

"Singing the words of the Lord on the altar and under the wedding canopy is not for money, Reb Brainin," David said, hearing himself sound like Brainin and noting but ignoring his mother's warning, reproving glance as she sat down across the kitchen table from Reb Brainin.

"But of course," Brainin replied, "what else? It is like I do." He picked up the old worn black bag from the floor next to his dusty shoes and shook it so that the muffled sound of coins emerged. "This too is praise of God's word. Charity. No?"

David did not answer, but his mother said for him, "What else? A man who spends his life collecting for the poor, for the unfortunate, can only do God's will and good."

David knew that half of what Brainin collected was for himself, for his own living, and who was there to watch his counting? True, he gave everyone a careful little receipt, and his father said Brainin was honest, a good Jew who worked not for himself, though *he* had to make a living too, but for charity, for widows and orphans and poor scholars of Talmud. And his mother said that even if Brainin did get half, at least those who were in need got the other half in charity; if Brainin did not do the job he did, they would probably get nothing.

"Would you like a glass of tea, Reb Brainin, and a few poppy-seed cakes?" his mother asked.

"Your poppy-seed cakes are known all over, Mrs. Freed. What then? Of course, I'll have them, and a glass of tea, too."

"Dovid," his mother said, "please go put up the water."

David made the tea and served the poppy-seed cakes his mother had baked the day before in spite of his father's warning to her not to overwork. She was no longer an invalid, she said. She hadn't been well for a week or so, but that was all over, and now she had to cook and bake as always. His father said she was stubborn, that they could live without poppy-seed cakes, but she baked them anyway, a celebration she said, though she didn't tell him of what, and when she was done, her face whiter, her movements hesitant and heavy, she went back to bed.

"Dovid, please, go get the *pishkas*," his mother said.

"What?"

"The *pishkas* for Reb Brainin. You know where they are," she said, unusually irritably.

David went to the food pantry where his father and mother kept their *pishka*, and then to his own room for his. Both seemed strangely light to him as he placed them on the table between his mother and Reb Brainin. "That's fine, Dovid," Reb Brainin said, waiting for his mother to open them and empty the contents on the table to be counted. He reached over, curled David's earlocks on his fingers, and said, "You are a good religious boy. You wear earlocks, and of course you put on the phylacteries, and you sing in the house of God. Such Jewish boys we need."

David disengaged his earlocks by moving out of Brainin's reach while his mother opened the back of the first *pishka* and shook out on the table a quarter, three dimes, and a nickel and four pennies. She stared at the small change, then opened the back of David's, and two half dollars, three nickels and seven pennies fell out. She turned both *pishkas* upside down, put her fingers into them and probed, but there was no more money. Her face flushed. Reb Brainin began to cough and drank some more tea. Slowly, very carefully, his mother counted the coins: "One dollar and eighty-six cents," she said, and pushed the money across the table to Reb Brainin. Then she turned and said to him, "Did you touch the *pishkas*, Dovid?"

"No, Ma," he said. He thought how he had considered offering Pop Vecchione his *pishka* money without asking her, and blushed.

"The truth, Dovid, did you take the money?" she asked again.

"No," he answered a second time.

Abruptly she rose from the table, shouting, "You're lying!" She slapped his face, and he felt as if his cheek had been burned by a hot iron. "I want you to tell me the truth."

He didn't move. "I told you the truth," he whispered.

She slapped him, first one cheek and then the other, her own face white and red by turns, yelling, "There was more than fifty dollars in your *pishka*. I know. I counted it myself a few weeks ago because—" She stopped, and slapped his face even harder. "The truth," she screamed. "I want the truth. What did you do with the *pishka* money?"

Each time she slapped him, harder and harder, David knew he would not cry, would not give her the satisfaction, or Reb Brainin either, though he knew if he did she would come to her senses. Something inside him hardened, like a fist clenched, and he did not cry. He looked straight at her, not moving, while she kept slapping his face, until she herself began to cry. "Tell me what you did with it. Tell me that you took it," she cried. "Do you hear, tell me!" But he said nothing, letting her rain blows on him, her face twisted with crying, almost hysterical, while Reb Brainin sat and drank his tea, broke a poppy-seed cake across, dunked it into his tea, and put it daintily into his mouth. Suddenly his nose bled, blood running past his mouth, off his jaw and onto his shirt, and she stopped when she saw her hands stained with his blood. Wearily, unable now to lift her arms, she dropped back into the kitchen chair and put her head in her hands. "Go," she commanded hoarsely.

He went, glad to be free, no longer feeling the tightness in his throat and hands, but unable to cry, though his face was painfully swollen, as if he were badly sunburnt.

In the kitchen he heard Brainin talking to his mother. "And this," Brainin asked, "is all? For charity?"

"I'm sorry," his mother replied in a choked voice. "I thought there was more."

"You have no other monies?"

"Things are not good with us now," she said.

"To steal is bad enough. To steal from charity is the greatest of sins," Brainin continued.

"I don't understand. He is a good boy. He never did anything like that before."

"You must remember," Brainin said, in a loud voice that David knew was meant for him, "the story of Jacob and Esau. For Esau despised his heritage and sold his birthright for a mess of pottage." Brainin went on to describe the story David knew so well and knew that his mother had known since she was a child and had herself told him so many times. Somehow, David had always sympathized with Esau, although Rebi Greenberg and Rabbi Deutsch had cautioned against such sentiments, because he thought Jacob had tricked Esau, swindled him. Finally, Brainin's voice rose higher, a warning and a prophecy: *"The voice is the voice of Jacob, but the hands are the hands of Esau,"* and David knew that Brainin had cursed him.

He lay down on the bed, covered his head with the pillow to shut out Brainin's high, scratching voice, and tried to sleep. He dreamed his head was a top, being spun on his shoulders by two palms slapping its sides because the top cord for spinning was missing, and then it was dusk and his father was shaking him awake, saying, "I leave you to look after Mama when I have a day's work, and where are you? Sleeping in the bedroom like a baby."

David got up, his face stiffer and more painful, as his father threw the light switch. "What's the matter?" his father asked, touching his face. "You have blood all over your face and your shirt."

"It's nothing," David answered. "I must have had a nosebleed."

"Sure, you had a nosebleed. But how?"

David began to take off his shirt, but his father's voice rose. "And your face is all swollen. You've been fighting with those Italian gangsters again?"

David shook his head.

"Then what?"

"Nothing."

"What do you mean, nothing, when I can see it's something?"

"Ask Mama, she'll tell you."

His father's mouth closed and his lips turned white. "Mama hit you like that?" he asked, his voice unbelieving. "Why?"

"She says I stole the money from the *pishkas*." As he spoke the words he began to cry, trying hard to stop himself, but he couldn't. He fell back on the bed, burying his face in the pillow until he was cried out and the sobbing was only an ache in his chest. When he got up again, the light was on in the kitchen, and the sounds he heard were of his father making dinner for them.

His mother went back to bed for a few days, as though slapping him had worn her out. Nothing more was said about the *pishka* money, but David knew that the matter was not settled. Someone had to have taken the money, and only three of them knew about it. His mother hadn't known that the *pishkas* were almost empty. Of that he was sure, although why she had counted the money in them he didn't understand. He had not taken the money himself, though he felt guilty because he would have for the Vecchiones to use for the mortgage or for Riso and the wagon, and he wouldn't have asked his parents' permission for it, either. That left only his father. But why should his father want the money? And why secretly? His father could just have asked, or told him, or his mother, that he was taking the money. . . .

One afternoon, when his father was at work and his mother taking a nap, he sat reading in his room and occasionally looking out of the window to watch the *boccie* playing. Pop Vecchione wasn't there, and David realized that he hadn't seen the Vecchiones in the weeks his mother had been in bed, and he wondered if anything had happened to them. The telephone rang, and David hurried to get it before it rang again and woke his mother. He picked up the receiver and heard the rich, faraway voice. "Dovid Freed? Here is Eleazar Flamm."

"Hello, Chazan Flamm," David replied, "how are you?"

"I'm fine, and you? Your voice is still the same?"

"The same."

"Not better?"

"You will hear it for yourself."

"Good. When do we talk?"

"Talk?"

"Of course. We must sign the contract for the High Holy Days. Soon rehearsals begin. You told your parents, of course, and Barrt?"

"Not yet."

"But why not?"

"It wasn't necessary. I will tell them now."

"Ah, you waited until you were sure of me. Clever. A Jewish head. Fine, fine. So I will come over tonight, and we'll sign on the dotted line, no? You and your parents and me."

"Tonight is all right, about eight o'clock."

Work had lasted only until two, and his father came home early in the afternoon. David told him that Cantor Eleazar Flamm would be coming to the house after supper.

"The Flame? Here? What for?"

"To see me."

"To see you?"

"Yes. I am going to be his soloist for the High Holy Days."

His father was stunned. "You didn't tell ... ask ... me ... or your mother," he stammered. "You didn't say anything." He walked to the kitchen window and turned his back. "You spoke to Chazan Barrt?"

"No."

He turned and came to the kitchen table again, staring and drumming his fingertips on the table top. Absentmindedly he asked, "Your mother is sleeping?"

David nodded.

"But why? Why?"

David shrugged. "Flamm offered me two hundred dollars for the holidays, not counting Succoth. Barrt offered me sixty."

"But the money is not everything. Barrt gave you lessons, he found you weddings, he taught you the cantillations," his father continued.

"I owe him nothing."

"He wasn't good to you?"

"Good?" David laughed. "He treated me like a victrola, something he wound up that sang like a record, by itself. I am not a victrola or a record; I am a man."

"A man you are?"

"I did not forget that he took *his* share of *my* money."

His father threw up his hands. "What difference does all that make? If you made up your mind already to sing with him," he asked angrily, "why does Flamm come here tonight?"

"Because you and Mama must sign the contract with me."

"Oho, then you are not such a big man yet? You are too young to sign the contract by yourself."

David nodded.

"And if your mother and I refuse to sign, then what?"

David thought for a moment. "I will sing with no one, not with Barrt or anyone."

"Dovid!" his father's voice was fierce.

"What is it now, Jakob?" his mother asked, coming from the bedroom into the kitchen, tying her bathrobe, her hair neat and brushed, so David knew she had listened from the bedroom, though her eyes were still filled with sleep.

"Dovid is going to sing with Chazan Eleazar Flamm for the High Holy Days. The Flame comes here tonight to sign the contract, and Dovid didn't ask us, or tell Chazan Barrt. What kind of respect is this to parents? What kind of gratitude to Barrt? What comes over him?"

"Dovid?"

David did not look at her directly. Their eyes had not met since she had slapped him in front of Reb Brainin.

"You do not like Barrt?" she asked gently.

"I hate him."

"If you hated him, why did you sing with him?"

"Why?" His laughter rang high-pitched in his ears. "Because Papa wanted me to sing on the altar, because he wanted to be proud of his son, and"—his voice sank to a whisper—"because you needed the money, since Papa wasn't working."

His father looked down at his hands, then took one of his small, dark cigarettes out and lit it. His mother walked to the kitchen window. The only sound was something bubbling on the stove, and then his mother turned down the light so that it too was silent.

"You didn't like the singing?" his father asked tentatively.

"Cantillations I liked, weddings I hated."

The quiet settled in the room, thick as cigarette smoke.

"You really *want* to sing with Chazan Flamm?" his mother asked.

"I don't know," David replied. "He treats me like a man. I like that. And," he went on grimly, "he will pay me two hundred dollars for the season."

"Two hundred dollars!" his mother exclaimed.

"It's not the money, Leah," his father argued. "It is whether it is the right thing to do. Dovid doesn't have to sing if he doesn't want to."

"Big shot! He has to sing. He knows and we know. What's to be ashamed of, that a grown-up boy has to sing to bring home a little money, to help in the house? He could have worse jobs: to shine shoes, or deliver telegrams, or sell newspapers on the street corners," his mother said angrily, but David couldn't tell if she was angry with him, his father or herself.

"You will sign?" he asked them.

"You want that?" his mother asked.

"It is my choice."

"Then we will sign," his parents said together.

David left the apartment and went down into the street, knowing he had won a victory but not enjoying it. He remembered Barrt's seven to his three and the sting of his mother's palm against his cheeks, her shame about the *pishka* money. He would sing with The Flame.

No one was in the backyard, the vegetable garden or the *boccie* alley. The door to the Vecchione cellar was unaccountably locked, the first time he had found it that way, so he couldn't go inside to listen to the records. He went to the schoolyard to look for a baseball or basketball game to forget the look on his parents' faces when he had told them, "It is my choice." A baseball game was already on when he walked through the gate, and then, too, in the corner shadow of the old red brick building, Pop Vecchione was sitting on a small, three-legged stool next to a green wooden wheelbarrow on which was a half-barrel of dry ice. Stuck into it was a frosted metal container like the big milk cans the trucks delivered to the grocery stores. Mr. McLean was standing next to Pop while the old man, bent and sitting so low that he looked like a hunchbacked dwarf, was lighting his corncob pipe.

"Hello," David called.

"Hi," Mr. McLean greeted him. "Haven't seen you here for a long time."

"Hello, Pop," David said.

"Hallo, David, where yuh stay?" Pop said coolly. "No seen you more'n two weeks."

"My mother was sick, and I had to help my father take care of her."

"You mother sick?" Pop was concerned. "Bad sick?"

"No. Not now. She's gonna be all right."

"Thassa fine," the old man said. "But why you no tella about you mother? Mama come up, help cooka meal fa you father, maka house nice an' clean. Why you no say somethin'?"

"Mama has plenty to do without that."

Pop stroked his hair and said to Mr. McLean, "He'sa my favorite boy, thisa boy David. Ver good boy, lika my Joe."

"Are you Joe Vecchione's father?" McLean asked.

The old man nodded.

"I know Joe well. A good man. We used to teach together."

"You a teach too?"

Mr. McLean nodded.

"Thassa good. You gotta steady job."

A kid came up, holding a penny in his dirty fingers. "Hey, Mister, gimme a penny ices."

Pop lifted the cover off the metal container, took a paper cup from a long, thin cardboard box, and with an old spadelike scoop filled the paper cup with white lemon ice. He handed it to the boy, took the penny, and put it into his pocket. "You no gotta sell ice fa penny to kids," the old man said, puffing his pipe as if he had not been interrupted.

Mr. McLean looked down at his black and white sneakers. "Nothing wrong with selling good lemon ice to kids. Kids are customers like anybody else."

"You think?"

"Sure," David said, before Mr. McLean could answer. "I'll take a three-cent one."

Pop gave him an overflowing cup of ices and said, "You keepa you money."

But David insisted and pressed the nickel on him. Finally, Pop gave him the two cents' change, but there was something strange in his eyes, and David wasn't sure he had done the right thing. Maybe it was better to let Pop give him the ices free, feel that he could give something away for nothing, a gift.

Mr. McLean took one too, a nickel's worth, and paid for it. Then two kids started to fight at second base, yelling, "He's out, I tagged him!" "He's safe, he's inta second before you touched him." Mr. McLean went out on the diamond to make peace. David sat down next to Pop's stool, his back against the cool brick wall, and looked out on the hot, sunny ball field. The ice was cool and lemony, not sweet, and quenched his thirst. The old man next to him puffed silently on his pipe and watched Mr. McLean talk to the kids.

"You lika him, David?" Pop asked, nodding toward the summer-school teacher.

"Yes," David answered, "I like him."

Pop hesitated. "Is somethin' funny inside, not right," he said.

They watched Mr. McLean settle the argument and back up home plate to umpire. The game began again.

"That's good ices," David said, when he'd finished the cup.

"I make myself," the old man said proudly. "An' I build thisa pushcart, too. I look fa you after I have to give upa Riso ana wagon. I want you say good-bye to Riso, but you nowhere. I no lika distoib you upastairs. An' I wanna you help me build an' maka ice."

"You gave up the wagon," David said, hearing the surprise and chagrin in his own voice, although he knew that that could be the only reason for proud Pop Vecchione sitting in the schoolyard, selling lemon ices to kids for pennies. Pop told him what he had already guessed, that the business had not made enough money, that he couldn't meet the interest payments, wasn't even making enough to cover the principal of the loan. Then—he hung his head—the bank called the loan in and—he looked up—only by *borrowing*—he emphasized the word—some of Joe's savings and selling Riso and the wagon could he pay the bank off. Vito and Johnny Strigari wanted him to go on relief, but he wouldn't. So he built the wheelbarrow and made the lemon ice, the way his Aunt Nella used to make it in Napoli, and he was in *biziness* again. Not so big business, maybe, but no bank loan, no interest, no principal: only few dollars for lemon and ice, sugar and dry ice. And he was doing okay, too, making, three, four, sometimes five dollars a day, most of it profit. It wasn't, maybe, just the kind of business he wanted, he didn't like to take money from kids for ices, but it was better than relief. With the ices money and his cabbages, lettuce and tomatoes, and a couple of rows of his garden corn, they'd make out until the Depression was over and he could go back to carpentering.

David remembered that Joe had said Pop was too old, that they wouldn't hire him back, so what would he do when the fall and winter came and he couldn't grow vegetables or sell lemon ice? For the first time, David regretted that fall and winter would soon be coming, the fall and winter he'd prayed for. Now he wanted the summer prolonged so that Pop Vecchione could have a little more time to stay in business. . . .

David had almost forgotten what Eleazar Flamm looked like. Sometimes he even wondered if he had really met such a man, but when he rang the bell that night and David opened the door for him and saw him, huge, filling the entire doorway, his red-gold beard and mane shining as if there were a light buried beneath the hair, David knew he had not imagined The Flame or the meeting. "Hello, Dovid," he boomed his greeting, "The Flame always keeps his word. Here I am."

"Come in," David said and then added, so that his parents, seated behind them in the kitchen, might hear, "I'm very glad to see you again."

"And I you," Cantor Flamm replied, giving his earlock a playful tug.

David introduced him to his mother and father, and they invited him to sit at the table and have some tea. His mother went to prepare it, and his father talked to Flamm about the August heat wave and the Depression, then asked where he had come from in the old country. The Flame told him that he'd been born in Galicia and had studied to be a *chazan* from the time he was a little boy, even younger, he said, than Dovid. For a time, when he was a young man, he thought he might leave the synagogue and go to Vienna to study opera, and though his father forbade it, he went. But somehow—he shrugged—there was something missing for him in the other music, or perhaps missing in him for the other music, something sad that belonged to him, and he had eventually returned to the cantillations and the altar, although many in Vienna assured him that he had a great career in opera open to him. His father nodded while he listened, as if he understood every word The Flame was saying, although

David couldn't see why Flamm had wanted to leave the synagogue in the first place, and why he couldn't do both if he did. When he asked, Flamm replied that he couldn't serve two masters, that the voice of man for him was to sing the love of God and the praise of Israel, not for the love songs of Italian peasants, German barbarians or French ladies of the street.

His mother served tea and poppy-seed cookies, and The Flame said the cookies were wonderful. He hadn't had a good glass of Russian *tchai* since Vienna, where he used to sing Russian folk songs in exchange for real Russian tea and *borscht* in a café owned by some Czarist refugees. When they had finished drinking tea and talking, the *chazan* said, "Your son, Dovid, has told you I want him to be my soloist for the High Holy Days?"

His parents nodded, together.

Flamm took the contract from his pocket, smoothed it open on the table, and turned it toward them to read. "I will pay him two hundred dollars for Rosh Hashanah, Yom Kippur and Slichos"—he looked at David—"as I promised. But you must sign, too."

"You know," his father said hesitantly, "Chazan Barrt, the man he sings with now, taught him—"

"Nothing," David interrupted. "I knew before I sang with him, and I learned more from the old man Vecchione's victrola records than Barrt ever showed me."

"Well," his mother added, "it is late for Barrt to get a new soloist for the High Holy Days. He is the cantor in *our* synagogue, and we have known him for a long time." She said no more.

"I know how you feel," The Flame replied, "but your son has a gold voice. It should not be hidden in a small synagogue with a *chazan* like Nathan Barrt. I don't mean that Barrt is not a good cantor, only he does not have the voice or the training for your son."

"And he doesn't pay me enough. He cheated me at weddings and probably in the synagogue, too," David interjected.

"Your boy is a very good businessman," Flamm commented admiringly.

"Too good a businessman," his father responded.

"Well," Flamm concluded, sitting back, "it is up to you."

"No," David emphasized, "it is up to me. Either I sing with you or I do not sing at all."

"You told Barrt?" his mother inquired.

"No. I waited for the contract to be signed. I'll tell him after."

"Some businessman," The Flame repeated, handing them his fountain pen. "A shrewd head."

His father took the pen and signed quickly, then his mother. They passed the paper to him. He read it through, signed, and gave it to Flamm. "Thank you," Flamm addressed all of them, "you won't regret it."

"When will I get the money?" David asked.

"A hundred dollars after Rosh Hashanah, the rest after Yom Kippur."

"And Succoth?"

The Flame grinned. "Separate payment, as we agreed." He stood up, almost, it seemed, touching the ceiling. "Remember, we start rehearsals next week." He turned to his mother and father. "Thank you. Of course, Dovid will spend the Holy Days away from home, since it is not permitted to travel."

"Oh!" his mother breathed.

"Where—" his father began.

"The members of my congregation take one or two choirboys each and put them up. I'll look after him. Don't worry."

His parents stood up, his father shook hands with Flamm, and they said good night.

David went to his last rehearsal with Barrt the next day. When he got there, Barrt told him that he would be a few minutes late, for David to wait in the "music room." Ilsa Kermitt was waiting too, sitting there smoking a cigarette. "Hello, Dovid," she called, showing off her Yiddish, "how goes it?"

"Okay, I guess. Not many weddings, though."

"Oh, so? Barrt gave me two, and a circumcision ceremony, and a *bar mitzvah* party last week. I made out pretty good, almost fifty dollars altogether," she said in English.

David was pleased she'd told him. He would feel even less remorse about leaving, about going with The Flame. Barrt had given him less and less to do since Ilsa Kermitt had come, and his income had shrunk proportionately.

"Well, well, how's my duet?" Barrt greeted them more cheerfully when he returned. "I was making another wedding for you, Ilsa, my dear, and arranging to begin the High Holy Day rehearsals for you, Dovid."

"I'm sorry, Chazan Barrt," David said quietly. "I won't be singing with you for the High Holy Days."

Barrt laughed. "Why not, you've got something better to do than make sixty dollars for a few hours of singing?"

"Yes," David countered, "I'll be making two hundred dollars for the same few hours' singing—somewhere else."

Barrt stopped laughing. "You're joking," he said.

"No. Today is my last time here. I only came to tell you that I quit."

"You can't quit," Barrt shouted.

"Why not?"

"But why, Dovid?" Barrt began to beg. Then he thundered. "I taught you everything you know. When nobody heard of you, I made you a *soloist* in the synagogue, then a *chazan*. I paid you monies when your father wasn't working, gave you weddings to sing—"

"Seventy percent for you, thirty percent for me," David said softly.

Barrt looked surprised. "I should have signed you to a contract, that's what I should have done. Instead, I treated you like a gentleman, a good Jewish boy. And what do you do the minute my back is turned? You run to somebody else who'll pay a few lousy dollars more."

Ilsa Kermitt sat smiling, flicking her cigarette ashes on the red rug.

"Nuh, so say something," Barrt yelled at him.

"There's nothing to say," David answered. "You took money for work I did. You milked this cow long enough. It's enough. You cheated me, you used me. I don't owe you anything, not even an apology."

"But where will I get a soloist so late in the season? It's almost Rosh Hashanah already," Barrt pleaded.

David shrugged.

"Look, Dovid," Barrt resumed after the silence, "I'll make you a proposition. Stay with me, and I'll give you a hundred dollars for the season."

David laughed. "I told you I was getting two hundred."

"I'll give you a hundred and fifty," Barrt offered.

David shook his head. "It's not the money. You cheated me. You brought her in"—he nodded at Ilsa Kermitt—"not that it's her fault, and you gave her most of the weddings, too. Because I didn't like your seventy for you, thirty for me."

"Two hundred!"

"No. I just don't want to sing with you anymore."

"Two hundred fifty, and fifty-fifty on the weddings."

Slowly, David got up and went to the door. He turned, smiling. "Good-bye, Chazan, I hope you enjoyed all those fivers and tenners you took out of my voice. Seventy for you, thirty for me."

Barrt's face turned bluish, his nose quivered, his lips shook. "Go to the devil, you pig, ungrateful dog. . . ."

David went out, then closed the outside door behind him, and though he could still hear Barrt's bass raving, he couldn't hear what he said.

David started rehearsals with The Flame the following week, a wholly new kind of rehearsal, in an old, dilapidated YMHA building near the bridge, and although it was a long train ride up and back from his house, and sometimes he had to rehearse very late at night, David didn't mind. Flamm had the whole choir there when they rehearsed, but it was not like Barrt's quick effort to get the choir to sing together in the right key and to respond to the *chazan* at the right time. Flamm went over the cantillations again and again, the way Barrt had done with the wedding songs, but more carefully and with patience. They rehearsed each passage until they were perfect, each voice, each section, and the entire choir blending into a many-colored single voice that David felt a part of. It was a good choir too, much larger than Barrt's: five sopranos, five altos, three basses, three tenors, himself as soprano soloist and *chazan,* and another boy, a little older, named Billy Fyvel, who was alto soloist. Flamm stopped often to explain the cantillations to them and to translate for those in the choir whose understanding of Hebrew was poor. He wanted them to *feel* what they were singing, know what it meant. "You must know what it means before you can sing it, make the same feeling in people who listen to you," he repeated again and again. "You are singing of the great things, the important matters of life: the love of God, the hope of justice, the destiny of His people. Now here," he said, "for example, each time I sing a line, you answer in chorus. I sing, 'Those who are strong in faith, with a loud voice say, the Lord reigneth.' And all of you must answer with the chorus, the line repeated over and over, 'The Lord reigneth: the Lord hath reigned: the Lord shall reign forever and ever.'

"That chorus is repeated twenty times or more, so you must make each time different, not only to keep it from becoming boring. but to connect it to what I have sung. Softly, loudly, diminuendo, crescendo, two-part harmony, four-part harmony, without harmony, with dissonance.

When I sing, 'The swift burning angels declare,' then your crescendo must have swiftness and flame. When I sing, 'They who inherit the precious law with rectitude,' your voices must be filled with awe and law, singing small and quiet together. Changing, changing, do you understand? So that the music and the voices say what is behind the words, in the words, around the words, yet letting the words speak for themselves, and still raise the meaning beyond the words with your singing."

David learned much about his own voice from The Flame too, how to improve his trill and tremulo, make his phrasing more distinct, increase the cleanness and sharpness of his voice in all pitches and volumes. His voice grew stronger and better, he widened his range, and he was able to do more with his voice, control it, project it better. It improved so much in the weeks with Flamm that the *chazan* himself remarked that it was even more beautiful than when he had first heard it. Sometimes when he sang alone, or in duet with Flamm or Billy Fyvel, David saw the admiration in The Flame's face and in the faces of the other members of the choir. From the duets with Flamm he learned with every turn and trill, and their voices, his soprano and Flamm's baritone, blended together well. Yet, there was something missing in Flamm's singing that Barrt, with his lesser voice and smaller skill, had had.

"He's a phony, like a three-dollar bill, that's what it is," Billy Fyvel said sharply when David asked him about it.

"A phony?"

"Sure. He doesn't believe a word of all that stuff. Prayer. The love of God," he mimicked the cantor's speech. "He knows how you're supposed to sing it, sure, every word, but he doesn't really believe it. And if you don't believe it, it don't come out right, no matter how good you sing, no matter how much training you got. You know what I mean?" Billy Fyvel was sneaking a cigarette in the hall while Flamm was rehearsing the basses and tenors separately and the rest of them had a break. "It used to be that way with me—when I believed."

"You don't believe?"

Billy Fyvel shook his head. "Nah."

"Not in God?"

"Nope."

"Or Jewishness?"

"Nothing. All bushwah. Baloney."

"Then why do you sing in the synagogue?"

"Boy, Davie, you're a dope. Same reason Flamm sings there: I need the money. I get paid to sing, don't I? And my old man and old lady don't make enough with their lousy newsstand, working from five in the morning to eight at night, to pay for the goddam rent." Billy dropped the cigarette on the wooden floor and stubbed it out with his sneaker. "Once," he went on, "I could sing . . . like you. Oh, maybe not as good, but with the *feeling, the* feeling, because I believed in it. Now I don't, and I can't sing like that anymore. And he," Billy said, as Flamm called them back into rehearsal, "he don't believe none of it either, so that's what's missing."

The rest of the choir, boys and men, didn't like either of them, him or Billy Fyvel, because they were soloists and got paid better, so David spent most of his time at the choir with Billy, and liked him. There was something kind about Billy under his rough talk, considerate under his coarseness, and funny in the way he would always talk about "the workers" and "the bosses" and how there was a "movement" that would fix all of this Depression with a "great revolution." The older men laughed at him, joking about "Comes the revolution, we'll all eat strawberries and sour cream," and then another would squeak, "I don't like strawberries and sour cream, I like strawberries and sweet cream!" And a third would always chime in with, "You'll eat strawberries and sour cream and like it!" But Billy never laughed. He tried to argue or got angry and shouted that they'd see, all of them, they'd get stood up against the wall and shot.

One night at rehearsals, when Flamm brought in the posters advertising the High Holy Days, David saw the choir's dislike and envy of him plain on their faces as they read:

TEMPLE BETH JUDAH
presents for the
High Holy Days
Chazan Eleazar Flamm
and
David Freed
Boy Cantor
with the
Famous Flamm Choir's Eighteen Fine Voices
William Fyvel, Soloist

"They give you some buildup, don't they?" Billy remarked.

David was embarrassed, but he took a few of the posters home and gave them to his parents, who looked and nodded, trying to keep the pride out of their faces and voices while they said, fine, fine, but he mustn't act differently from the other boys, because after all, his voice was a gift from God.

A few days later, David met Rebi Greenberg on the street. The *rebi* called to him from across the way, "Dovid, Dovid, what's the matter, you're such a big shot now you don't say hello anymore?"

David crossed the street and apologized, said that he hadn't seen him.

"And you didn't come into the Talmud Torah all summer, even to say a word to your old teacher? So, all right, you're on vacation, maybe, but you'll come in the fall to study Rashi and maybe a little Ram Bam, hah?" Rebi Greenberg plucked his earlock, not painfully, as he used to when David didn't have the place, but gently, almost proudly. "Then, when you're a big *chazan*, maybe I'll be able to say, '*I* taught him Rashi.'"

Small and so slight in his black summer caftan, his blue eyes still serious behind his glasses even when he was joking, Rebi Greeberg seemed terribly frail. David tried to think of him as Uncle Joe had pictured him, banging people's heads together, leading strikes, speaking at street-corner meetings, but he couldn't.

"I saw the announcement from Temple Beth Judah," Rebi Greenberg said.

"You did? Where?" The Flame had said that they weren't going to distribute the posters until September.

"On the bulletin board in the synagogue. There's one in the Talmud Torah, too. Everybody saw them. Your father put them up, I think. After all, he's entitled to a little *nachas*, no?"

Though he regretted that his father had done that, he was touched too, but the guys would think he was showing off, and later, when Sonny and Nadie and Maxie razzed him about it, not much, he could see that they were really impressed by the posters. "Bet you'll get your name in the newspapers," Sonny said.

"You must be makin' a pile of money," Nadie added.

"Yeh, and all the girls'll be runnin' after him now," Maxie commented, nudging him with his elbow.

One morning, David took a poster down to Pop Vecchione and found him in the cellar, making the day's lemon ice. The old man read the poster carefully, shaping the words with his lips and speaking them in a hoarse whisper. "This fa me?" he asked. David nodded. "Come on," he said, "I gonna show you somethin'."

They went into the victrola room, and from one of the big chests Pop took old, yellowed squares of folded paper and spread each one carefully on the floor. There were six-foot and eight-foot-high picture posters of Caruso in *Traviata*, *Pagliacci*, *Trovatore*, at La Scala, at Covent Garden, at the Metropolitan. As Pop unfolded each one and laid it flat on the floor, David understood why The Flame had wanted to sing opera, why he had gone to Vienna. The Flame, too, had sung all over the world, but he was known only to Jews, and there was a great world beyond the synagogue that knew Caruso and Martinelli and had never heard of Eleazar Flamm, would never hear of him or any other cantor unless he came to them and sang their music in their opera houses and concert halls.

"You like?" Pop asked.

"I like." David looked at each of the posters for a long time, wondering what it would be like to sing arias in Rome and London, in Milan and Buenos Aires, listening to the bravos and encores. Then he knelt down and began to fold the posters up, carefully, smelling the age in the paper, feeling its stiff yellowness and crumbling softness between his fingers, flecks of it coming off on his hands like skin.

"I like you keepa thisa one," Pop said, holding up a poster of Caruso singing *The Pearl Fishers* at the Paris Opéra.

"Oh, no, I couldn't take it."

"Of course you can." It was Toni, heavier, her walk flat-footed, bigger in front. "He never even offered one to anybody else. Especially not *that* one. It's one of his favorites."

"Somebody calls fa you?" Pop hissed.

"Yes, David did," Toni replied. "I haven't seen him for a long time, and we're friends."

You love each other, David wanted to tell them. Why do you talk like that, snapping at each other like two dogs in the street? Please, for me, because I like you both, don't. It hurts me when you hurt each other, and I can't do anything or say anything. But he kept quiet and they went on talking.

"Always spoila everythin' with you big mouth," the old man said, and dropped the poster on the floor. "Fa!" He walked past her, stepping around her as if she were a dirty puddle, and went into the next room. As they stood there, looking at each other, the lemon-ice mixer in the next room began to crank. Toni looked at the poster, which had floated down flat on the floor, and then crouched down, and began to fold the other posters neatly into squares, one on top of the other, crying. David touched her shoulders and patted her hair. "Oh, David," she sobbed, putting her arms around him and her head against him, "I'm so unhappy I could die."

As the summer drew to a close, it seemed as if he were never home, never saw his parents or talked to the Vec-chiones, or played ball with the gang or read, or listened to Pop's victrola records. Flamm's rehearsals grew longer and later as the time until the Holy Days grew shorter. He worked them until they were hoarse and irritable, until their singing fell apart like a tired discord, but the next day they were always better. David rehearsed with The Flame in the afternoons and with the choir in the evenings, so that he left the house after lunch and often didn't return until midnight. In the afternoon rehearsals Flamm sang his part, but in the evenings, with the choir, he only whistled his part. When David, only half-joking, commented that his grandfather used to say that only teamsters and Gentiles whistled, The Flame roared that he was *not* a common man, that he *was* a good Jew and didn't care about what anybody's grandfather said.

Billy Fyvel nudged him and whispered, "He's saving his voice, you dumbbell! Think he wants to use it up, like you and me?"

At home his father was more restless than ever because there were even fewer workdays than before. "August was always bad, slow," he explained hopefully, "even when times were good. You remember, Leah, how it was?" His mother nodded. "Maybe things'll pick up a little after the High Holy Days." The portions on the table grew smaller, the farina and soup thinner and thinner, and his parents' faces longer and more nervous, until he went to see The Flame and said, "Look, I'm working more than eight hours a day, sometimes six days a week, rehearsing. I have to pay carfares, and most of the time I have to buy some food, because after our rehearsal, choir practice begins. *I need money*."

"Your father isn't working?"

"No."

"So why didn't you say something? I'll get you some weddings."

"I want to get paid for rehearsals."

"Paid for rehearsals! You're crazy or something, Dovid? Who pays for rehearsals? Even in the Metropolitan Opera they don't pay for rehearsals."

David didn't get paid for rehearsals, but Flamm did arrange some weddings and parties for him and let him skip rehearsals when he had to sing on the outside. Though David hated those weddings as he had hated Barrt's, at least he got full pay for them and there was some money coming into the house, but he had even less time for himself.

Coming home from one of the late choir rehearsals, David was aware that he was muttering and humming only when some of the people sitting near him in the subway stared at him strangely and then changed their seats, moving farther away from him. In his head he was singing the *Umipenay Chatoenu* they'd been practicing all afternoon and evening, Flamm's baritone and his own soprano, and still it wasn't right. He thought over the words:

But because of our sins were we exiled from our land, removed
    from our country,
And we are unable to go up to appear and to prostrate our-
    selves before Thee,
And to fulfill our obligations in Thy chosen house, that
    great and holy Temple which was called by Thy name,
Because of the hand that has been stretched out against Thy
    sanctuary. . . .

He got out at his station, wondering if maybe Billy Fyvel was right, if The Flame had forgotten what the words meant: to be exiled, to be removed, to be unable to worship in the house of God.

The night was hot and windless, with a faraway snow of stars that melted and reappeared against the cloudless navy-blue sky. His throat was dry, the rest of him hot and wet, his clothing pasted to his skin. Uncomfortable and intent on listening again to the song in his head, David didn't even hear their first shouting, "Hey, David, wanna ride?" until they pulled up to the curb next to him in the big yellow Auburn touring car. "Looka that guy, he don' even know where he is, or where he's goin'," Nadie Rosen said.

"Spend alla time countin' his money," Banana Nose added.

"How you like our car?" Maxie Jonas asked, sticking his head out.

"It's a beauty," David replied. "Yours?" he asked Fonzi, who was at the wheel.

"Naw," Banana Nose cut in, "it's me brudder Joe's."

"Come on, hop in," Fonzi invited.

"Yeh, we gonna Coney for a hot dog, gitta custard, mebbe go for a ride on the Cyclone," Banana Nose said.

"It's late," David said, half to himself, thinking how cool it would be on the boardwalk. "I oughta go home and sleep."

"Yeh, look under the boardwalk for the lover boys." Maxie guffawed. "Hah, Fonzi? You better come along and learn, Davie. You're way behind already."

They all laughed.

"Too hot to argue. You wanna come, come," Fonzi said, racing the motor. "It's cool down the Island, and maybe we go for a bare-ass swim and get this hot sweat off."

Nadie opened the door, grabbed his elbow, and yanked him into the back seat. Fonzi pulled the car away from the curb. "Plenny power, this buggy, huh?" Banana Nose grinned back at him from the front seat.

The wind flowed in, cool and soothing, and David sank back in the seat, feeling suddenly relaxed. Fonzi drove carefully, stopping for lights, signaling for turns. At the Island they had a couple of hot dogs, and David realized he hadn't eaten since lunch. He treated them with some of the money he had left from the weekend's weddings, and they all slapped him on the back and said he was a pretty good guy after all, even if he was a little sissy about cracking chewing-gum machines. Banana Nose wanted to go on the Cyclone and Thunderbolt and Tornado, but they didn't have enough money. Besides, Maxie Jonas said, it was too damn hot. Instead, Fonzi drove down to the end of the boardwalk and parked so they could go for a swim.

"You got trunks?" David asked Nadie.

"Naw."

"Come on," Fonzi called. "We go bare-ass. Just follow us."

When they got under the boardwalk, they took off their socks and sneakers and carried them. They walked carefully, the light from above making dim yellow stripes through the boards over their heads, their eyes not yet used to the dark. Banana Nose elbowed him in the ribs, "Getta load of that, will ya?" A boy and girl stood against a post, pressed close to each other, swaying like trees in a wind. Watching them, David tripped over two people lying on a blanket. "Oh, excuse me," he mumbled.

"Fa Crissakes, whyn't you watch where you're goin?" the man grated.

A little way farther, someone called, "What the hell you kids lookin' for?"

"Me mudder's cat, Mistah." Maxie Jonas' voice was plain in the dark. "You seen her?"

They all laughed.

Out under the sky they walked down toward the water, and close by, Nadie pulled his shirt off, dropped his pants, and yelled, "Last one in is a rotten egg."

They undressed quickly, throwing shirts, pants and underwear down on their socks and sneakers and then racing for the water. Though there was no one on the beach, David hesitated about his undershorts, then dropped them and ran after the others. The water was cold and sent shivers up his back. Then his feet danced over the sharp, broken shells, and he dove into the white waves. The water closed over him, cool and soft and salty, and he saw little lights in the dark waters. He swam underwater, feeling the pulse in his head and ears and the big bursting feeling in his chest that was like holding a high note beyond breath and hearing. When he came up gasping for air, the others were around him, splashing, shouting, diving, swimming, floating. He felt good and strangely clean.

On the way back Banana Nose drove the car, and as soon as he got behind the wheel, David knew something would go wrong. He tore the car away from the curb, turned the corner so that the tires screeched, drove through two red lights, skidded past another car coming through the intersection, and then just missed two people who had stepped off the sidewalk to cross the street with the lights. "Some buggy," Banana Nose kept grunting as he drove, "hah?"

"Look," David called out finally, "if you want to give this car back to your brother in one piece, you better take it easy."

"Joe don't care anyway," Banana Nose chortled. "It's hot, and he already used it for a job. Whatsamatta, Davie, you afraid?"

"You dumb jerk," Fonzi said quietly, "always shooting your big mouth off."

"The car's stolen," Maxie Jonas said to Nadie, surprised.

"Well, whaddyu expect," Nadie answered, "a chauffeur and a new limousine?"

"The cops'll be looking for the car, so you better slow down and quit passing those red lights," David advised nervously, as Banana Nose went through another red light. "And when you stop," he added, "I'm getting out."

"Yeh, me too," Maxie said. "No hot cars for me. Anyway, you're driving crazy." His voice shook.

"Get out anytime you want," Fonzi said, lighting a cigarette, but Banana Nose didn't slow the car down.

The siren started right after they went through another red light and were only a few blocks from home. It began with a low moan, and David thought it might be Maxie or something scared inside himself, and then it rose to a high scream.

"Cops," Nadie said, looking behind them.

"Step on it," Fonzi ordered Banana Nose. "Get off the avenue and cut down the side streets."

Banana Nose spun the car off the avenue, raced it down the dark side streets, slammed the car screeching around, shot it up another street, down a third, taking the turns almost on two wheels. But the lights of the police car followed them like two white eyes and a scream.

"They're catching up," Nadie called.

"Listen," Fonzi turned to them from the front seat. "We're gonna pull this car into that empty gas station—you know, the one near the schoolyard?—and we're gonna ditch it there. Get it? Everyone gets out of the car as soon as it stops—fast! But don't run. They'll look for guys running and be on our tails. So walk, walk slow. And get on the side streets as quick as you can."

Banana Nose turned the Auburn sharply, throwing them against the sides of the car. "Wahh!" he cried.

"Remember," Fonzi warned, "if the cops catch any of you"—he looked at David—"you don't know nothing, see!" He turned, facing front, and flicked his cigarette out of the car, a long sparking arch.

They roared into the gas station, Banana Nose stopping the car a little late so that the fenders and bumpers slammed into the back of the garage building, and David felt his teeth shake and his head snap. The car lights went dark. David opened the door and was shoved out by Nadie and Maxie Jonas behind him. Banana Nose and Fonzi were already halfway up the block, walking very fast. The three of them ran after them and caught up. "I told you to cut out the running, you dumb bastards," Fonzi gritted, grabbing David by the back of the shirt and holding him back. "Slow down! Walk!"

The five of them walked together, forcing themselves to go slow. David looked over his shoulder and saw the police car race into the gas station, its siren dying but its lights still on the yellow Auburn. The policemen jumped out and ran to the Auburn, one on each side of the car. "Don't turn around," Fonzi said, digging his fist hard into David's back.

"Ouch!"

"And shut up!"

"The cops are there," David whispered.

"Whaddyu think they was, Boy Scouts?" Banana Nose countered.

"Pipe down. You done enough harm already," Fonzi said. "Your brother's gonna beat the hell outta you on accounta this."

"Oh, yeh?"

"Yeh!"

"No time for arguin' now," Nadie said. "Keep walkin'!"

"Who asked ya?" Banana Nose said. "When I call for toilet paper, you roll in, see!"

Ahead of them, David saw a man trying to keep his steps straight, but walking in big, loose loops, from the curb to the darkened storefronts, as if he were wearing roller skates and hadn't learned to control them. He fell against one of the store windows, and for a minute, David thought the crash of glass would bring the police right after them. The man roller-skated to the curb and leaned against a streetlamp in front of them, and suddenly Fonzi let go of his shirt, leaped out to the man, and put his arm around the man's shoulder. "Hi ya, Mr. McLean, how're you?" he asked.

In the lamplight, Mr. McLean turned a white face and bloodshot eyes to them. "Hullo. Who're you? Oh, I didn't recognize you." He tried to pull himself up straight and propped his back against the streetlamp. "David," he said, "what are you doing here?"

Fonzi glared at him.

"Just taking a walk, Mr. McLean. Too hot to sleep," David answered.

"Nice to see you all . . . out of mischief."

Nadie laughed and Maxie, too, high, frightened laughter.

Mr. McLean's head perked up, his nostrils went wide, as if he sensed that something was wrong, and he moved out of the lamplight back into the shadows of the storefronts. Behind them the low moan of the police siren began again. "You in trouble?" he asked, his voice suddenly sobered in the shadows. No one answered. "David?" he asked. The headlights picked them up and the siren grew louder. Still no one spoke. The police car pulled up next to them and two policemen were standing one on either side of them, an older fat one with a gun in his hand, the younger, thinner one with a club.

"Okay," the fat one said, with a thick Irish brogue, "now, where do you think you're going?"

"We were just walking, officer," Fonzi said in his best school voice.

"I'll bet you were, just out promenadin' at midnight in that yella Auburn back there, at sixty miles an hour, like a bat outta hell, weren't yuh, now?" the fat policeman continued, waving his pistol at them.

"The boys are okay, Brady," Mr. McLean said, moving out of the shadows.

"Oho, Jocko McLean, it's you, is it?"

"Well, shure it ain't yer grandmither," Mr. McLean said, mimicking the policeman's brogue.

"Yuh never can tell, Jock," the thin cop spoke up. "She took her few drops, too."

"A little of Bushmill's Irish never hurt no one, Marty Tilton," Mr. McLean said. "Did it now, Brady?"

"Not that I ever seen." The fat policeman smiled.

"There was a car stolen this afternoon, Jocko," Tilton said. "They knocked off a gas station with it, in Queens somewhere, and they used it"—he pointed his club back toward the yellow Auburn—"for a getaway car."

"Did the gas-station people describe the holdup punks as kids?"

Brady shook his head. "No, Jock, they were older."

"You know the way descriptions are, Jocko," Tilton said.

"Well, I can tell you that all these boys were playing ball in my schoolyard this afternoon," Mr. McLean avowed, "except him." He pointed to David.

"And where were you?" Tilton asked.

"Singing, at choir practice," David replied.

"Over at St. Joseph's?" Brady inquired, putting his pistol back into the holster.

"No," Mr. McLean answered for him. "He sings in the synagogue."

"Oh, a Jew boy," Brady said.

"Look, Jocko," Tilton said, still not quite convinced, "if you're sure these kids were with you, we better be movin' on."

"Well, be off with yer, then," Mr. McLean grinned, "and Brady, I'll be savin' a drop of that Irish the next time yer up to the house."

"And don't think you won't be seein' me, either," Brady said.

The policemen walked back and got into their car. Tilton stuck his head out of the window and remarked, "You kids are plenty lucky that Jocko McLean is with you. Otherwise, we'd book you for sure."

"Okay, kids," Mr. McLean said, "it's late. Now go on, beat it. Go home to bed."

They began to walk off, and the police car pulled away and turned back to the gas station and the yellow Auburn. David turned the corner with the others, and there Mr. McLean caught up with them. They all breathed their thanks together, and even Banana Nose complimented Mr. McLean. "You wuz pretty good with them flatfeet."

"Were any of you in that gas-station heist?" Mr. McLean searched their faces in turn. "No," he answered his own question, "all of you except David were playing ball this afternoon." They nodded. "But you *were* in that Auburn. I saw you. Whose car was it?"

"It was . . ." Maxie began.

"We found it near the gas station," Fonzi interrupted him, "with the key in the ignition, so we took it for a ride."

"Just like that." Mr. McLean snapped his fingers. "You saw a car with a key in it, so you just took it for a ride. You kids better listen to me. I lied for you back there. I don't like lying, and I don't do it often, either, especially to the police."

"Who asked yuh?" Fonzi said softly.

"Yeh, who asked yuh?" Banana Nose seconded.

"Oh, so it's like that, is it?" Mr. McLean said quietly. "Okay, then, beat it. Next time I'll know better."

Fonzi and Banana Nose, Maxie and Nadie disappeared, almost without a sound, as if they had turned into shadows on the street. David stood and watched Mr. McLean take a pint bottle out of his shirt and drink. Carefully he put the bottle back into his shirt, just over the belt. It was a good place. You couldn't even tell he was carrying anything there; it just looked like the way the shirt fell before it was tucked into his belt. "Well," Mr. McLean asked, "what are *you* waiting for?"

"I wanted to say thanks."

"Okay, you said it. Now beat it."

"Look, Mr. McLean, I'm really sorry."

"Yeh?"

"I didn't know the car was stolen. I was coming home from choir rehearsal, and it was hot, and we all went to Coney for a swim." He stopped. "What's the use? You know what I mean."

"Sure, sure," Mr. McLean said after a minute. "I'm just a little off my feed. If they booked all of you, though, and found your fingerprints all over that car—and they would have—you'd have had a holdup and a stolen car to explain, and you'd all end up in the reformatory."

Without talking, they walked through the quiet streets, the only sounds the faraway hum of cars, the dim rustle of the night wind in the trees, like skirts above them, and the sound of a lone dog baying the half moon. When they reached his house, David said thanks again, but Mr. McLean replied, "Look, don't thank me. If you really want to help me, help me clean up that gang of Forty Thieves."

"There's no way I can help."

"You can tell me who's in the gang, how they tie into Georgie Harvard's mob, you can tell me a lot."

"But I don't know such things, and—"

"And even if you did, you wouldn't tell."

David didn't answer.

"You can help me, David, don't you understand?" Mr. McLean whispered hoarsely. "You can help me." He leaned down, held David's arms against his sides and kissed him on the mouth. Then, quickly, he touched him, and David pulled away and ran up on the stoop. His mouth felt as if he had touched a darkness and a flame, and both ran down through his spine and stomach and left him shaking. Suddenly, he leaned over and was sick in the garden beneath the old branches of the bare magnolia tree.

Mr. McLean was looking straight up at him, the moonlight shining on his eyes so that they were like big white tears in his face. "I'm sorry," he said, "I'm very sorry." Mr. McLean sat down on the curb, his back shaking, and

David heard him crying. He pulled the bottle out of his shirt, threw back his head, and drank.

"Good night," David called, not thanking him again.

Holding the bottle with one hand, Mr. McLean waved his other hand, as if he were putting a light bulb into a socket with it, a funny wrist-twisting motion. Then David left him there on the curbstone, still crying and still drinking, and shaking cold inside, David took himself up to the warmth of his bed.

From the moment the Rosh Hashanah ceremonies began, from the opening sounds of "The King who sitteth upon a high and lofty throne," David felt he spoke directly to God, singing His praise, pleading with Him to end this Depression, to make things right with his family, with the Vecchiones, with Nadie Rosen and Maxie Jonas. His voice rose up strong and clean in his own ears as he sang the opening *Shir hamalos:*

Out of the depths I have cried to Thee, O Lord.
Lord, listen to my voice; let Thy ears be attentive to the
    voice of my supplications. . . .

His own solo followed The Flame's and his mouth tasted of burning tears. When he was done there was the muffled burst of applause in the synagogue, until the *shammos* called out to the congregation in a hoarse whisper, "Ssha, let there be ssha! This is the house of God, not a cabaret." Only once before had David, in all his years in the synagogue, heard that spontaneous applause, and that had been when his father had taken him years before to hear the great Yossele Rosenblatt, but then the applause was thunder. Now the rustling handclapping was for him and for The Flame, and David saw Flamm's face red with the exertion of singing the *Shir hamalos,* but his eyes shining, and there was envy in Billy Fyvel's face and in the faces of the rest of the choir. The Flame nodded and winked at him, and though David knew what it meant, it did not seem proper on the altar of the synagogue on the first day of the New Year.

When they sang their first *Shema* together, David couldn't contain the mounting happiness that rose in a column of song, and the words sang themselves, as if for the ears of the Lord alone:

Hear, O Israel: the Lord our God, the Lord is One. In

silence, Blessed be His Name, whose glorious kingdom is forever and ever.

And thou shalt love the Lord thy God with all thine heart, and with all thy soul and with all they might. And these words, which I command thee this day, shall be upon thine heart: and thou shalt teach them diligently unto thy children, and shalt talk of them when thou sittest in thine house, and when thou walkest by the way, and when thou liest down, and when thou risest up. And thou shalt bind them for a sign upon thine hand, and they shall be for frontlets between thine eyes. And thou shalt write them upon the door posts of thy house and upon thy gates.

A fierce and terrible joy almost choked him and rang deep in his singing, and he knew why the *Shema* was *the* prayer of Jews everywhere and always, in their time of trouble and in their time of joy. He had been blessed because his father had diligently taught it to him, had taught him to bind it on his arm and head with the phylacteries, had shown him how to kiss it on the *mezuzahs* of the doorways of houses, so that each word was a friend, as familiar as his name.

He was grateful for the little of God's fire that had descended into his throat and heart and head. He didn't care about the look of delight on The Flame's face or the reluctant admiration of Billy Fyvel and the choir, or even the open pleasure on the faces in the congregation. He cared only for singing the prayers, for the feeling that carried him over their heads up into the vaulted ceiling of the synagogue. Each time he sang the *Adonai sfawsi*—"O Lord, open Thou my lips, and my mouth shall declare Thy praise"—it was a truth he knew, living and singing.

Four or five little bursts of handclapping had to be silenced by the *shammos*, but the choir and Flamm were caught up with him, and they sang together as he had never heard them sing before, as if they were possessed with the *Shechinah*, with the very spirit and presence of God, their words and music rising to the final pitch of his solo: "Thou hast heard my voice; hide not Thine ear at my breathing, at my cry."

Everything would be all right. David knew, he knew. He was sure. His father would get regular work again, and his mother would be cured of the little red animal, and the house would be as it used to be. They would both know and tell him that someone else had taken the *pishka* money. Toni would have the baby, and she and Johnny Strigari would be all right. Pop Vecchione wouldn't have

to peddle lemon ice anymore, but he'd have his old job as
a carpenter back, and Joe would be able to marry Regina.
The police would finally catch up with Georgie Harvard's
gang and with the Forty Thieves, and then Vito and
Maxie and Nadie and all the rest of the boys Mr. McLean
was worried about would be fine. Everything would turn
out. God would hear his voice; God would not hide His
ear at his cry.

On the altar, the tall old man blowing the ram's horn
held it as tenderly as if it were made of bones older than
time. The old man's face knotted, the cords in his thin
neck stood out, and he blew:

> *Tekeha, Teruha, Tekeha,*
> *Tekeha, Teruha, Tekeha,*
> *Tekeha, Teruha, Gedolah!*

The sound was quavering and reedy, somewhere between
the cries of pain of a man and an animal, and sent shivers
down his back. He remembered suddenly the way the
priests of Israel had blown the rams' horns at Jericho and
how the walls had fallen before them. The notes were as
sharp as if the final cry of the curved horn were the end
of all their cries and cantillations to the Lord, and something more. Then the first day of the New Year was over.

The choir's dressing room was noisy and David tried
not to listen, but the other boys and the older men and
even Billy Fyvel were talking about him. "You were
great," Billy said.

"Thanks," David said and took off his choir robe and
folded it.

"Honest, I mean it," Billy repeated, "you were wonderful today."

David didn't want to talk about it, didn't want to hear
anyone's praise. What difference did it make whether *he*
was wonderful? What was wonderful was to feel the
strange flowing thing crying upward out of you to heaven,
and knowing, knowing, that the Lord was listening to your
heart, hearing your mind.

The Flame stormed in and swept him high off the floor
into the air, as though he were a child weighing only a
few pounds. "Oh, you wonderful boy," Flamm chanted,
"you golden throat! One should kiss your hands, no, your
feet!" Flamm kissed him on both cheeks, then put him
down. "Good I knew you were," he went on, looking
down from his great height, "but magnificent I didn't

know. I didn't even imagine. Do you know what you did there?" He turned to the rest of the choir, as if they were an audience, a congregation. "He doesn't even know what he did out there. Someone should tell him, no? You made us *all* sing like a chorus of angels," Flamm said, turning back to him, "of cherubim and seraphim at the foot of the throne of the Lord."

The choir burst into applause; even Billy Fyvel, standing in front of him, clapped as if he really meant it. Then, luckily, members of the congregation began to come into the dressing room, and the applause died away. The members of the congregation came to Flamm and shook hands, and then to David, too, and stood around as if waiting for an encore or an announcement. Flamm quickly assigned the choir singers to the members of the congregation who waited. Billy Fyvel and David were introduced to a fragile, tiny old man whose name was Martz and whose pale yellow face was like a canary's. "Come," he whispered into David's ear, "let us please go out into God's silence. It is too noisy here for an old man."

"And for a young man, too," David whispered back, instantly liking the canary-faced old man. He tugged Billy Fyvel's sleeve, and they followed Mr. Martz out of the synagogue into the evening. "Come, come." The old man motioned them to follow, and led them to an old-fashioned, two-story house with big glassed-in porches on both floors. "You see there?" he pointed. "That's where you'll sleep. First you'll meet Mrs. Martz, and we'll make the blessings and have a meal, and then, maybe, we can talk a little."

Billy Fyvel nudged David. "Oh, we gonna pay for this one just like in a hotel," he whispered, as they followed Mr. Martz up the stairs. "Talking and singing and making the blessings. Fa God's sakes, they'll have us playing pinochle with 'em for their lousy bed and *gefilte* fish."

"Sssh! He'll hear you."

"So what do I care? Let him hear me. What does he want from us?"

It was a big quiet apartment that smelled of camphor and old clothes, clean and faded. An old woman, even thinner and more fragile than Mr. Martz, wearing the traditional perique and looking like a starved sparrow, met them at the door. "*Lishonah tova* ... May you be written in the Book of Life for the New Year," she greeted them, her false teeth clacking.

"*Lishonah tova*," they replied together and followed her

through several rooms, a hall, a kitchen and dining room, another hall, and finally past a study to the glass-windowed front porch where an old big brass double bed was made up, sheets turned back, pillows fat and clean, and all smelling of mothballs.

"Here you will sleep. Come on, come on"—Mr. Martz' canary face smiled—"take off your jackets. Be comfortable. Dinner will soon be here."

David felt at home in the Martzes' dining room. It had a big table, was clean, with a starched cloth and candles burning in the menorah, and the food home-cooked and tasty. Mr. Martz talked to them about the service, how much he liked the choir and Flamm, and both of them, of course. He asked about their singing, but he did not have them bless the wine; he did it himself. Billy Fyvel was embarrassed and offered to sing the *kiddush* himself, and while he sang, his soft alto quiet but penetrating, David saw tears run down Mrs. Martz' lined face.

When the food came, David realized how hungry he was. Flamm had insisted that he sing without eating beforehand. "One must have an empty stomach to have a full voice." Perhaps hunger had made him light-headed, and he had only imagined that he was singing to the Lord, that things would turn out right. He felt uneasy, as if some of the food had gone sour in the eating and the thinking, but perhaps it was only the strangeness of the house, or the wine, or the day-long hunger and tiredness.

Later, on the darkened porch, the feeling still haunted him, and he tried to tell Billy Fyvel about it as they lay next to each other in bed. He tried to explain about the Vecchiones and Mr. McLean and the Depression, but he couldn't talk about his parents. "Why?" he asked quietly, looking out of the porch windows at the moonlight and the streetlamp, both yellow among the trees' late leaves. "Why does it happen so bad?"

"Why I don't know, but it happens."

"But if God knows, how does He let it happen?"

"Maybe," Billy suggested softly, "he doesn't know."

"But He knows everything," David protested.

"Look, whaddyu want from me?" Billy said. "If He knows, then He's a louse for letting things happen—"

"Ssh! Don't talk like that!" David warned.

"—and if He doesn't know, then He's a dope," Billy concluded. Then he turned his back, pulled the sheet over his shoulder, and in a few minutes he was snoring quietly.

Why? David kept asking himself. Why? Why? until the

why grew into a huge question mark painted on the sail of a boat rocking through waves that leaped white-footed on the deck. The boat pitched and rolled and he was suddenly awake, not knowing where he was, with windows all around him, yellow lamplight outside, and the hushed talk of leaves beyond the glass. Then he remembered and at the same time felt the movement next to him. He saw Billy Fyvel, face twisted, eyes closed, holding himself in the moonlight, his hand a moving blur, his body tense until abruptly his back arched, and he groaned and held himself with both hands.

When Billy opened his eyes he was looking straight into David's eyes. "Oh, so you're awake," he said. "Whatsa matter, you jealous?" he asked when David didn't say anything. He held out a cupped hand. "Look," he said, "betcha you can't do that much."

"What is it?" David asked.

"You never done it?" Billy was surprised. He moved his hand swiftly again, as if to remind David of what he had done, but David shook his head. "You're fooling," Billy said, "that's what makes babies."

Billy got out of bed, holding his hand in front of him, still cupped, as if he were carrying a saucer. From his trousers, hung on the chair he drew a dirty handkerchief and wiped his hand. Then he came to bed again and explained, but though David tried and tried again after Billy, having watched him and laughed, had fallen asleep again, nothing happened. He couldn't do what Billy had told him everyone did to be a man, even his father and his uncle, what made men fruitful and able to multiply.

For a long while he couldn't fall asleep, but lay there listening to Billy Fyvel's breathing. Was something wrong with him? He thought about what Billy had told him, how children were born, and he thought of his father and mother, of Johnny Strigari and Toni, and his stomach rolled as if he were still dreaming of that boat. His mouth was dry but his palms wet. Quietly he got out of bed without waking Billy and tiptoed to the kitchen for a drink of water. In the dining room he came face to face with Mrs. Martz. She sat at the dining-room table playing solitaire, laying one card on another, moving cards from one pile to another, tears running down her birdlike face. In the quiet, David heard their quiet splash on the cards, like tiny raindrops on dry leaves. He nodded to her when she looked up, but she didn't see him, her eyes on something in the far distance, her hands shuffling the cards automatically.

In the kitchen Mr. Martz sat reading an old Bible at the table. He looked up, not surprised, and nodded. "You couldn't sleep," he said, stating a fact.

David shook his head.

"Sleep doesn't visit this house often, now," the old man said. "Your friend, he sleeps?"

"He sleeps," David replied, "but your wife?"

"She is waiting up for her son."

"Oh," David said, "will he be coming home so late?"

"No," the old man answered, rubbing his reddened eyelids, "I don't think so."

"Then why does she wait for him?"

"*She* thinks he will come."

"And *you* don't?"

"No, my boy," Mr. Martz said, "he will never come."

"Never?"

"Never. He's dead. He died a long time ago, during the Great War, in France, at a place called Argonne." He said the last word in Yiddish, pronouncing it as if it were English so that it sounded like "a gun."

"And still she waits?"

"Still. She does not believe that he would not come home, that he will not come home. After all," he said wearily, "he is her son." Mr. Martz leaned his face in his hands, and David turned away to the water tap. When he had drunk and turned back, the old man stood next to him, smiling. "Sleep now," he said calmly, "it is the New Year, and tomorrow another day of singing. Go to bed and let that golden voice sleep too."

When David returned home after Rosh Hashanah, it seemed he'd been away for a very long time. Summer was over without any preliminaries, and he could taste autumn in the air. A new wind in the trees dropped the leaves to the dark ground, burned red and yellow and brown, until the trees were bare-limbed. As he walked up the street toward his house, he felt like a stranger returning from a long voyage to another country. But when he saw his mother and father, and they kissed him and wished him a happy New Year, written down in the Book of Life, he was happy to be home.

"We heard about your voice even here," his father told him after lunch.

"Here?"

"What else?" his mother asked proudly. "Over the radio, on the Yiddish station, they announced in the news that there was a new boy *chazan* singing at Temple Beth Judah with the famous Eleazar Flamm. They even said the congregation in the synagogue applauded, though it is not allowed and a shame in the house of God."

They were even prouder that afternoon, when his father brought home the Yiddish paper and there was an article about "Dovid Freed, the Golden Voice of Beth Judah" on one of the back pages. It told how he had sung the services not only with his voice but with his heart, with such heartfelt piety that even Eleazar Flamm said he had never heard better from a boy and not often from grown-ups, either. David stopped reading and handed the paper back to his father.

"What's the matter?" his father asked. "Don't you like that?"

"It's not right. I sang for the Lord, not for newspapers, or radios, or even for the congregation." His voice trailed away and he knew he couldn't explain, but he saw his parents' faces even prouder. Later he went to the Vecchione cellar and listened to the Caruso recordings again and the aria from *The Pearl Fishers* twice, and knew how small and poor his own voice was.

Flamm worked them hard, and he told David that there would be no rehearsals that week, that they would only go stale if they overworked. He wanted them to be at their best for the Yom Kippur services, he said. That was always the hardest, because they had to sing all day without eating and drinking. Fasting and singing didn't mix, he said, even if fasting and praying did; but Flamm looked angry when Billy Fyvel remarked that feasting and singing didn't mix, either.

Although David had to practice at home, he realized that he had a vacation, probably the last one before school started again. He got up early, practiced in the morning, especially the *Kol Nidre*, and again after he came home from synagogue with his father, and then he could spend the day as he wanted. He sat with Pop Vecchione, selling lemon ice, or helped the old man to make it, or worked in the garden with him. He walked with Joe and Regina in the park and listened to the band concerts with them, or even went swimming at Coney Island with Nadie and Maxie and Sonny. Sometimes he sat with Toni and Mama Vecchione, shelling peas and cutting string beans, while Toni sang "Ramona" or the "Cuban Love Song" or "Wedding of the Painted Dolls."

The whole week was like that, calm and restful. He read some of the books Joe Vecchione gave him, he looked at the Ram Bam his father had bought for him to study in Talmud Torah, and tried to remind himself that everything would turn out right; but he felt uneasy and unquiet. The autumn wind blew cool and steady with a certainty he wished he had in his heart.

One morning, David awoke to the sound of a rooster crowing, and thought he was dreaming of that summer he and his parents had gone to the mountains, where he had every morning been wakened by roosters and the lowing of cows. Only when he was fully awake did he remember it was the morning before Yom Kippur, his vacation was over, and it was time for *schlogen kaporos*. The rooster was tied to the faucet in the bathtub, and it began to screech like a bad *shofar* while he washed and brushed his teeth.

"Ssha!" his father commanded, coming in to see why the rooster crowed. "Your time is short," he said to the bird. "Soon you will be at peace," but though David saw that his father intended it as a joke, he did not quite feel like laughing.

After breakfast they brought the rooster, still crowing, into the kitchen for the ceremony. His father began and they read together:

> Children of men, such as sit in darkness and in the shadow of death, being bound in affliction and iron, He brought them out of darkness and the shadow of death, and broke their bands asunder. Fools, because of their transgression and because of their iniquities, are afflicted. . . . Then they cry unto the Lord in their trouble, and He saves them out of their distress. He sent His word and healed them and delivered them from their destructions. . . . If there be a messenger with him and interpreter, one among a thousand, to show unto man his uprightness: Then He is gracious unto him, and saith, Deliver him from going down to the pit: I have found a ransom.

As his father read, he held the rooster by its yellow legs and slowly turned the rooster around his head three times, and the words in his father's mouth were a promise even as the rooster's scarlet comb shook. All would be well, everything calm and quiet as that week had been, and as they finished the *kaporos* together, David felt sure:

This is our change, this is our compensation, this is our redemption. This rooster is to be killed while we shall be admitted and allowed a long, happy and peaceful life.

They took the rooster back to the bathtub, and while David held it, his father tied it to the faucet once again. In his hands the rooster was quiet, not making a sound, as if it already knew it was doomed, as if it were half-dead with the weight of sin and atonement for his family. The scapegoat for the Freeds.

In the kitchen, afterward, they sat at the table, and his father smoked one of his dark cigarettes, and then spoke softly. "Dovid, I have something to confess to you and to your mother."

His mother bowed her head and looked at her hands, and so did his father, and David was sure that his father had already told her what he was about to tell him. His father blew thin streams of smoke and his mouth made motions of speech, but no words issued. After a very long time, in a low, reluctant voice, he said, "It was I who took the *pishka* money."

"It was not my intention to steal it," his father continued after a pause, and David saw the effort in his face, the whiteness of his knuckles, and wanted to cry out that he need say nothing more, that it was enough. "I meant only to borrow it. I needed it for ... for Mama's ... operation." He looked up from his hands. "I should have asked my brother, Uncle Joe, for the money, but I was too proud. I couldn't. I thought there would be time, more days' work, before Reb Brainin came to collect from the *pishkas*. And then I'd be able to return the money before he came. I didn't want your mother to know. When I gave her the money, she thought I had borrowed from your uncle. That's why"—he slumped down in his chair and his voice was a lost whisper—"she slapped you. She thought you took the *pishka* money. She didn't know. It wasn't her fault, it was mine."

It was like seeing his father naked, as he had seen his mother that day of the red animal, when she lay uncovered on the bathroom tiles. He was sorry he'd seen both, and not sorry, too.

After a time his father straightened up again and said, "I wanted you to know, my son. I didn't want to go to the synagogue on the Day of Atonement with this on my conscience."

There was another long silence until his mother, impatiently gesticulating, said, "Nuh, Dovid, say something to your father!"

But he couldn't. There was nothing to say.

The rooster crowed suddenly from the bathroom, and they looked at one another and laughed, but the laughter was close to weeping and their eyes shone with tears that did not fall.

The evening of the Day of Atonement began the same way the New Year had, but right from the beginning, David knew something had changed. He sang the opening *Kol Nidre* with all his heart and voice, but although there was once more the congregation's hushed applause and the sexton's "Ssha!" he felt as if Flamm were holding his mouth, as if Billy Fyvel were dragging him down, as if the whole of the choir were choking his voice, damping his feeling. He kept trying to pull them up, then trying to rise above them, up to the heights he'd felt on Rosh Hashanah, to the feeling that the Lord had opened his lips, that his mouth was declaring God's praise, but his voice seemed tied to his teeth and buried in his throat. Something was missing in Flamm, in Fyvel, in all of them, and he felt it like a burden.

When the congregation came to the *Al chait,* he remembered how during the *duchanin* the year before he had looked up and been afraid to be blinded by the finger of God, by the very presence of God. What a dumb kid he had been then! Billy Fyvel said that God didn't know, didn't care, was blind. That was funny. Instead of being the way it was when he was a kid, the finger of the Lord blinding you if you looked up at His presence on the altar, God was blind when He looked down from the altar if you pointed your finger at Him. He caught himself up. Was he crazy? Was he listening to Billy's foolishness? He believed, he knew he believed. He knew God was real, He was good, and He would listen to the pleas of His people. But when he came to the prayer he read the words like a plea:

Answer us, O Eternal, answer us. . . .
Answer us, Thou who are clothed in righteousness, answer us. . . .
Answer us, Thou who are just and upright, answer us. . . .
Answer us, O God of our Fathers, answer us. . . .

and each time he read the line, he felt impelled to shout out the "answer us."

After services, at Mr. Martz' house, David asked Billy Fyvel what had happened in the singing. "Nothing," Billy growled.

"Aw, come on. You heard them too."

"Well, whaddyu expect," he asked angrily, "that they'll sing like angels every time?"

"Don't get mad," David said. "I was only asking."

"Sure, sure, don't get mad. You're just asking." He pulled his nose. "Why shouldn't I get mad? You think everybody's dumb, like you, believe all that crap? I told you, you dope, you gotta believe it to sing like that, you hear! And nobody, none of 'em, believes it, can't you see?" Billy began to cry and turned himself away in the bed, covering his head with the blanket, sobbing until he fell asleep.

David awoke from a choking nightmare he couldn't remember and went for a drink of water. Only when he got to the dining room and saw Mrs. Martz sitting at the dining-room table playing solitaire and heard the dropping of her tears on the cards did he recall that it had all happened before. When he came into the kitchen, Mr. Martz' canary-yellow face was where he expected it would be, over the black Bible, and David knew he wasn't dreaming.

"Good evening," the old man said, laying aside the Bible and taking a gold watch from his vest pocket to look at the time. "It's a little late, no?"

David tried to answer but no words came.

"I told you that sleep doesn't come here often," the old man said. "It is like the Passover, as if someone had rubbed the blood of a lamb on the door so that the Angel of Death would pass over and kill only the Egyptian firstborn. Only with me it is a little different, hah? The blood is my first and only son's, and the angel that doesn't stop here is the Angel of Sleep."

David nodded, not sure he had heard him right.

"You wanted something?"

"A glass of water." He went to the sink.

"You're not fasting?"

It was the Day of Atonement, a fast day. Sleep and the dream had left his throat and mind cottony, and he'd forgotten. "I forgot," he apologized. "Thank you for reminding me."

The old man began to read his Bible again. David watched his narrowed eyes flicking from right to left on the page, his pale yellow fingers turning the leaves, and he remembered Fonzi and Banana Nose making fun of his "backwards" Hebrew books. For the first time, watching Mr. Martz' eyes and fingers, it looked backwards to him too. "Don't you ever sleep?" David asked.

Mr. Martz looked up, as if he'd forgotten he was there. "You're still awake?" he asked, and David wasn't sure whether the old man was surprised or disappointed. "Yes, I sleep sometimes. A little nap here, a little dream there."

"You're not tired?"

"I'm tired all the time, very tired. But there'll be plenty of time to sleep soon, only to sleep. And I have been tired for a long, long time," Mr. Martz said, his face as it had been when he spoke about his son's being killed in the war.

David wanted to say that things would turn out fine, that the Angel of Sleep would come to his house, but he wasn't sure. He went to Mr. Martz and patted his dry hand where the veins stood high and blue in the old tight skin. He hadn't seen the presence of God before; perhaps he'd imagined the spirit of the Lord shining in his voice. Maybe Billy Fyvel was right. . . . His thirst grew as the thought shook him. Maybe God didn't know, or care. He wet his lips with his tongue and said good night, and went back to bed past the sounds of Mrs. Martz' tears and solitaire without seeing her.

In the synagogue the next morning, his voice was husky and his mouth dry. His skullcap seemed too tight on his head, and the fringes of his prayer shawl were tangled and wet as his fingers closed and opened over them. He was impatient to get the service over with. His head was hot, and he felt the sweat run from his armpits over his chest and stick where his belt was tight against his waist. He started to worry about getting sick. The prayers seemed only words, heavy, unfriendly, too familiar words that he was bored with, that lay like leaden weights on his voice. His singing, he knew, was still clear and precise, but not better than the choir's or Flamm's, and Flamm looked sharply at him as once his voice almost went flat in one of their duets.

After the morning service, David went back to the choir dressing room with the others. His head still ached and he felt dizzy. When the boys in the choir began to yell and the men to argue, he took off his robe and prayer shawl and went out for a walk. He walked quickly away from the synagogue, the fresh air against his face begin-

ning to wipe away his headache and to rinse the taste of
fasting from his mouth. The autumn leaves stained the
sidewalks and he suddenly felt he had sung enough, he
didn't want to go back. But he knew he had to. It was the
last day of Yom Kippur singing, but he would still have to
sing for Succoth. Flamm hadn't paid him yet for Rosh
Hashanah, but he had promised that he would give him all
the money for the High Holy Days the next week, and
then maybe he'd be able to rest. Even as he thought it,
David knew he'd have to continue to sing as long as his
parents needed the money, as long as he had a voice.

He walked for a long time and then hurried back, went
through the rear door of the synagogue into the choir's
dressing room, and slipped quietly inside so that if he were
late he wouldn't be noticed. The sun was shining through
the dressing room's high windows and fell like a dusty
spotlight on Eleazar Flamm in his cantorial robes and
white skullcap with Ilsa Kermitt sitting in his lap. They
were at a small table with paper plates that had a whole
roasted chicken, hard-boiled eggs, slices of *challah*, red
tomatoes and green pickles, and a bottle of red wine that
glowed in the sunlight. All of the food looked as if it had
tumbled out of the big brown marketing bag that lay at
the end of the table.

The Flame had a chicken leg in one hand and was
gnawing on it, while with his other hand he held Ilsa
Kermitt in his lap and stroked her behind. Laughing, she
sat and fed him slices of egg. "Good?" she was asking in
Yiddish. "Oh, Eleazar, you're a pig. And on Yom Kippur,
too."

Shocked, David stood silently in the doorway. A *chazan*
eating and drinking in the synagogue on Yom Kippur!
And with a *shicksa* in his lap. Sacrilege. And Ilsa Kermitt,
what was she doing there? Did she know Eleazar Flamm
too? A foolish question. It was clear she knew him—and
very well.

Flamm nuzzled his big, bearded face into Ilsa's bosom
and she giggled. "No, not here, Eleazar, not now. Stop."
She ran her hands through his red beard and red mane,
fingernails shining an even brighter scarlet. "Come on,
now," she said, as he burrowed his face into her breasts,
"have some wine. You'll be thirsty until after the evening
prayer." She twisted in his lap to reach the wine bottle and
saw David. For a moment she sat there, her hand outstretched but not touching the bottle and her lipsticked
mouth an O. As she got up out of Flamm's lap, smoothed

her dress and picked up the wine bottle, Flamm said, "Where're you going, Ilsa? I still have time. The boys are already out on the altar. I sent them out a little early so we could be alone and enjoy a little."

"We're not alone," she said in English.

"Good holiday," David greeted them in Yiddish, for want of anything else to say. "I didn't know you knew each other so well."

The Flame turned to him, drumstick in one hand and the other opening and closing, until Ilsa Kermitt put a glass of wine into it. Automatically, Flamm gulped some of the wine, then wiped his mouth on the back of his other hand. "You're here?" he asked finally. "Why aren't you on the altar?"

"I had a headache, so I went for a walk, for some fresh air."

"On Yom Kippur you leave the synagogue to go for walks? What kind of *chazan* are you?"

"On Yom Kippur you eat and drink in the synagogue?" David replied. "What kind of *chazan* are you?"

Flamm suddenly discovered the chicken and wine in his hands, looked around him as if for a place to hide them, then put them down on the table with the rest of the food.

"It was no accident that we met that night?" David asked.

"No," Flamm replied.

"It was her?"

Flamm nodded.

"Why?" David turned to Ilsa Kermitt.

"Because you had a beautiful voice," she answered, "because I knew you needed the money, because I thought Eleazar—Chazan Flamm, I mean—would teach you and train your voice, because I liked you—"

"And because," David interrupted, "you got more weddings and made more money with Barrt if I was not in the way?"

"Yes, that too." She bit her lip.

"Why couldn't the great Eleazar Flamm get you weddings? More than Barrt could?"

"It's ... well ... he and I ..."

"And who made you the rabbi, to give judgments and ask questions?" Flamm interjected angrily. "Get out, do you hear! On the altar!"

"As soon as I am dressed," David said. Slowly he took off his jacket, put on his robe, his special skullcap, kissed the fringes of his prayer shawl, blessed it, and put it on. They stood watching him, not moving, not speaking. As he walked to the door, to the corridor that led to the synagogue proper, Flamm called, "Dovid?"

David turned.

"You won't . . . mention this? Ilsa . . . and this?" His hand took in the food and wine, but his voice, and his anger, failed him.

David shook his head. "No, I won't mention it." Then, because he was hurt, and wanted to hurt The Flame too, he went on, words brimming over his lips. "But that's why you are not a great *chazan*, why you're not a Rosenblatt. You don't believe here"—he touched his temple—"or here"—he touched his chest over his heart. "You have the voice, the skill, the training, but not the feeling, not the understanding of prayer. You don't believe. You know the words and the music and how they go together, but you can't hear what's behind them, what really joins them together." He saw the pain filter through Flamm's face, into Ilsa's, as she watched him, and then he turned and went out.

The rest of that day they sang as if again they were possessed. David sang with a bitterness and disappointment he couldn't have put into words, but that cut into the music. The flurries of applause the *shammos* had to quiet told him he was singing well, but Flamm sang better than David had ever heard him before, as if he were trying to prove something, and every time he sang a passage well, a turn, a trill, a falsetto, a roaring crescendo, he looked straight at David.

The shadows were long in the synagogue; the voices of the congregation dry and tired by the time they came to the closing prayer. David felt he couldn't sing another solo at all, as if his voice, like the day, had faded away, but he wanted to show them, The Flame, Billy Fyvel, the choir and the congregation, and he felt his bitterness rising in his throat like a belief as he began the *B'rosh hashanah.*

On the First Day of the New Year and on the Fast Day Atonement, it is inscribed, it is sealed and determined, how many shall pass by, and how many be born: who shall live and who shall die, who shall finish his allotted time, and who not; who is to perish by fire, who by water, who by the sword, and who by wild beast; who by hunger, or who by thirst; who by an earthquake, or who by the plague; who by strangling, or who by stoning; who shall be at rest, and

who shall be wandering; who to remain tranquil and who
be disturbed; who grow rich, and who become poor; who
shall be cast down and who exalted.

David sang the first line again, struck the high note of "it
is sealed and determined" in full voice, and there was a
sudden quavering trill of pain in his throat. His voice went
reedy shrill, then broke and sounded like the old man's
breathless blowing of the ram's horn. Flamm's head
sprang up like a jack-in-the box to stare at him, and Billy
Fyvel's face fell toward his chest. David caught himself,
fought the shaking in his throat, and brought his voice
back in clearly and in tone, and he could see Flamm's face
relax and Billy's thin mouth flatten into a smile. But by
the time they blew the ram's horn to indicate that Yom
Kippur was over, that atonement was over, David knew
his voice was changing, for in the soprano he had heard
not only the first alto tones, but the uncontrollable shrill-
ness that told him he was beginning to lose his voice.

When David came home that night his voice was a
harsh whisper, his throat ringed with pain. Fever and
chills shook him, and his mother put him straight to bed
and dosed him with hot tea and lemon, *schnapps* and
aspirin. But the fever lingered and made his eyes burn
beneath his heavy eyelids, and his head felt packed with
mud. He slept heavily, without dreams, and when he
awoke, always found his mother waiting there with tea or
hot farina, or warm milk and crackers, her face pinched
with worry, her nervous hand feeling his forehead for
fever. His mother kept the window shades down, and
when he awoke he didn't know whether it was day or
night, and he didn't care. The darkness seemed a friend,
and each time he awoke, to eat or drink or go to the
bathroom—he would not accept the bedpan, and fought
until at first his father carried him and then his mother let
him go by himself—he felt as if he had come from a
black restful world into a shrill bloodshot one, and he was
grateful when sleep returned, swift and dark as a blanket
over his face. He cared about nothing except the sleep and
the dark. Not even about the money. Let them worry. He
was tired. He was sick. He had to stay in bed, sleeping, to
get better.

One day he opened his eyes and the shades were up.
The sun shone through the window, and outside the old
men were playing in the *boccie* alley and the leaves from

the twisted fruit trees floated to the ground. The world looked clean and blue, and he realized that autumn had arrived, that soon he would have to go back to school. He wondered if school had begun yet and asked his mother when she brought him some soup, but she told him he'd been sick only for a week and still had plenty of time. He'd been in bed a week, an entire week, but it seemed as if he'd spent a month there. He wanted to get up, dress, go outdoors, but when he tried to get out of bed and stand by himself, his head whirled, his knees went weak, and he fell back on the bed, panting with the effort.

The next afternoon, when his father was playing casino with him, David asked, "Nobody came to see me?"

"No, Dovid. You had a very bad grippe, and Mama didn't want anybody should come near you."

"Nobody called?"

"Yes, Chazan Flamm. Twice. He will call again."

"Did he say anything?"

His father shook his head. "Only that he would call again." His father played the good deuce. "He paid you?"

"No, Papa, not yet," David answered. "You're not working?"

"No," his father replied, and looked down at the cards. He played the ten of spades, and his father took it with the good ten, and picked up an eight of spades and the good deuce at the same time.

"Didn't the Vecchiones ask for me?" David said after a while.

"No."

"Did they know I was sick?"

"They knew."

"And they didn't come up?"

His father laid the deck down on the bedcovers, paused to light one of his brown cigarettes, and said, "One of the old one's sons was taken by the police."

"Which one?" David asked wearily, already sure he knew.

"His name I don't know."

"The one with the long black hair, dark, you know, the painter?"

His father nodded. "That one."

David built three sevens, one a four and a three, and took them. The police had arrested Vito. What for? But even as he asked himself the question, he knew it had finally come, knew it had only been a matter of time. He hoped it would be okay, but he knew it wouldn't be, yet he wasn't surprised; he'd expected it all the time. The Forty Thieves and Georgie Harvard's boys had fixed it—and Vito had gotten caught.

The first day David was outside the weather was cool and clear, and he found Joe Vecchione reading in the backyard.

"Hello, David," Joe said. "Say, you look awful. Pale and skinny. What's the matter, don't want to go back to school next week?"

"No, it's not that. I've been sick."

"My father asked about you, and Toni. They said you weren't friends with the Vecchiones anymore since you had become a famous singer."

"Oh, that's not so, it's—"

"I was only teasing, David. Take it easy." He moved down on the bench. "Here, come on and sit down. Want to hear some Italian poetry, Dante?"

"No. I want to hear about Vito."

"Oh."

"My father said something about the police."

Joe put a marker in his book and placed the book carefully on the bench. He stood up, wedged his arms between the pickets, and looked out at his father's field, the *boccie* alley, the fruit trees. "Vito wouldn't listen," Joe said softly, "not to me, not to Toni, certainly not to my father." His shoulders moved as if he had a chill.

"What happened, Joe?"

"He got tied up with some of Georgie Harvard's hoodlums, Mario Pastore and Joe Russo—"

"I know, but what happened?" David interrupted impatiently.

"You knew?"

"I told him he'd get in dutch if he kept running with those guys, but—"

"He wouldn't listen to you, either."

David nodded.

"How'd you know?"

"I used to see him hanging out with them on the corner, and once he helped me when they were after me," David replied.

"They were after you? What *they* and what for?"

"The Forty Thieves, and then Mario Pastore because I punched his brother Banana Nose."

"The Forty Thieves? What are they?"

"They're kind of the kid gang of Georgie Harvard."

"Banana Nose, you mean that little hooknosed kid brother of Mario's?"

David nodded.

"What did they want?"

David told him of the night Vito had let him slip out of the alley and away from Mario Pastore and Banana Nose, Fonzi and Nadie Rosen, told him about the chewing-gum machine, his singing money, but again brought the conversation back to Vito.

"Vito went with Mario Pastore and Joe Russo on a job. They pulled a job," Joe said sarcastically, "a job, just like the movies. Hot stuff. Big-deal operation, they robbed a little grocery store in Bay Ridge and cleaned out the cash register. But the poor groceryman and his wife tried to stop them—and Mario shot them."

"They're not . . ." David tried to say *dead,* but the word wouldn't come.

"No. The woman was wounded in the hip, but the man has a bullet in the chest. He might die and if he does, then they're up for murder."

"But Vito didn't shoot him, did he?"

"No. He didn't even have a gun. Only Mario had a gun. A rod, Vito called it, a rod. Can you imagine? Too many gangster movies. Joe Russo had a knife, but Vito had nothing. He was there, though, he was there."

"Sure he was, whaddyu expect?" It was Johnny Strigari. He and Toni walked up the steps from the cellar and stood at the bench with them. "Vito ain't got no job, ain't got no money. Whaddyu expect him to do? Sit an' read books like you, or go an' sell lemon ices like his old man?"

"Isn't that better than being in prison with a bullet in the shoulder?" Toni asked quietly.

"That's your crazy old man's fault, nutty bastard, callin' tha cops. And on his own son. Madonna, I would'na believed it if I wasn't here and seen it with my own eyes."

"Pop called the police?" David asked Joe.

"After they shot the grocer and his wife, they tried to get away in a car," Joe said slowly, still looking out at the *boccie* alley. "But people heard the shooting, saw them running, and called the cops. A police car chased them. Vito was driving, and one of the cops shot him through the shoulder. He stopped the car and the three of them scattered, and the cops lost them."

"Vito came home, down to the cellar, and the old man is there an' sees him bleedin' all over his clothes on the floor, and what does he do? Crazy, crazy! Dumb old bastard! His own son shot, and he goes upstairs, to your house"—Strigari pointed to him—"an' calls the cops."

"Pop put Vito on the couch downstairs," Joe said finally, as if Strigari had never interrupted, "and bandaged him up. Vito told what happened and who was with him, and Pop used your folks' telephone to call the police."

"And they came and took Vito," Toni added.

"So now he does time," Johnny Strigari said, "but if your old man keeps his big trap shut, the whole thing blows over and nobody gets hurt."

"Except the groceryman and his wife," David said.

"But they already got it, anyhow. What difference it makes? Vito goes to jail don't do them no good."

"Maybe," Toni said, "if Vito gets away with it this time, next time he kills somebody. Then they give him the electric chair."

"Sure, sure," Strigari said sarcastically, "it's okay a man turns his son over to the bulls because it's your old man."

"You think it's easy, Johnny? You think my old man doesn't love Vito? Vito's his son. You think that doesn't cut him up, tear a piece out of his life?" Joe asked. "Only, my father knows he's helping Vito more by turning him over to the police, even if he hurts himself."

"You Vecchiones, you're all nuts, alla you," Strigari said. "Have a little fun"—he looked at Toni's swollen belly—"gotta get married. Can't getta job, but can't go on relief. Your boy gets shot and cops go lookin' for him, so you call them and hand him over like a sheep. You Vecchiones are crazy. You still think you're livin' in a small guinea town, makin' pasta and keepin' goats. This country's not like tha old country. Gotta cut a few corners just to keep goin', make a buck." He looked at them but no one answered. "Aw, whatsa use, you all just plain nuts." He went back down to the cellar and slammed the door behind him.

"My father told the cops Vito was out with Mario and Joe Russo, and the cops picked them up, too. They're all down in the Tombs, and in a couple of weeks they go to trial," Joe said, completing the story.

"For murder?"

"No," Toni whispered, "the groceryman's still living."

"And even if he lives, then maybe they'll get five to ten years," Joe said bitterly. "With time off for good behavior, of course."

"*You* wouldn't have called the police?" Toni asked him, and David noticed how thin and pale her face was.

"No." Joe turned from the fence to face her. "No, I wouldn't. Vito's not a bad kid. He got in with the wrong crowd, and this would have taught him a lesson. A bullet in the shoulder and being chased like that, that's plenty of lesson. What do you think will become of him in prison? He'll learn to be a gangster, so when he comes out he'll be just like Mario Pastore and Joe Russo, bad, rotten, mean."

"But the groceryman and his wife," Toni protested softly.

Joe's shoulders slumped, and he looked down at his shoes. "Yes, Toni, I know. How about them? But Johnny was right, Vito's going to prison doesn't help them even a little bit." He turned his back and shook the picket fence so hard it rattled. "I don't know! I don't know!"

"Papa did right," Toni insisted, "he did right."

"Papa's always doing right," Joe said, "but maybe you can't do right all the time. Maybe sometimes you have to be easier, more human, not so right."

David found Pop Vecchione in the schoolyard in the corner shadow of the old red brick building, in the same place he always used to be. It looked as though he'd never moved, never gone away. He was alone, sitting on the tiny three-legged stool next to his big green wheelbarrow of lemon ices, lighting his corncob pipe. David sat next to him on the ground, his back against the wall, and said nothing. The old man nodded and puffed his pipe awake, then silently leaned back against the wall with him. They sat there watching the kids practice indoor baseball until Mr. McLean came out of the building and started a game on the diamond.

When the game was going, Mr. McLean came up and bought a nickel's worth of lemon ice from Pop Vecchione. "Hello, David," he said, not looking at him. "Haven't seen you for a long time."

David remembered the night Mr. McLean had touched him and cried, "You can help me," and he felt sick to his stomach. Mr. McLean's face seemed to be a stranger's, dark hollows under the eyes, freckles like discolored sand under his skin, lips twisting like snakes. David turned his face away without answering, but he felt guilty. Mr. McLean had always been good to him before, yet now he felt that Mr. McLean was dirty, that if he touched him once again he'd never be able to wash the stain off.

Mr. McLean stood there for a long time, looking from him to Pop Vecchione, letting the lemon ice melt in his hand, before he went back behind home plate to umpire the ball game.

It was late in the afternoon when Fonzi and Banana Nose came into the schoolyard with Petey and Sal. They walked over to Pop Vecchione's wheelbarrow, and David felt the hair on his neck rise. As they ordered nickel lemon ices, David inched himself slowly to a standing position, his back against the wall. Pop filled the four paper cups and handed one to each of them, saying "Thatsa twenny cents."

"Twenny cents?" Fonzi said. "For this stuff?" He licked the ices once, then dumped it all over Pop Vecchione's shoes. Suddenly the schoolyard was quiet; no sounds of bat and ball, no running, no yelling, and David knew everyone was watching.

"What crap!" Banana Nose said, and turned his ices over Pop's gray head.

Petey threw his at Pop's face and missed, slopping ice over the old man's shirt. David blocked Sal's hand so that his ices slipped out of his hand and fell all over his own pants.

"You stay outta this, Davie, yuh hear?" Banana Nose warned.

"This ain't your business," Fonzi said.

Pop wiped his face with a big blue plaid handkerchief and shook the ices off his head onto the concrete. He didn't get up and didn't look surprised. "Whatsa you name?" he asked Banana Nose. "You Mario Pastore's brudder Joseph, no?"

"What's it to yuh?" Banana Nose answered.

"You gangster lika you brudder," the old man said. He stamped his foot, and immediately the four of them backed off and had knives in their hands except Fonzi, who had a small black thing like a thick piece of licorice hanging from his wrist by a leather band. "Whatsamatta, you scare?" Pop Vecchione asked. "I only brusha tha ice offa my shoes."

David saw the four of them spread out, Fonzi and Banana Nose in the center, Petey and Sal on the sides, and they began to edge in closer again.

"Get up, quick," David said hoarsely, and was surprised

at how fast the old man was on his feet, the three-legged stool steady in his hands in front of him.

"No fool with me," Pop said. He put one of his hands out. "Giva the twenny cents an' g'wan."

"Listen to the old guy," Fonzi called. "He wants his twenny cents, Banana Nose. Whyn't you give him his twenny cents?"

"Give money to stool pigeons? Naw. Cops give stoolies plenny. This guy's a big stoolie. He got plenny now," Banana Nose jeered.

"How much yuh think he gets fa your brudder?" Fonzi asked.

"So much," Banana Nose grunted, and lunged at the old man with his knife. Pop caught the blade on the stool and his other arm swung sharply, the open palm catching Banana Nose's face with a sound like water splashing on pavement.

David felt sick of it, felt like running away. He was tired of fighting, always fighting. He felt his sickness still weak inside of him, shaking like a chill. What was the use? It was the same thing over and over again, until one time Banana Nose or Fonzi or somebody just like them, jumped you with a knife and stuck it through you. They just never let you alone, never. He heard Pop Vecchione's voice from a great distance, saying, "You get outta heah, David, go home." And he felt as if the old man had slapped him, not Banana Nose. Even if it was no use, you couldn't run, you couldn't just walk away. The four of them swam back into his vision, blurred at first, as if he were looking at them through water, and he realized that tears of anger and weakness were in his eyes.

"I warned you once," he heard himself saying, "that the next time I'd kill you."

Mr. McLean's voice came from his right hand. "And if you think he doesn't mean it, I do. David," Mr. McLean called out sharply. David spun and Mr. McLean threw him a baseball bat. David caught it, choked it, and was ready to use it. "First one of you starts anything gets his head busted, you hear?" Mr. McLean said quietly, working the bat backward and forward a few inches at a time. "Now, go on, drop the pigstickers and beat it."

Petey dashed in, grabbed the can of ices, and threw it and the wheelbarrow over. The ices can bounced out, fell on the concrete, its cover rolled away like a wheel, and the ices spilled all over the ground. Then Fonzi was swinging the small black stick. He hit Pop's wrist and the old man dropped the stool, grabbed his arm, and bent over in pain, his lips sucked in over his teeth, his pipe falling from his mouth. Fonzi's face was shining, as if it were covered with sweat, his eyes soft and wet as if he had smoke in them. He picked his arm up again, this time to hit Pop Vecchione's bent head, and David realized the black thing was a blackjack. He was so surprised that he just stared at it. A blackjack!

Mr. McLean jumped in front of him. With one hand he brought his baseball bat down sharply across Fonzi's forearm, and the crack sounded like a ball hit to center field. Fonzi's arm fell, the blackjack dangling from his wrist, and David knew Mr. McLean had broken Fonzi's arm. He heard Mr. McLean grunt and saw Banana Nose pull his knife out of Mr. McLean's shoulder. Mr. McLean dropped his bat, and David, with a fierce joy bubbling like a stifled scream in his throat, swung the bat with all his might at Banana Nose's back. He caught him across the shoulder blades and followed through just as if he were hitting a ball, feeling the strain go up from his wrists through his arms into his back and shoulders, and watching Banana Nose go down on his face as if he had been pushed off a diving board. "All right," he heard himself shout, as he put himself between them and Pop Vecchione and Mr. McLean, "anymore you want? The next one gets it across the face!"

They stared at him and at Fonzi looking at his broken arm as if he couldn't believe it, and Banana Nose lying face-down on the concrete, his breathing like a sick dog's. Fonzi picked his right arm up with his left and, hugging it to his body, cradled it as if it were a baby. Petey and Sal pulled Banana Nose to his feet. His knife, pearl-handled and bloodied, lay on the concrete, and no one bent to pick it up.

"I'm gonna kill you, McLean," Fonzi said. "I'm gonna find you someday and kill you dead!"

"The next time, Alphonse," Mr. McLean said, using Fonzi's school name, "you better make sure you get it right, because there isn't going to be any second time." He held his hand over his shoulder, the blood leaking through his fingers.

"You plenty brave because you got the cops on your side."

"And you've got the Forty Thieves and Georgie Harvard's hoodlums."

"You friggin' fairy!"

Mr. McLean flushed and bent for his bat.

"Pansy, pansy!" Petey jibed.

"My brother likth it, but I can't thdand the stuff," Sal lisped, putting one hand on his hip, the other behind his head, and shaking his behind like a girl.

"Queer as a tree-dollar bill," Banana Nose gasped.

"You his pretty boy, David?" Petey called. "You like that stuff?"

"Betcha he does," Fonzi said. "You get yours someday too, Davie."

"You talka plenny. Now g'wan," Pop Vecchione said. He plucked Mr. McLean's bat and Banana Nose's knife off the concrete in a single swoop. "You heah? I breaka you face!" They backed away, but Banana Nose spit a long arch of spittle that landed at the old man's feet.

"Agghh!" Pop yelled, raised the knife and bat over his bent body, and charged them.

They ran before him and he chased them all the way to the schoolyard gate. They stopped outside, he inside. They raised their arms, cut stiff palms into the crooks of their elbows, and shot their arms out as if they were jabbing at the old man, yelling, *"Bafangu,"* together. Only Fonzi, holding his arm, turned and walked away.

When Pop came back, he asked Mr. McLean if he was hurt bad, and when Mr. McLean shook his head, the old man tore his shirt sleeve off and looked at the wound. The top part of the shoulder was cut and bleeding. Pop slit the sleeve with Banana Nose's knife and bandaged the shoulder. "I better see a doctor, eh?" Mr. McLean asked, while the old man soaked the rest of the sleeve in the melting ice in his wheelbarrow and wiped the arm clean of blood. The old man nodded. "How's your arm?" Mr. McLean asked.

"Mebbe sting a little before," Pop replied. "Be okay now. You wan' I go with you to tha doctor?"

Mr. McLean shook his head. "No, thanks. And thanks for the bandage, too."

"No, Mista, I thanka you. You no gotta nuthin' to thanka me fa."

Mr. McLean shook his hand and then put his hand out to David. "Good-bye, David."

David shook his hand and let it go. "I'll see you next summer," he said, feeling ashamed of having dropped the hand so quickly, and wanting to say something nice because he was grateful for Mr. McLean's courage and help.

"I don't think I'll be back next summer, you know,"

Mr. McLean said, looking away. "I'm going to take a little trip, I think. Maybe I won't even teach anymore, either." He shook himself. "We'll see. Good-bye, now, David, and God bless you."

He turned and walked back to home plate, where the kids still stood frightened in a circle, and yelled, "Okay, what are you waiting for, is this a ball game or isn't it?"

Together, David and Pop Vecchione got the wheelbarrow straight and the ices can back into it, and together they wheeled it back to the fence. When they looked back the baseball game was already under way once more, and David saw Mr. McLean take his jacket from the door handle where it hung and sneak a quick drink from the bottle in the pocket. He put the jacket over his wounded arm, and then, when he saw them watching him from the gate, he waved his good arm to them. Across the ball field he looked very small and thin, and his voice was almost lost in the distance. "Good-bye," he called, "good luck."

As they pushed the wheelbarrow toward the house, Pop Vecchione put his arm around his shoulder. "You *not* lika that, lika him?" the old man asked him, embarrassed. "Not lika whata the boys say?"

David shook his head. "No," he said, shivering. "Thank God, I'm not."

School had begun, and David got up in the mornings, hurried to the synagogue, and then walked to school. He was so busy that he had little time to remember that his father wasn't working still, that Pop Vecchione now couldn't sell his lemon ice and couldn't get another job, that Vito was in jail. School was better, though he missed having Toni there and was angry when some of the kids teased him about where his girl was this term. He spent more time in the library listening to symphonic and chamber music in the record room, and he liked that even better than opera, though he still went to the cellar when he could to hear Pop's old records. The books and music kept him from worrying about his parents, the Vecchiones, his voice.

The Flame called him to come to be paid for the High Holy Days. Ilsa Kermitt opened the door of Flamm's apartment when he rang the bell and said, "Hello, David, come in." David followed her down the hall to the big living room and sat down next to the piano. "Would you like some milk, tea?" she inquired. He refused. "Eleazar will be a minute," Ilsa said, and went out.

The Flame came in and asked him how he was. Fine, he said. And his voice? Flamm asked. It was still the same, David answered, why? "Because," Flamm said abruptly, "I think you should stop singing."

"Stop?"

"Yes. Your voice is going. I heard it on Yom Kippur, just the beginning. Come here," he said, and went to the piano. He sat down and played the opening bars of the *Kol Nidre*. "Now, try that." David sang it but his voice went out of control, slipped from soprano to alto, to baritone, back to soprano, then cracked into a reedy falsetto.

"You see?" Flamm said. "You mustn't sing for a long time."

David went back to the couch and put his head in his hands. What would his family do for money? He looked up as Flamm put a cigarette into his holder and lit it. He wanted to ask Flamm what to do, but he couldn't. He remembered Yom Kippur and The Flame's being fed by Ilsa Kermitt on his lap.

"The choir is beginning to rehearse for Succoth. If you want, if you need the money"—Flamm hesitated—"you could sing with them."

"In the choir?"

Flamm nodded.

"If I can sing at all, why not as a cantor, a soloist?"

"Because alone I can't rely on your voice. In the choir, if it breaks, the other voices will cover it. Alone"—he shrugged, and blew two distinct streams of smoke from his nostrils—"it's no good."

David stood up and began to pace.

"It's hard for you, I know," Flamm said. "But it would be better if you do not sing at all. If you want the voice should come back beautiful, you must not sing or shout. You must take it quiet for a few years until the voice returns, rested and new. I will give you the name of a voice teacher who will help you to take care and do the right exercises—"

"Just like that!" David snapped his fingers. "No more voice. Yesterday I was a cantor; today I am something for a voice doctor."

"In life it is like that," Flamm said. He tried to change the subject. "You know that all the Yiddish papers and radio stations said you were a wonder, a new Rosenblatt?"

"That's all they know!" David said angrily. "A new Rosenblatt! A little Yossele! Can't they say anything else? And I'm not. I'm not. Now I don't even have the voice of David Freed anymore."

"The voice will come back."

"How do you know?"

"If you take care of it and treat it like the gift it is, it will return."

"And if I don't?"

"Then you will be like others, like most men, without a beautiful voice."

Clouds of fog rolled through his throat. He heard himself opening his mouth and a hoarse, croaking sound came out, not music, but a harsh groaning. He didn't want to lose his voice, just yet, not now. It wasn't just the money, but something more, something he couldn't explain; his voice made him feel bigger, more secure that things would, in time, turn out well, more hopeful, somehow, that God would look after him.

"It's not so terrible," Flamm said. "You must not act like it was the end of the world. Your face looks like sackcloth and ashes."

"For you it is easy to say."

"You are foolish, Dovid. You talk like an unthinking child." He stopped, unwilling to continue, then forced himself to go on. "Don't you think it happened to me, too? And didn't I worry for four years until the voice came back? It has advantages, too, you know, the voice going away."

"Advantages?"

"Yes. It is the sign that you are becoming a man."

"I am a man," David replied.

"That is another, a different, kind of man. You will soon see."

"Eleazar," Ilsa Kermitt called from the other room.

"Yes, Ilsa, right away," Flamm called back. "Now, I suppose you want your money." He took his wallet out and counted some bills onto the piano. "Here," he said, "count it, two hundred dollars, as we agreed."

David counted the money and pocketed it, but he didn't say thanks.

"And here's another twenty-five," Flamm added. He handed him two tens and a five. "The congregation asked me to give you a present. They said it was the finest High Holy Days singing they ever heard."

David felt the blood in his face. "Thank you . . . them," he stammered.

Together they walked down the corridor to the door. David opened it, and they shook hands. "Good luck, Dovid," Flamm said, "I will remember you for a long time."

"And I you."

"Thank you for giving me the best High Holy Days since I was a young cantor," The Flame said, almost in a whisper, as if he didn't want to hear himself. "Take care of your voice—and your belief."

"And you yours," David answered, knowing the unkindness of the remark and seeing it burn into Flamm's face. He put the twenty-five dollar bonus in his pocket, and said good-bye.

"Good-bye, Dovid," the cantor said. "If you ever need any help, let me know."

When David came down into the street, he sat on a curbstone and cried. He took out the twenty-five-dollar bonus and saw that there was a card there with the name and address of a voice coach embossed on it, and he didn't know whether he was crying for his lost voice, or for the lost cruelties to Eleazar Flamm and Ilsa Kermitt that he could never take back.

David awoke in the middle of the night, feeing his heart beating like the knocking on the door, and only when he heard his father call out, asking who was there, did he realize that someone was at the door, that he wasn't dreaming.

"It'sa me, Mistah Vecchione," a voice called back.

David was out of bed, his robe over his pajamas, and into the corridor before his father had the door fully open, and Pop Vecchione, all dressed, looking smaller and even more bent, came in. "Please," the old man said, "I likea use your telephone. My daughter, Toni, she gotta go ina hospital."

"Come in," his father invited.

"What is it, Jakob?" his mother's voice came from the bedroom. "Something is wrong?"

"Nothing, Leah, nothing. Stay in bed. It's Mister Vecchione from downstairs. He wants to use the telephone." His father took Pop to the telephone in the kitchen and put the light on. "You're up," he said, surprised, when he saw David.

"Yes," David replied, "I heard the knocking. He turned

to Pop Vecchione, fumbling with the telephone, and offered to dial for him. Pop nodded. "You calla fa me, David. Saint Xavier Hospital." While he found the number and dialed, Pop was at his elbow, saying, "Tell 'em come ina hurry up, right away." David called the hospital emergency service and gave them the name and address, then hung up. "They'll come soon," he told the old man. He had never seen Pop Vecchione like that, his white hair almost leaping from his head and his eyes spinning around in his face as if he were trying to look everywhere at once.

"Don't worry, Mr. Vecchione," his father said, "soon you'll be a grandfather."

Pop Vecchione looked up at and through him. "No," he said to himself, but out loud, "No. It'sa not go right. I no like. I no like." His head shook as if it were going to roll off his neck. Slowly, like a sleepwalker, he went to the door, and just outside, turned and thanked them for the use of the telephone. "Don't worry," his father answered, sounding reassuring, "everything will be all right."

Everything will be all right. That's what his father always said, always believed. Even when he'd come home and told them that he was losing his voice and couldn't sing with Flamm any longer, even then, his father had nodded and said it was all right, everything would be all right. God would look after everything. His mother had been upset and angry and said, "Nuh, Jakob, so if you're not working and David neither, so where will the money come from? How will the cat cross over the water?" He hadn't seen much of God's work in this Depression, in the schoolyard, with the Vecchiones, or with the Forty Thieves and Georgie Harvard. Or even in the synagogue, with Barrt and The Flame.

"You want me to go with you?" David asked Pop Vecchione, who was still standing at the head of the stairs as if he didn't know where to go, what to do.

"It's the middle of the night," his father objected. "You must go back to bed."

The old man nodded. "You betta go sleep." He turned and went, heavy-footed, down the stairs.

David lay in bed, listening for the sound of the ambulance siren, worrying about Toni. He loved her. Yes, yes, he loved her. What was he saying? Was he going crazy? Toni was married to Johnny Strigari, she was going to have his baby, be a mother, but he knew that made no difference; he loved her anyway. He strained his ears for

the siren, but heard nothing. He got out of bed and looked
out of the window. The lights were on in the cellar, and
square yellow patches surrounded the house. He watched
for a long time and heard only the low moaning of the
wind, and saw the bare trees twisted in the moonlight
beyond the *boccie* alley. Then the cellar door was opened
and a man came out, back first, holding something heavy.
It looked like a sled, and then he saw two men and knew
it was a stretcher. Toni was on it, all wrapped up in
blankets that covered her like shadows, but then, as they
tilted her to carry her up the cellar stairs, he could see her
clearly, throwing a huge shadow on the ground like a bird
with giant wings, and he turned up to see if there really
was a bird above them. In the moonlight, he saw her
beautiful dark face crumpled with pain, her blond hair
wild on her head.

"Toni," he called from the window, "Toni!"

Her eyes opened and she looked for him; then she saw
him and smiled, her teeth like a slice of moonlight. "David," she said in her summery voice. "David. Hello."

"I love you, Toni," he cried, not caring about the two
men carrying her, whose faces were also turned up towards
him.

Her face was serious then, the smile fading like the
moon behind clouds, and when she smiled again, it was
only with her lips. "I love you, too," she replied. The men
came to the top of the steps and turned the stretcher to
carry it down the alley. "Good-bye," she called, and tried
to take her arms out to wave, but she couldn't, and then
her white face was gone.

Strigari, Joe, and Pop Vecchione came out and followed. David watched, but didn't call to them, and listened until their footsteps faded. A motor started, there
was the low wail of the siren, then silence, and he remembered he hadn't waved good-bye.

In the morning before going to school, no one seemed
to be awake at the Vecchiones'. When he came home
from school, David knocked at the upstairs door, then the
cellar door, but still there was no one. While he was eating
lunch, he asked his mother if she had seen the Vecchiones,
and she said she thought they were all at the hospital.
After all, it was the first grandchild, even if—

"Even if what?" he shouted.

"Why are you screaming?" his mother asked. "I can
hear you when you talk quiet, and your father—thank

God!—has a day's work in New York, so he can't hear you even if you yell louder."

"Even if what?" David repeated, controlling himself, but still angry.

"Even if it's from such a young girl, and with a no-good for a husband," his mother replied calmly.

David went back to school. Twice, in Latin and in algebra, the teachers caught him not paying attention and gave him zeroes, but he didn't care. The final bell was a relief, and he raced home as fast as he could. He didn't wait to take his books upstairs but went straight to the Vecchione cellar. The door was open, and in the parlor Pop Vecchione stood in front of the victrola, carefully taking the records from the cabinet one by one, breaking them in half, and flinging them against the wall. Joe was leaning against the other wall with his face buried in his arms, his body turned away, and Johnny Strigari was sitting on the couch, his face in his hands. None of them spoke. Quietly and systematically, Pop Vecchione broke the records, one after the other, and David, stunned, could not speak or move to stop him. Then the old man took the opera posters from the drawers, tore them savagely across, twice each, and pitched them against the wall, until, floating down, they looked like yellow snow over the records. When he was done his arms fell from his shoulders, dragging as if they were broken. *"La commedia è finito,"* he said hoarsely, and then David knew that Toni was dead.

Joe whirled from the wall, his face covered with tears and red, as if someone had scratched it. "No, that's where you're wrong again. The comedy isn't over. The comedy's over only when you're dead. Toni's dead, but the baby's alive. You're alive. We're all alive. The comedy'll go on."

The old man stood in the center of the room, his face stone, his body shaking, his hands trembling.

"I told you we could get a doctor to take care of it. No! You knew better. You had to make her marry. And now she's dead, oh, God, she's dead." He began to cry aloud, sobbing between the words. "You knew, you knew! You knew with Toni. And you knew with Vito. You were right, but she's dead and he's in jail. So what good was it? You're a stubborn, thickheaded old man. Stubborn, stubborn, stubborn!"

"All your fault, ya crazy bastid," Strigari muttered to the old man, his face coming out from behind his hands, automatically searching for a Di Napoli cigar and putting it unlit into his mouth.

"You keep your mouth shut," Joe turned on him and shouted. "I should've killed you before I let him marry you to that poor kid. I should've killed you with my bare hands." He ran to Strigari and smashed the black cigar into a shredded, tobacco-colored flower against Strigari's face. Joe lifted him off the couch by the throat, choking him and holding him up at the same time, until Strigari turned blue. "You scum! He may be a crazy, pigheaded, old-fashioned man, but you had to fool with a little girl. You hot-blooded bastard! You couldn't keep it in your pants, even in a house where you were treated like a son. You had to show your guinea cock pride, show you could do it, even to a kid. It makes you a man, doesn't it, a big man!" Suddenly, Joe let him go and Strigari fell to the floor in a heap, holding his throat. Joe looked down at him and kicked him in the ribs. Strigari fell over, groaning, and crept along the floor. "And even then, you couldn't treat her right. You had to make her feel like something the old man palmed off on you, something spoiled and dirty, so she didn't care whether she lived or died." Joe kicked him again, and Strigari moaned and crawled.

The sound came out of the old man's mouth like a tree cracking in a storm. David turned and saw Pop Vecchione begin to bend at the knees, as if he were going to kneel and pray, and the the old man pitched forward on his face so that he lay flat and stretched out, looking very long and tall, his white head only a few inches from Strigari's black-haired one. They lay on the floor, the old man not moving, not making a sound, Strigari squirming and making little yelps like a kicked dog.

Joe went to his father and turned the old man over on his back. His face was white, his lips blue, but he was still breathing. "Give me a hand with him," Joe said. "We'll take him upstairs."

David moved to help, took the old man's legs, and Joe took him under the shoulders. As they began to lift, Joe saw him. "No, David, not you," he said. He turned to Strigari. "C'mon," he bit out, "get your dead ass off the floor and give me a hand."

Strigari got up slowly, kneeling first, then pushing himself up with his hands as if he didn't have the strength to stand. When he was up, Strigari shoved David aside and took the old man's legs. "Okay," he said, his eyes down, "let's go."

When they were gone, David stood staring at the yellow posters covering the records. Spots of color peeped out, here the nose and one eye of Caruso, there the background picture of the hunched back and twisted form of Rigoletto, and under it all the black of the records themselves and the torn spots of red and blue labels that told what music they played.

Slowly, David went to the victrola and looked into the record cabinet. It was bare. Not a single record remained. He opened the victrola top, and there one record was left on the turntable. David reached in and plucked it out; it was the Caruso aria from *The Pearl Fishers*. He took the record between his fingers, feeling the grooves irregular beneath his fingertips, and threw the record with all his strength against the wall. Like a bird it flew through the air and smashed into bits against the wall, dropping with a blank, waxen sound on the rest of the records and the posters.

They brought her home from the hospital two days later and laid her on a bier in the upstairs apartment. When he told his parents he would have to pay his respects, David was surprised that they asked to go along with him. The three of them went downstairs together and knocked at the door. Carmine opened it, and for a minute David saw Toni's face in his, tan, brown-eyed and blond, alive and quick, but the moment passed. Carmine took them into the parlor where the bier was. It was dark wood, with flowers all around and something that once was Toni in a white dress, its hands folded around a dark wooden crucifix. It wasn't Toni, but anyone, anywhere, a figure like a wax dummy in Coney Island, the dark wood and the white flowers making his head ache with their odor.

There were people David didn't recognize, and their faces turned to look at them, at his father's beard and mother's perique, at their earlocks and skullcaps. David searched for Johnny Strigari but couldn't find him. Pop sat by the frosted window, looking out, his back turned on the bier and the people in the room, his breath misting a ragged circle on the window that melted and misted, melted and misted. Mama Vecchione sat next to the bier; Regina, next to her, was holding her hands. Joe was there, too, and he and Carmine wore black bands sewn on their left sleeves. Only the old man, in his worn gray sweater, wore no black, but his face was as white and blue-lipped as it had been when it lay on the floor of the cellar.

Joe came across the room and shook hands with his mother and father, thanked them for coming and asked if they would sit down, but they said they could only stay for a little while and would rather stand. After a little time, they went to Mama Vecchione and talked to her, and shook her hand. Then to the old man, but he didn't look at them or talk or take any notice of his father's outstretched hand. His parents came back and whispered to him, "You'll come back up soon?"

David nodded and they left.

Carmine came and stood by him, and David asked where Johnny Strigari was. "Gone, I guess," Carmine replied. Then he shrugged.

"Gone?"

"Joe didn't want him here anymore, and I guess he didn't want to stay anyhow, after . . ." His voice broke.

"But the baby?" David asked after a time.

"Joe's bringing her home day after tomorrow."

"It's a girl?"

"Yeh, looks just like Toni, Mama says."

"Doesn't Johnny care about the baby?"

"Naw. He doesn't give a damn about anybody. You know him. He didn't even want to see her. Says we're all nuts, all the Vecchiones, and the baby'll be just like us. Joe made him sign some papers, and now she's a Vecchione, not a Strigari."

The Vecchiones didn't ask him to come to the funeral, and David was relieved that they didn't. He wanted to remember Toni alive, not being buried. The day of the funeral was dark, and there was no sliver of sky or sun visible through the low, heavy clouds. The gray hearse and the long black cars waited outside of the house for the Vecchiones, but Strigari wasn't there. When they were all in the cars and had driven away, David knew that Toni was really dead, that they would put her yellow hair and summer laughter and lovely face in the ground and that he would never see her or hear her again. And every night in the weeks that followed, he awoke shivering from a dream in which he and Toni lay in a dark snowbank that froze them together so they could neither move nor warm h other, until something inside him, day and night, seemed frozen gray forever, and then the nightmare stopped.

One day after school, David went into the backyard, and Pop was at the fence, looking out at the fields and the *boccie* alley, his face dead, the only sign of life the thin curl of smoke from his corncob pipe. David stood next to him, but the old man didn't even seem to know he was there. He leaned against the pickets, more bent than he'd ever been, saying nothing. Even when David heard the baby crying inside, the old man's face didn't stir, his eyes didn't blink, and the frozen gray thing inside him chilled him more than the cutting October wind that blew through his jacket.

David tried to talk to him, that afternoon and many other times, but it was like talking to a statue, the eyes two dead stones. The old men he'd played *boccie* with came across the hard ground to call to him by the fence, but he never answered them or even noticed them. When they had talked for a long time and grown silent and uneasy, their birdlike hands drooping at their sides, he'd turn his back without a word and go down into the cellar. Not even old fat Ferrara could get through to him.

One day, coming home from school, he met Nadie Rosen on the corner. Nadie had a new suit and a gold key chain that he kept swinging, and told him that Vito had gotten five years, Joe Russo and Mario Pastore ten to twelve. The grocer didn't die, he said, so they were lucky. They'd be out before, with good behavior. Georgie Harvard's lawyer took good care of his boys. David asked if he was still hanging out with Fonzi and Banana Nose.

"Sure," Nadie answered, "why not?"

"Well, if you don't know by now, I sure can't tell you," David replied, before he walked away. But he knew he didn't care anymore, knew that it didn't make any difference, and that he was afraid.

Another evening, he saw Regina come running past him out of the alley, crying so that she didn't even see him. He went down into the cellar to see what had happened, forcing himself to go, because he felt that the gray and ice in him were turning to stone. Joe was sitting at the table reading, the naked yellow light bulb over his head and a bottle of whiskey on the table in front of him. He took a swallow of whiskey and then said, "Hello, hello. Come on in, David. Where you been keeping yourself?" David saw that he'd been drinking for a long time. "Don't look at me like that, you young puritan. Just like my old man, a puritan. Dyed in the wool. What's the matter, don't you approve of my drinking? Well, what if you don't? A man must have something, mustn't he? Or must he?" He had another swallow from the bottle. "Come on, sit down, I'll read you some fine poetry by another puritanical wop called Dante."

David sat, and in a voice that reminded him of the cantillations Joe began to read:

> Upon a day came Sorrow in to me,
>   Saying, 'I've come to stay with thee awhile';
>   And I perceived that she had usher'd Bile
> And Pain into my house for company.
> Wherefore I said, 'Go forth—away with thee!'
>   But like a Greek she answered, full of guile
>   And went on arguing in an easy style.
> Then, looking, I saw Love come silently,
> Habited in black raiment, smooth and new,
>   Having a black hat set upon his hair;
> And certainly the tears he shed were true.
>   So that I ask'd, 'What ails thee, trifler?'
> Answering he said: 'A grief to be gone through;
> For our own lady's dying, brother dear.'

Joe slammed the book closed on the table. "You like that?" he asked. He drank again and said the poem by heart, in Italian, sadder and angrier, but somehow more beautiful, though David couldn't understand the words.

"What's the matter, Joe?" David asked, knowing the words were hopeless, that it was not a question.

"Nothing, David, nothing. What could be the matter? My only sister's dead, my brother Vito's in the jug for five years, my father's gone crazy. Doesn't talk to anybody, doesn't recognize anybody, just sits. And I've just told my girl—you remember Regina, don't you, David?—that we're all washed up. Why? Why, you ask. You *should* ask why? Because Joe Vecchione is a *good son*. He's got to take care of his mother and father, his dead sister's infant daughter, because Joe Vecchione is lucky, he's got a job, and no one else has a job in the Vecchione family because there's a Depression. The *Depression*. Depression."

Carmine came down the stairs. "You better go to bed, Joe," he said.

"Sure," Joe said, "I better go to bed. Everybody's telling me what to do. I gotta stop drinking. I gotta go to bed. Sure, but what's the use? I can't sleep."

"You got enough of that stuff in you to make an army sleep," Carmine said. "C'mon."

When his father came home and said he had a new job, a steady job, it didn't make any difference anymore. His father came in, smiling, took his mother's hands and said, "Leah, God has been with us."

"What happened, Jakob?" his mother asked.

"My brother Joe knew the union delegate to a shop where they needed another presser. The old one"—his smiling face went solemn for a moment—"had a heart attack and died."

"Oh, God forbid such things from happening," his mother wished fervently. "Was he a young man?"

Sobered, his father nodded, then brightened again. "But, Leah, steady work, fifty weeks' pay a year. For us the Depression is over."

David was pleased to see them happy, embracing, and he laughed when his father shouted, "For a whole year I don't want to see a plate of farina now," but he knew it didn't make any difference. Even for that piece of luck, of God's luck, a man had to drop dead. "And now"—his father turned to him—"you can go back to studying with Rebi Greenberg, hah? He was asking for you again."

"I'm not going back," David said flatly.

His parents exchanged looks. "But why?" his father ased. "Now we'll have the money. It'll be all right."

"I don't believe in God, that's why."

"Dovid," his father roared. "I don't want even to hear such words in my house."

"Then don't ask me why."

"Do not ask? Am I no longer your father? Do I not have the right to ask?"

"You have the right," David said softly, "but I must speak the truth in answering, then. There's nothing, nothing."

"No, Dovid," his father said, so softly he had to strain to hear. "You are too young to say that. You don't know."

"I know, I know."

"You can't know."

"I *do* know. It's all nothing, nothing but old wives' tales and old men's dreams."

Later, in the smoky dusk, David saw Pop Vecchione sitting in the backyard smoking his pipe, his eyes blue and faraway. When David, so close to him he could touch him, said hello, Pop didn't even see him. What was the old man staring at with those terrible eyes? Toni's grave, Vito's cell, Strigari's hatred, Joe's anger? David didn't know, couldn't imagine, and that somehow seemed to be the end of it, the only thing he was sure of.

Slowly, David turned away and walked down to the drugstore. He still had some money left from what Flamm had paid him. He bought a razor and some blades and went back home. Upstairs, he slipped the door open quietly and went to the bathroom, catching only the fragment of his father's saying to his mother, "Nuh, Leah, it's all right now, hah? Everything's all right?" He closed the bathroom door, soaped his face until there was a white froth over it, and then put the razor blade into the razor. Quickly he shaved the first hairs off his chin, his cheeks, under his nose. Carefully, then, he took his earlocks in his fingers and stretched them to their full length. He looked at them in the medicine-chest mirror for what seemed like a very long time, and then, with quick impatient strokes, he shaved them off. He took the two long, thick plaits of hair, squeezed them dry, and laid them carefully on the washstand to dry. He cleaned the razor, put it into the medicine chest, and ran his palm up and down the new smooth sides of his face. It was a new face, a stranger's, older somehow, and not cleaner for being clean-shaven. Finally, he picked up the earlocks, threw them into the toilet, and flushed them away.

When he came to the dinner table, his father sat waiting and his mother was getting the soup and farina. His father looked at him twice, and his face seemed to fall into little shaking pieces, and silently he began to cry, tears running down his face into his beard. His mother came to the table, and David heard the plate crash and felt hot soup splash his ankles. She stood looking from him to his father as if she couldn't believe either of their faces, and when David couldn't stand their silent staring any longer, he put on his jacket, and without eating, went out. He thought he'd go down into the backyard, but he remembered the old man siting there like a chunk of stone, and instead he climbed the stairs slowly up to the roof.

The night was clear and deep blue, the stars tiny and unblinking, the moon a white face that looked freshly shaven. He leaned over the edge of the roof and saw the little wisp of gray smoke in the pool of darkness below that told him Pop Vecchione was still sitting in the yard.

The light went on in the cellar, and Mama Vecchione came out, smaller and thinner than he remembered. She took the old man by the arm, and without speaking, led him down the steps back into the house.

On the roof, looking down on them, so small, so frail, walking slowly, as if they would otherwise shatter, David wanted to sing, to scream, to cry out to God to hear his voice, to hearken to his plea. The *Eli, Eli* rose up in him like sickness and nausea, and he sang it over and over again until his voice was torn, and he tasted the thick blood in his mouth and felt it in his throat:

> Eli, Eli, why hast Thou forsaken me?
> Eli, Eli, why hast Thou forsaken me? . . .
>
> Hear my plea! Listen to my cry!
> Only you can help, you alone.
> *Shema yisroel adonai elohenu, adonai achod.*

When he was finished, the hoarse croaking of his throat and the mumbling of his swollen, bitten lips no longer made any sounds that were song. And he didn't care. He didn't want his voice, that voice, back. It was gone, lost, done with; his voice was dead, as a whole part of him was dead and would never return; but in that time that lay ahead, and without his old golden voice, he would still have to make a new life.

SIGNET
BOOKS

Other SIGNET Books You'll Enjoy

☐ **H.M.'S RAPTURE (The Stranger in the Snow) by Lester Goran.** A splendid portrait of a self-made failure and his attempts, alternately jaunty and sad, to come to terms with the specter of guilt that haunts him.
(#T3694—75¢)

☐ **I, ROBERTA by Elizabeth Gray Vining.** Set in Victorian Philadelphia, the poignant story of the self-revelation of a lonely woman. (#P3620—60¢)

☐ **THE ECSTASY BUSINESS by Richard Condon.** The author of The Manchurian Candidate weaves a wild satire of the movie industry, revolving around Hollywood's most beautiful couple. (#T3615—75¢)

☐ **THE BROTHERHOOD by Lewis John Carlino.** The compelling drama of two brothers caught in the death-grip of the Mafia. A Paramount Picture, starring Kirk Douglas.
(#T3658—75¢)

☐ **I NEVER PROMISED YOU A ROSE GARDEN by Hannah Green.** A beautifully written novel of rare insight about a young girl's courageous fight to regain her sanity in a mental hospital. (#T2592—75¢)